Iva Pekárková

TRUCK STOP RAINBOWS

Iva Pekárková was born in 1963 in Prague, where she studied biology before leaving Czechoslovakia in 1985. She spent a year in an Austrian refugee camp and then came to the United States. In addition to writing, she now enjoys working as one of New York City's few female cab-drivers. *Truck Stop Rainbows* is her first novel; she is currently working on her second novel, *The World Is Round*.

INTERNATIONAL

TRUCK STOP RAINBOWS

Iva Pekárková

TRUCK STOP RAINBOWS

TRANSLATED BY

David Powelstock

Vintage International

Vintage Books

A Division of Random House, Inc.

New York

Library of Congress Cataloging-in-Publication Data
Pekárková, Iva, 1963–
[Péra a perutě. English]
Truck stop rainbows / Iva Pekárková; translated by David Powelstock.
— 1st Vintage International ed.
p.   cm.
ISBN 0-679-74675-7
I. Title.
[PG5069.P44P4713   1994]
891.8′635—dc20   93-6257
CIP

Author photograph © Bohumil "Bob" Krčil

To my father and the memory of my mother

I would like to thank the people who helped me with this book: O.S., my former boyfriend, who cooked for me when I was typing away; all my friends who read it and offered critical advice; Mrs. Zdena Salivarová of Sixty-Eight Publishers, who was the first to publish this book in Czech; and also my agent, Lisa Ross; my translator, David Powelstock, and Elisabeth Dyssegaard, the best editor I ever met.

TRUCK STOP RAINBOWS

1

Life is a one-way dead-end street with no stopping or stand-ing, it occurred to me that day.

I rode along in the bus, chewing this formula over in my head. I liked it—the insatiable hitchhiker in me liked it. I liked it as the beginning of a story (which would then have to develop to a happy ending), but I wasn't sure it wasn't just pretentious and shallow.

I thought about Patrik. He would know.

From time to time, the bus linking the Garden City housing complex with my home braked with a wheezing sound; going around turns it shuddered and threw me across the seat, almost into the arms of my sweaty neighbor. I as-sociated the shaking with a pleasurable feeling between my thighs and thought about Freud. Each in the series of artful tremors was like the well-aimed touch of someone's hesitant but knowledgeable hand. It was especially exciting when translated into words or ideas—but I couldn't recall whether and how powerfully I had felt that good feeling even before reading Freud. (One benefit of a training in psychology.) Through diligent practice I'd learned to provide my body with these slight but essential gratifications, modest releases from the everyday grayness—and you couldn't guess it from my body, see it on my face, or read it in my eyes.

Of course, psychologists are really supposed to help their fellow men. How many times had my friends (or, more accurately, my classmates) from high school come to me: You're that *psychiatrist*, that analyst, that doctor. Advise us, tell us what we should do about our husbands, about our children, what do you think about my mother-in-law . . . At first I listened—even though I'm neither a psychiatrist nor a doctor. But then, when I tried to give advice, I would learn my lesson: What can you, a single girl, even begin to know about our problems, the problems of married women and mothers?!

These girls pronounced the word "mother" in the precise spirit of the posters and banners on the streets that to me were just obstructions that blocked my view of the world. The mother is the pinnacle of womanhood, the socialist reproducer of socialist offspring. Mother—the obedient female, unflaggingly producing ever more and more khaki soldiers who will one day fall heroically in the struggle for a better world.

I don't believe that a better world could ever exist. And if there exists a less hideous, a less gray and expressionless world than this one in which we live, then I'm convinced the search for it is more a question of space than of time. Which, of course, is something I keep to myself.

Most attempts at discussion during our teachers' lectures ended with a condescending reference to the text, or directly to the Holy Trinity of Marx-Engels-Lenin. The university, which was supposed to teach us love for our fellow man, was slowly and persistently turning us into a flock of well-read, imperious misanthropes. I still kept trying hard to grind away, but the future after school, which was already unpleasantly near, no longer offered even the slightest glimmer of scarlet sunrise morning. No, it wasn't that I had a black view of reality. It was gray, gray, like a badly contrasted amateur photo. Gray, as gray as the spring around us.

2

Oh yes, it was spring. Or, more precisely, early spring. The sooty tits twittered, hopping around in the sooty brush. Buds were bursting on the sooty branches of the forsythia in the little garden in our neighborhood: the radiant yellow blossoms lit up the world for an instant, so that we could, a couple of days later, trample the little flowers, translucent and limp, severed by the first spring rain. The birches pushed out little spires of leaflets as freshly green as innocence itself, this year's leaflets, which hadn't yet tasted the Nusle fallout of ash and sulphurous wastes.

My classmates, the Married Women and Mothers of Their Children, dragged their seedlings through the redolent streets with a gusto unheard of the rest of the year—and in forced conversations (forced on my part) they recited their problems, which, at this time of year, instead of appearing in the form of threatening mothers-in-law with rolling pins, were more likely to take the shape of unfulfilling husbands. You wouldn't know, instructed the enlightened wives and mothers. You're not married. You don't have children. And however unentertaining these laments were, in the end I still listened to them. These outpourings brought me satisfaction, for they convinced me over and over that being free and on my own was the best thing that could happen to a woman of twenty-five.

Spring had no effect on me. I was just as free in the fall; in the summer I would be free, say, in a haystack; in the winter—in an apartment, in a car, or in some broken-down shack, because the one time I'd made up my mind to be free right in the snow, it cost me a bladder infection. I couldn't imagine settling down and wisening up, as my grandma used to call that reduction of all the world's spaces to the kitchen, marriage bed, and damp, diaper-filled bathroom. I couldn't imagine living any other way than I did, having someone to whom you have to explain, make excuses, or lie, having just one spade in the garden, as the saying goes, and a compulsory one at that. Not to be married off at my age, not to have children, not to strut around hanging on the arm of someone who hasn't been replaced for a few weeks (so there's hope he'll marry you), or not at least to brag about the broken heart that followed in the aftermath of some ancient Great Love—that, in this narrow, gray, planned, normal, and normalized world, was a punishable offense. If it hadn't been for Patrik, I probably would have started to doubt my own sanity.

3

Patrik was a wild-animal madman with perfectly chiseled mental convolutions. He was a vessel of sin and a fountain of wise words.

Professional womanizer and amateur poet.

University-educated plumber and self-appointed researcher into all forbidden fields of knowledge.

Writer writing for the drawer, and painter drawing for his friends.

Photographer of life, who more than once had the film ripped from his camera by the cops and ended up signing a statement about his conduct at the police station.

Awkward mountaineer who fell from cliffs, and discoverer of old mines, in which he regularly got lost.

Patrik was talented and industrious but undisciplined. He could have done anything he wanted, as his poor unhappy mother would say.

The problem was that the things Patrik really wanted to do, he couldn't do. And Patrik (like me) was infinitely attracted to things that weren't allowed; things that weren't amoral but still couldn't be done—and consequently, the range of his interests was boundless.

For me, Patrik was a human being—something infinitely rare in a world gone gray with tedium. He was the only person who never bored me, and I could always count on him. In other words, my only true friend.

4

It was Mrs. Fišer who answered the door that day. It was always Mrs. Fišer who answered the door, even though nobody but me ever came calling on Tuesdays in the early evening. She'd scurry to the door before Patrik even had time to get out of his little cubbyhole, and that was only so that she could welcome me with a smile so coldly formal and a joy so badly acted that a kick in the rear would have been less expressive of her feelings for me. "It's you?" pronounced Mrs. Fišer, and she opened the door wide. "So you've come to visit us again! P-a-a-a-t-r-i-i-k!"—she called with her thick and saccharine teacherly condescension in the direction of her twenty-seven-year-old son's cubbyhole—"you have a v-i-i-i-s-i-t-o-o-o-r! Viola has come to see us . . ." I slipped inside and disappeared as quickly as possible into Patrik's room. I hate the toothy social smiles of women and girls, and I can't imitate them either—even psychology hasn't taught me how to feel at ease when I'm not welcome. Besides, I hate it when anyone calls me Viola.

"Hi, Fialka!" Patrik welcomed me and I already felt comfortable in his cubbyhole. In contrast to the rest of the apartment, which was morbidly scoured and smelled permanently of the kitchen and big Laundry Days (I don't know how Mrs. Fišer managed to generate such enormous laundries in a family of only three members), Patrik's cubbyhole was a fragrant oasis of dust, books, posters, and the old photos he had stuck up on the walls. Patrik slept on a sofabed, in whose bowels he hid officially banned books, obscene photographs, and bottles of white wine, and over his head he had hung both halves of the face of the moon. On the opposite wall shone the sun with a protruding tongue of fire. The cover on the bed wasn't much good anymore (Patrik slept directly on top of it, under a blanket, without any sheets); it was worn through in a number of spots, and the place where Patrik put his head bore vestiges of his rarely washed hair. Patrik didn't really give a damn about beauty. But he had this specific scent which apparently had its effect on women. I gathered this from the fact that it affected me, too. While we talked, I would usually lie on the bed, greasing up the still relatively pristine wall beneath the sun with my socks and listening to Patrik with my head on my palms. He sat in a little chair without any back, elbows on his knees, chin cupped in his hand, and articulated his thoughts through his extended fingers. We spoke quietly, because the walls have ears (especially in the prefabs), and behind a sound-screen of Pink Floyd, all of whose albums Patrik had borrowed and taped and who, to the meager delight of the musically (and otherwise) conservative Mrs. Fišer, howled from the squeaking, almost completely trashed tape player.

I'd known him for a long time, but it was not until recently that Patrik had succeeded in winning himself a little living space of his own. Mrs. Fišer concluded that "Viola had a hand in this, too," and I won't rule out the possibility that she was right. I supported her no longer young child in his shenanigans and in his attempt to be independent—and after all, that enormous rusty lock he insolently used to lock his *disgusting hole* had been my gift to him on his twenty-fifth birthday.

Patrik was two years older than I, but in so many ways he was refreshingly helpless and impractical! And that was exactly what attracted me to him. It was strange, because I'd always been attracted to people who were genuinely older. Experienced and worn smooth around the edges. People who had already more or less lived life and were in a position to evaluate it as a whole . . . But Patrik actually had a lot of different lives. In some of them he'd fully matured at the age of fourteen, in others he'd refused to grow up altogether. This strange mix of maturity and childishness, grief and persistent naïveté, transcended Patrik's years.

Of course, Patrik wanted to move away from his parents. This desire, at first an adolescent dream, gradually grew into a perfectly natural longing to gain his independence, but one without hope of realization. Many of his peers had gotten married and built their nests, but Patrik's thirst for freedom and peace couldn't be quenched by going that route. And so he stayed holed up miserably on the fifth floor of the prefab, that hated *box*.

There was no great reason to hope he would succeed in getting his hands on an apartment in Prague; he had too few acquaintances in the right places. The simplest thing of course would have been to find himself some woman who was ripe for it and move in with her, but Patrik could never have reconciled himself to that. He also could have moved out of Prague and gotten a job at some enterprise that provides housing for its employees. Or gone looking somewhere in the Most district in northern Bohemia, a moonscape plagued by sulphurous rains and respiratory illnesses, where it's easy to find a free apartment. Where terrified, earnest environmentalists celebrate each and every dandelion that sprouts in the dumps.

But Patrik didn't know how to live without Prague, just as I didn't—probably none of the people close to us did. He had parents with a so-called oversized apartment in Prague (two little bedrooms, entry hall, and kitchenette) and so he wasn't entitled even to a studio apartment. A clear and unresolvable situation; unresolvable, at least, by the means we knew.

"Mother is angry with me again," remarked Patrik with an infantile tinge to his voice as soon as he'd put on Pink Floyd. "When I went out this morning, I left my cocoa mug in the sink and a *disgusting* dirty pan from my eggs. Mother sentenced me to vacuum twice a day for a whole week."

I laughed.

Mrs. Fišer was a teacher whose job it was to accompany a single group of little kids from first through fourth grade over the course of four years. Then she got a new group of first-graders. As a result, every four years Patrik matured from a first-grader to a fourth-grader, only to revert over the summer vacation and start the whole cycle all over again. At the moment he was in second grade.

"And Mother told me she's coming to inspect this disgusting hole of mine, because the earwigs have started crawling out into the apartment."

Every time I came to visit, little schoolboy Patrik would make some new claim. One time, he'd dared to set foot in the living room in his boots and for two months he had to water his mother's 350 or so African *Saintpaulia*, watering can in hand and suffering on his face. Another time, he'd left a ring in the tub and was sentenced to a big Laundry Day. Patrik accomplished this mission with a cunning all his own, of course: he piled up layers of sheets, bedspreads, socks, and variously colored T-shirts in the tub, covered everything with a generous coating of laundry powder, and turned on the hot water. Later, while soaking parrot-colored shirts and sheets in bleach, Mrs. Fišer apparently decided that never again would she entrust anything of the kind to her dim-witted son. Obviously he could have pulled something similar with her collection of African violets, but—since they were living creatures—he had mercy on them.

Patrik never dared not to fulfill the tasks assigned him. And so (for the sake of familial peace) he was vacuuming at least once a day—before leaving for work, while the parentals were still asleep. Every day, as soon as he staggered out of bed, he would grab the vacuum from the closet, turn it on, lay it down on the carpet, and lie down right next to it. Then he put his hand over the mouth of the pipe and used it to regulate the pitch of the sound until he got just the right howling, so that it sounded as if he was really going over the carpet.

Mrs. Fišer, though no doubt startled from her sweet sleep each morning, listened and was satisfied. And Patrik, still halfway lost in limbo, with eyes closed and a half smile on his drowsy face, vacuumed and vacuumed with relentless determination.

5

The Garden City prefabs.

We'd stared at these gray rectanguloids in Patrik's housing complex often enough. We tried to understand why they had to take such a monstrous form—which was a pretty sad task, as was for that matter the effort to understand almost anything around us. It was as if objects and human relations were coming asunder, crashing down and forward toward that bright tomorrow that we all—it was compulsory—had supposedly been anticipating since time immemorial. Looking forward, longing, and making the best of it, until—until one day, when . . .

Nobody had any rosy visions of the socialist tomorrow anymore, but people, altogether independently, still aimed their minds toward the future: kids couldn't wait until they were sixteen or eighteen. Happy families looked forward to getting a cooperative apartment, or to the possibility of affording a car.

But the future didn't lure Patrik and me with its spell. We didn't want to get anywhere, attain anything, patiently wait in line for prosperity. We wanted to live, live for the instant, to taste to the fullest those scarce moments that still had color and flavor.

And all around us some mysterious force was commanding humanity to build hideous things. Senseless things. Medium-gray things which struck a population thinking in gray as only a little out of the ordinary.

The environmentalists' posters in glass cases pictured flowers and animals and posed the following rhetorical question to anyone who still bothered to raise his head while passing the store: Will they survive to the year 2000?

Will our forests and rivers, our mountains and flowers, will our countryside survive?

The "silver-foaming Vltava" hasn't foamed silver since the pulp mill in Větřní was built; the Elbe rolls along her course toward the West, just as in the primordial days of Ur-Father Čech, and with Old Czech equanimity takes unto her bosom the chemical wastes and toxic runoffs from the fields. The sickly forests are turning into naked clearings, the mountains are quietly dying beneath gray deposits of fly ash and floods of acid rain. And the people live in reinforced-concrete bunkers, above each other, below each other, next to each other, in rationally constructed units, all drinking from one pipeline and shitting into the same pipe that descends through the prefab from asshole to asshole.

The brontosaurus didn't survive, the environmentalists pointed out, why should we?

I didn't know and I didn't even care.

But still, I had this awful wish that at least Something would survive. Something that would push its yellow-and-green antennae out from under the filthy ruins and radioactive fallout. Something that would blink its eyes on their stalks and take off like a flash, to live, fuck, and love. A colorful, spontaneous, living Something. The Something Patrik and I had been looking for for years.

6

Garden City, of course, was the name of a section of the city filled with everything but gardens. Strašnice (from the word *strach*, "fright") and Hrdlořezy (meaning "cutthroats"), in their morose gloominess, seemed to me to suit their respective neighborhoods on the outskirts of Prague, and as for the rest, even Bohnice and Pankrác, whose names by association were now linked with an insane asylum and a certain fairly notorious prison, somehow belonged to Prague. But "Garden City" was a parody of itself. Between the recently constructed prefabs (so uniform that practically no untrained visitor ever found the street, block, and entryway he was looking for) there stood only little Škoda MBs in the driveways and dumpsters full of garbage; here and there a naked little shrub or a severed tree trunk reared out of the ground—and the rest was filled in by mud. The mud here—with a persistence that varied according to the most recent weather conditions—had persevered for years, and every year it was promised that the next year it would be changed into lawns, flower beds, or children's playgrounds. Which, needless to say, would never happen; and every day the residents still squelched their way to the bus stop through the mud along Strawberry, Jasmine, and Clover Streets, the women gossiped on the corner of Sour Cherry and Bilberry, and in order to reach Spořilov you had to drive through the intersection of Blackcurrant and Sweet Cherry.

I won't rule out the possibility that you might come across a couple of trefoils on Clover Street on a summer afternoon, but even the old-timers here had never heard of any currants or sour cherries—and sweet cherries and strawberries were things you stood in line for at the produce store down the hill, when they were in season.

Patrik lived on Blackberry.

A redolent and dark purple name, which unfortunately belonged to a street occupied by squat concrete blocks with gaps between the panels joined with black tar. An identical box stood across the way, and one on the left and one on the right, and when you looked out the kitchen window, whether toward Strašnice or toward Spořilov, the same picture greeted you. Garden City embraced an entire hillock in sullen lifelessness.

The view of the opposite windows all lined up in hideous uniformity and the little human shadows on the curtains tormented Patrik—but he was tormented far more by the fact that he himself lived in an identical concrete cube, by his own anonymity. Because maybe somewhere in one of those windows someone stared out night after night with a disgust tuned to the same wavelength as his—but Patrik didn't know him and never would know him, would never pick him out of the crowd.

Over the door of the cubbyhole hung one of Patrik's artworks. He had divided a quarto into equal squares, which he'd drawn with lines fading out into the background—and in each square, in each little stall big enough for a pair of small animals, an identical large-breasted female copulated stereotypically with an identical potbellied male endowed with an enviable penis. (Patrik was undeniably a bit phallocentric.) Noncommittal and immobile children, mutually indistinguishable from one another, multiplied fruitfully in each square—and at the bottom Patrik had attached a slogan (in yellow lettering on a blood-red background, like the majority of slogans) proclaiming: The socialist family is the foundation of the state. Each stall had its own color; Patrik drew them with pastels, using his particular style of short fine lines and shading, a style already somewhat old-fashioned but which nevertheless superbly captured the sense of exitlessness. He had turned his keen sense of color inside out to produce such a repulsive series of tints for those family stalls that by comparison the view of the gray apartment block across the way seemed almost natural.

At first I didn't understand how anyone could want to adorn his apartment with such a portrait of idiocy. But Patrik didn't seek beauty. He sought understanding. And he went after it head-on—like he went after everything else.

The facing block had nine identical entryways. To each entryway belonged seven identical landings, and on each landing were the doors to three identical apartments. It follows that in the facing block there were 189 nearly identical residential units, each supplied with assembly-line furnishings and inhabited by assembly-line people. Assembly-line families with assembly-line fathers, but above all, assembly-line mothers and assembly-line daughters.

Patrik decided he would fuck them. In assembly-line fashion.

An absurd and cynical plan. A self-destructive plan. A senseless plan. A plan I had tried in the course of long arguments to prove would not work.

But Patrik outgunned me. It worked, and for a while he even fancied himself in the role of a prefab Don Juan.

7

First of all, Patrik chose age boundaries. The upper one according to his personal taste and the state of preservation of the subject, the lower one at a level such that he wouldn't wind up in jail. So in practice Patrik was willing to fuck girls and women from fifteen to forty-five.

Then Patrik chose a method.

This was not so difficult. After all, Patrik was a plumber. He had gotten his degree in architecture but was so disgusted by the rift between theory and practice that he gave up on the useless struggle for a cushy sinecure and started making a living with his hands. He reserved his head for thinking. Patrik the plumber, then, made the rounds (both during and after business hours, which was pretty much all the same, since no one in the enterprise ever checked much to see whether anyone was actually doing his job) of the entire adjacent rectanguloid. He visited one apartment after the other, called systematically at every door, and, saying that he was from Central Repair, inquired whether anything in the apartment might need fixing.

The inhabitants cheered, thanked him, rejoiced, and, if Patrik actually carried out any maintenance, were not stingy with fifty-crown notes for the kind plumber who was sent to them so unexpectedly from above, like a star from the heavens.

And Patrik examined the feminine specimens present, discreetly asked about the quantity and kind of the remaining members of the family, and casually set to work. The rest then depended only on Patrik's personal charm and ingenuity. He certainly couldn't complain about any lack of those. And so Patrik might have become a successful conqueror. If he had wanted to.

But at the time Patrik only tested his method, evaluated it—and lost interest.

Mrs. Fišer was right: Patrik had no end of ideas. But he never followed up on anything.

8

The evening I'm describing, that evening in early spring, when the wind carries the thoroughly palpable wetness of cracking ice and melting snow in the mountains, when spring (still) taps on human souls and awakens longings we don't expect, that evening as the flaming televisions from the half-fucked prefab across the way shone into the windows of Patrik's cubbyhole like blue-gray stars—Patrik suddenly grabbed me by the fingers and gripped them tightly.

Such gestures were not the norm between us; on the contrary, almost programmatically we maintained about a six-foot sociable distance between us, because as man and woman we were hardly important to one other, but our companionship was absolutely necessary.

Patrik grabbed me by the fingers and I slowly raised my eyes toward him.

I didn't want to.

Just then we had been experiencing one of those private moments when Patrik would put a shitty recording of Kryl on the tape player at barely audible volume and we would listen religiously to make out the words to the Song of Songs among the squeaking, popping, and undulating chirping of the jamming towers.

Patrik had tapes that had been shittily recorded a dozen times over on a dozen shitty tape players from Radio Free Europe broadcasts. Patrik certainly would have spent days sitting by the radio, but was unable to do any such thing. Garden City was in a region perfectly and safely disinfected from ideological diversion. In fact, if he leaned just a little way out his window, Patrik could even see the Spořilov jamming tower.

Kryl sang from the tape player with that agitated voice that always—and painfully—persuaded me that we had to *do something, go somewhere.* That voice was so enormous and resonant that I didn't care at all who Kryl was, how he made his living, whom he was sleeping with, or how he lived; I didn't care about the rumors that he'd supposedly let his hair grow long and was producing nothing but trouble at Radio Free Europe . . . I didn't believe them and I didn't care. I knew that I'd never be able to tell him how much I loved him just on account of that voice and those tenderly cynical songs he sang—all of which I knew by heart.

> *In spring there the leaves all turn yellow*
> *And shower the flowers like snow*
> *And horror goes 'round with a lute,*
> *A chrysanthemum crown and a bow . . .*

We both knew all those lyrics perfectly; more than once I'd caught myself humming one of his defiant melodies in the metro or on the bus—and still we listened over and over again, because over and over again we felt the pain in those songs, and in that pain we found strength.

Patrik grabbed me by the fingers, forcing me to raise my head.

"I'm turning this off, Fial."

I shrugged.

When the room was filled again with Pink Floyd's howling, Patrik began: "Listen, Fialka, have you . . . ever . . . say, you go to bed with a guy and—"

"Really, Patrik!" I delivered this in the spirit of our favorite little game. "How can you, in light of my thrice-renewed virginity, even conceive of such a thing, that *I*—"

"Hm." (Over the years Patrik had learned to put up with my game.) "Hm. Have you ever . . . well, have you *ever* heard about, say, a guy who sleeps with a girl and he just can't get it up—and she tries everything, but he still can't get it up . . . so—"

"Certainly. Impotence, as it's known. We distinguish between long-term, or permanent, impotence and short-term, or temporary, impotence. Impotence caused by psychological influences and impotence caused by physical influences. Impo—"

"Fine." Patrik inhaled, and steadily released his breath

with a hissing sound, as only he could do. "Fine. So, next time someone calls me an impotent fuck, I'll go shake his hand and thank him for the diagnosis, is that it?"

I snuck a furtive glance at Patrik's jeans. An ordinary but telling blink of the eye that no one would have registered. Of course, Patrik noticed, and he made a face. I probably blushed a bit. We could always talk about anything, sure, but our actual bodies remained taboo.

Anyway, for a pretty long time I'd been thinking that a little lesson wouldn't do Patrik any harm. Somehow he was having just a little too much success with the ladies. So it was probably the blind envy in me speaking, since I'd never had the kind of luck with guys that Patrik had with women. And I have methods of my own.

But a person's got to know when to quit teasing. I asked for the details.

9

A Monstera had a part in it.

The Monstera was one of the housing-complex flowers that slowly grew and grew until they eventually forced a fateful showdown with the tenants: the inhabitants either had to throw the Monstera out the window or jump out themselves.

Mrs. Fišer had one in her apartment as well, a highly developed one.

(All the symptoms of housing-complex stupidity were represented in Mrs. Fišer's apartment, and all of them were highly developed.)

So it's no wonder that Patrik, in his long pursuit of assembly-line fucking, liked most of all to fuck in living rooms, right beneath the Monsteras, on the dark red or reddish-brown carpeting that the builders had used to furnish most of the living rooms in the apartment block Patrik was systematically fucking his way through. Beneath the Monsteras, whose gigantic, perforated, fleshy leaves formed for Patrik's fucking an appropriately morbid silhouette of growing problems.

Some of the Monsteras were childlike and budding, some were fairly large and menacing, and some of them in the apartments Patrik visited approached critical proportions.

Patrik even knew one Monstera, a monstrous and usurping Monstera, whose single leaf blocked half the picture window in its owner's apartment, and her children had gotten used to seeing the world below their window only through the holes; with eyes full of childish wonder, they stared at the gray world through a lattice of green.

Patrik knew all sorts of Monsteras.

He made drawings of them.

He compared the temperament of the Monstera with the characters of the people who had allowed it into their apartment. For Patrik these enormous Monsteras were symbols of human smallness.

10

But this one was *hers*.

That girl with the body of a cat, with promising eyes green as algae and the face of a truly degenerate seventeen-year-old.

She was actually fourteen, but Patrik had no way of knowing that.

One of those precocious, clinging nymphets that we girls over twenty can't stand.

She snuggled up to him in some bar, not quite the very worst kind of bar, where Patrik had ended up with his camera, apparently entirely by coincidence, since he always went looking for life exclusively in the very worst dives.

She snuggled up to him and whispered one of the usual professional lines, one that Patrik probably should have recognized, but which nevertheless, and God knows why, insanely turned him on.

Her hair smelled of gel and shampoo, her face of lipstick and powder, her armpits breathed cheap deodorant—and when Patrik went probing beneath her skirt (which was short, of course) he detected the unmistakable smell of sperm.

This excited him.

Even though he'd longed to for years, Patrik had never actually known a real whore. He certainly could have remedied that easily enough, but he had no intention of buying one of those made-up downtown hookers masquerading as ladies; those women and girls without a past didn't attract him; Patrik longed for red-and-blue duskiness, for honky-tonk piano and a blind fiddler, for a *chambre séparé* and black lingerie on well-fondled professional bodies, bodies that had stories to tell.

In other words, since he was sixteen he had wanted to visit a true, unadulterated whorehouse. A good old-fashioned Old Prague whorehouse with a madam and her girls, an honest-to-goodness respectable whorehouse from the thirties.

There weren't any whorehouses in Prague, however.

And prostitution, from its noble heyday, had metamorphosed into thousands of different shapes and forms that not just anyone could distinguish—but then again, they weren't for just anyone.

Patrik longed for contamination and despised sterility. The smell of someone else's semen from under the clothing of a girl who wanted to be his, that was an invitation to unknown, undreamed-of regions it would have been a sin not to visit.

He went with her—and when she said a hundred, he gave her two, so he must have come off either like a big shot or else like an idiot.

Or perhaps the girl didn't think in those terms; if she thought at all, Patrik said, then it was on a completely different level, a level that was immature and undoubtedly simple, but so unfamiliar as to be tantalizing.

The girl brought out a provocative mixture of longing and disgust in him; she didn't know how to put on rouge yet and there were little black strips of mascara under her eyes: she'd put too much on her lashes, and whenever she blinked, little black worms of it peeled off. She didn't know how to put on makeup, and this made her look less clichéd and more childlike; from time to time, a little grimace crossed her face, really more of a tentative half smile, like a nervous tic—and Patrik longed to feel those sweet dark purple lips on his mouth.

The girl was a temptation and a threat: her entire body, undulating to the rhythm of some mute song she sang to herself, appeared so open, accessible, and communicative that through her he longed to know other men, and himself, too; the girl could have been jailbait (in fact, she was), she could have filed a paternity suit against him or given him one of those well-known diseases that make the rounds of the Prague demimonde.

Patrik knew all of that, of course.

But the *unknown force* that he spoke of so often, and which he'd grown accustomed to submitting to, dragged him after her, in the form of that childish hand with its broken pink nails and three rings on each finger.

The unknown force drew him.

And Patrik followed.

And followed . . .

Followed meek as a lamb.

She lived in a tenement house and with someone who apparently posed no threat of returning.

She modeled for Patrik's camera (she was young and hadn't figured out yet that posing for such photos usually doesn't pay)—and in each click of the shutter Patrik heard the clang of a prison cell door.

He photographed.

He lay down on the floor and she straddled him proudly. Of course, all fourteen-year-old girls wore miniskirts panty-less, just like that, over their naked bodies.

Their beautiful, sinful, naked bodies.

Patrik photographed—and it was better than if he'd felt her body all over with his hands, because he knew the value of the image; he could somehow take an ordinary shot and stretch it to encompass all kinds of meanings: he felt smells and textures, flavors—even heat and coldness—from photographs. So at the time, by photographing her, he was *taking* her for himself—but she didn't know that. She surrendered to Patrik's power with a kind of indifferent naïveté and struck poses she had probably seen in smuggled magazines and which she considered seductive.

In actuality they were childish; they struck Patrik as incestuous. In spite of the fact that he still hadn't touched her, he already felt the skin of that young body on the tips of his fingers, its resistance, its firmness, its electric charge; availability linked with the impossibility of possessing her.

The girl *knew*.

Since he was a boy Patrik had wanted to *know* as much as he could (just as I had)—and (just as I did) he felt the impossibility of knowing everything. Although he certainly lived within the boundaries of the possible, he was always haunted by the consciousness of everything beyond; it wasn't possible to have a thousand lives—and somehow Patrik was unable to choose the one that would have most satisfied him.

Things were simpler for the girl. She had no choice between lives, most probably because she'd never seen the brilliant spectrum of possibilities of being. Certainly she was foolish, not much of a challenge—available—but still you couldn't be sure what she would think of you once you got her.

Patrik wanted to show her how good he was, but he wasn't at all sure how she would rate his performance. He felt afraid of her experience, or more accurately, her degeneracy, because true experience carries understanding with it.

Only when installed between her thighs did he realize that he didn't want to make love to her, he wanted to own her; that he didn't long to be hers but wanted her to belong to him.

That belonging didn't mean that any memories of her would remain with *him*. Possession for Patrik meant the opposite: that he could forget her (and had a responsibility to) as soon as he walked out the door. Possessing her meant occupying her mind with his presence—and Patrik saw how tiny a space in her little brain he could occupy. She was fourteen, but how late Patrik was! She probably didn't have much space in her head—and this was the most painful thing: at an unbelievably early age she already had the little space he might have penetrated choked full of something, inaccessible; there was no room for Patrik, and perhaps it was impossible to possess her.

What's more: she had a Monstera.

There was something morbid about it.

The apartment in the prewar tenement exuded a decrepit odor, slightly moldy; you might say the odor of a specific generation. In any case, the odor wasn't prefab and it harmonized with the lustrous, dark green leaves in some kind of transsensual relationship. This Monstera was no housing-complex flower: in this environment it acquired the symbolic values of life and moisture. Even this fourteen-year-old sensed this symbol subconsciously, and she cultivated it.

She let herself be photographed naked among its leaves and, with a matter-of-factness that puzzled him, lay down on the beige carpet.

No, the able-bodied stud of the prefabs was no conqueror here. He was being taken advantage of; in his day he'd
made enough attempts to get all kinds of girls into similar
situations, so it was easy for him to judge her level.

But here *his* level was to be judged, the situation prepared for him was almost out of a textbook; the girl surrendered with the same (seductive) moves to every man's
embrace and in the same aforementioned place. In that very
space *Patrik's* level was to be judged, judged against the floor
itself—and perhaps the girl didn't even know that. Patrik
knew it very well, and burdened with a furious and crushing
sense of penitence, he submitted to her advance.

It goes without saying that he wasn't sufficiently aroused.
A situation that a loving woman would understand (if
she isn't rating the man), but she didn't forgive him. She
fought her way into his pants; her touch was defiant and
devoid of all tenderness. So it wasn't long before Patrik found
out that he was an impotent fuck and that he might have
gotten more for his two bills.

11

Patrik played with the knob on the tape player, causing Pink
Floyd to fluctuate decibels louder than might have been the
band's own wish.

"And it's never happened before?" I asked in disbelief.

"No . . . well, actually, yeah," Patrik admitted. "But
that was a totally different situation. I knew that time, I
understood . . . but this time . . . I just don't know."

"But, Patrik, aren't you just making a big deal out of
nothing? You couldn't get it up—so you couldn't. Screw embarrassment; there's really nothing to be embarrassed about!
Fine, so she won't think you're the world's greatest lover. So
what, you fool. Next time you'll get it up and everything'll be

fine." (Oh yes! I knew how fine everything could be when a man got his cock up.)

"Unfortunately, that's where you're wrong," said the fool. "I still can't get it up. No matter what I do, I can't do a thing about it."

He ran his finger down his fly so reproachfully and guiltily that I was afraid he might take the little invalid out and wave it in my face.

We didn't really say much else in particular on that evening. I provided Patrik with a semi-scholarly, useless lecture about how the harder a person tries, the worse it usually makes it, for the world is shackled with chains and tangled up in vicious circles of actions and reactions. I advised him, as any "respectable sexologist" would have done, "not to think about it" and to relax. I couldn't take my advice seriously. And, of course, Patrik couldn't either.

So the whole mess remained unexplained. It was strange. I'd wanted to see Patrik taught a little lesson for a long time, but this wasn't it. And later, while I was riding home in the bus that shuddered and caressed me, I felt how ready *I* was, how nothing like that could happen to me; how my equipment responded to stimuli perfectly, perhaps a little too flawlessly; I thought thankfully about how it had never betrayed me yet, and for the first time in a long while I appreciated that decision of Chance or Nature or God, or God knows what, that made me a woman.

12

I didn't worry much about Patrik's problem after that. The essence of our relationship rested not in the mutual resolution of our problems but rather in the fact that we never let them get to us. The only real concern we shared was how we could raise some kind of rainbow over the grayness of the life imposed on us. The rainbow was sacred to us. When we managed to raise one, it didn't matter where we had managed to steal the colors for it. We could arrive at those pure, translucent colors by entirely impure paths, and still the result was as fresh and inspired as your first drop of mother's milk. The rainbow was born in clashes of opposites: from the meeting of rain and sunlight, from an oil slick on the water's surface; Patrik saw the rainbow in the bluish veins on women's breasts, and I looked for it (and found it) in an endless series of incidents and adventures, not all of which could be put into words.

The rainbow is the quintessence of unpossessible beauty. We searched for it all over parking lots in puddles covered with motor oil, in the foul-smelling froth of chemical waste, in dangerously sharp shards of broken glass, in the sperm that shoots skyward in passion and arcs back to the earth to die . . .

We walked without umbrellas through the poisonous rains and watched it grow over our heads. We freed it with our hands from fountains buried under dead leaves. There were many rainbows in our gray world, but few people ever saw them. Patrik and I learned how—day after day, from year to year, we learned to see them better and better.

Of course, we were also getting older.

1

Red splashed through the rain-speckled cutout of the world, which the wiper cleared with the regularity of a metronome. It ran in pink blotches on the dewy arc of the front windshield and filled the droplets, illuminating half of each one and lazily flowing together with them across the glass.

"Shit!" swore the veteran driver. "It's the troopers!"

And it was.

The Liazka sent a puddle showering into the air as it rolled down onto the shoulder, and the black night gave birth to a drenched cop, looking like a wet hen, a flashlight clenched in his frozen fingers.

"Identification Booklet, comrade."

The driver opened the door a little and handed the officer his documents.

The flashlight beam scanned searchingly around inside the cab and came to rest on my hair. Disheveled, I sat up straight in the seat and blinked blindly. The long arm of the law was shining its light on me.

"What's this?" said the light to the driver.

"A hitchhiker."

"Well, miss, can you show me an Identification Booklet?"

"Certainly."

I was already pulling my ID out of my bag. Wherever and however you traveled, the first and most important item was the Citizen's Identification Booklet. I never let it out of my reach.

It was raining urgently and relentlessly; the rain amplified dozens of highway odors and drummed loudly on the roof of the cab. It was warm inside. Comfortable.

From behind the wheel the driver watched with shining eyes as dirty water trickled from the truck door onto the officer's flat cap. It had made a little puddle in the creased crown and was already flowing down his neck and the back of his uniform when the cop raised his eyes toward me.

"Just where is it that you're employed, comrade?"

"I'm a student."

"Your booklet isn't stamped, comrade. You have no stamp whatsoever in here. Where are you employed?"

"I—am—a—student."

The cop shivered from the chill; I guess the droplets had reached some part of his body sensitive to cold.

"But you have no *stamp*," repeated the comrade with growing suspicion. Of course. If you haven't got a stamp, you aren't to be trusted. Even the driver seemed suddenly infused with suspicion.

"Our school doesn't stamp IDs, comrade," I said calmly. "No school in Prague stamps IDs. Would you like to see my student ID?"

"Of course."

I dug out my university record booklet.

Needless to say, I didn't like the idea of his wet fingers smudging its pages. But the situation was taking an ugly turn and, with almost straight As, my record booklet made a good calling card.

Clutching all the documents, the comrade ran around

the truck, rapped on my door, and made as if he needed to get into the cab.

"Pretty wet, huh?" I couldn't resist saying, as I slipped a dirty rag from the floor under his ass.

I winked at the driver, who already had that knowing gleam of approval in his eyes again, and we were both pretty amused when the cop settled down without hesitation on the stinking rag. I guess he didn't even notice it, since at the moment his mind was fully occupied with comparing the entries in my two identification booklets.

"Your name is . . . ?" he blurted.

". . . right in front of you, of course," I said brazenly (and the driver almost lost it right there). "And you even have it there in two places, so I don't see why I need to spell it for you."

I'd overdone it. No psychological subtlety. In my dealings with the state police I overdo it every time. What's worse, my calm self-confidence gives the impression that I'm a seasoned little bitch, a graduate of dozens of stations, mentioned in hundreds of police records. Which, of course, only complicates matters.

The offended arm of the law stopped in the middle of copying down my personal data and looked at me with an expression of frank sadness on his rather inanimate face.

"Comrade," he said, in an unofficial tone but using all the official words, "miss, insofar as you are traveling after sundown by means of hitchhiking and moreover cannot produce a valid Citizen's Identification Booklet, it is our responsibility to detain and cite you . . . In our state, as you are aware, every citizen is required to work—and you have no stamp *whatsoever* in your ID. Would you like to go with me now to the station or not? It is your decision."

I looked out into the rainy night. Little wisps of steam rose from my gloomy companion, and they emitted the unmistakable odor of soggy uniform.

"I suppose I have no choice," I observed. "But I'm a
contributing associate of the —————— *News* [I named a certain
famous Prague rag], and I'm on assignment to cover the Liberation celebration in Spiš. I was hoping to get there in time.
The document is in my ID."

The comrade leafed through the booklet. Suspiciously.
The comrades do everything suspiciously.

But there it was. The necessary document fell out into
his palm:

"To all organs of state administration and security. Miss
Viola Jourová, b. on such and such a date, is a permanent
contributing associate of the —————— *News* and has been assigned to report on the Liberation celebrations in your district. Thank you for your understanding and assistance in
helping her to fulfill this important assignment. Signed, the
editor-in-chief."

The crumpled paper was adorned with about half a dozen
crimson rubber-stamp imprints of various shapes, and the
three copies I had of it had already saved my neck on several
occasions. I particularly liked the phrase "in your district." It
made it possible to use this document in any of the 168
districts in our country. For at least the whole spring I could
use it anywhere, except perhaps for towns which had been
liberated by the Americans. And it actually worked throughout the summer and even on into winter, since very few cops
knew exactly when our homeland had been liberated. That
grubby piece of letterhead, with its painstakingly accumulated collection of rubber stamps, was my most powerful
weapon. Aside from my innocent eyes, of course. But my
eyes didn't carry weight with everyone.

The cop finished reading.

He had acquired a sudden respect for me.

"You're . . . you're a reporter?" he said in alarm.

"I'm only a contributing associate. Shorter articles, you
know. But this assignment is quite important."

He dumped the documents into my hand and jumped out, leaving behind a wet spot on the seat, with that filthy rag imbedded in it.

He saluted. "You may proceed," he announced to the driver, and he courteously pushed the door closed himself, so enthusiastically that it slammed shut with a loud bang.

"You didn't tell me you're from the paper," the trucker said to me a little reproachfully as we got moving again.

"I'm not. Drop it."

I settled myself again across the front seat. A lock of my hair (serendipitously) spread out over the gearshift, for I knew this would be pleasant for both of us. The dark violet night was little by little unfurling into morning. Snorting and straining, our truck, the driver's and mine, lurched forward; it lazily cut away slices from the highway, licking the milestones with its yellow headlights and beaming cones of light like beacons into the hushed, wet countryside.

It shuddered and puffed; in my imagination it stroked me in tender places, humming a lullaby.

I didn't know what would happen or not happen, and I didn't feel like thinking about anything. I let my thoughts be gently bundled up in dreams and myself be rocked into sweet, safe sleep.

I knew this truck and I knew this road, because I'd already ridden this way in dozens of identical trucks. I knew the slight odor of dust in their cabs, and in the purr of their motors I could detect the slightest suspicious sound. I knew exactly how to get comfortable in that seat, where to put my legs, what to put under my head to get a good sleep.

I could balance myself against the jolt of the brakes unconsciously—and the sight of the blue-black sky when I sat up blinking from my horizontal position was reassuring.

As reassuring as the firm, tender touch of the drivers' hands, to whose will I was (sometimes) so glad to entrust myself. I knew the silken feel of my hair in a stranger's hand,

and it seemed to me that each little strand sent out toward the gearshift was an advance scout that knew how to appreciate that hand.

I knew the roads from anywhere to anywhere else.

I knew the truckers' routes across the republic, and I knew the pubs and rest areas where I hooked up with drivers going my way.

I knew the drivers' souls and their truckers' hands.

I knew what it felt like to sleep on the road.

I knew . . .

As almost nowhere else, I felt at home on those roads.

2

I was twenty-five and I'd been living nearly seven years with my grandmother in an enormous, three-bedroom, financially almost unmanageable apartment. Of course, my grandmother refused to move anywhere else on principle; the place where she had lived since her wedding was the place where she intended to die, which—she promised—would be before too long if I continued to torment her as I had so far.

At that time my grandmother was my only material worry. I don't mean to imply that I would have wished her an early passing. Hers wasn't the type of personality that I could wholeheartedly love, but I also wasn't looking forward to laying her in her grave. Although since Grandfather's death she'd had a pension so minimal that more than half of her income came from me, I appreciated the way Grandmother solved for me the majority of those loathsome everyday worries. Grandmother knew when they delivered crescent rolls and milk to the store (so that I didn't have to carry that information around in my own head), and every morning she got up a little after six and by seven was already standing in front of the butcher shop so she would be first in line when they brought the meat at nine. I appreciated how Grandmother simply loved lines, no matter what they were for, and was actually drawn to them, so that, even in winter, she would bring home almonds and oranges; then, frozen to the bone by her three-hour wait in subfreezing temperatures, she would crawl into her featherbed and treat herself with hot tea.

Of course, she had a few bees in her bonnet, which is why I can't say I genuinely liked her. But in any case, I understood her, and I wanted somehow to help her through her old age, that period of external and internal disintegration when a person no longer has anything to look forward to.

Or, to be more precise, when what one has to look forward to is precisely nothing.

True, Grandmother was religious. She was a Catholic. Not a very common phenomenon in Prague anymore, even among older people. It was actually the young who went diving headlong into those semi-legal evangelical societies, but it seemed to me that for them it was a means of escape, that they were just trying to displace the dogma of Communism forced into our heads from kindergarten with the diametrically opposed dogma. Nevertheless, Grandmother was a sincere believer; every Sunday, dressed in her black mourning outfit (in honor of Grandfather, who had been dead twenty-seven years), she went to the little church in our neighborhood and—fondling the rosary handed down to her by her own great-grandmother—made a big black mark on my political security file.

Which, of course, I couldn't have cared less about.

Actually, much more effective in steering me toward the true faith than Grandmother and her undying efforts at my conversion was Comrade Řeháková from the Neighborhood Vigilance Committee, who, after running into my grandmother decked out in her Sunday best on the street, would inevitably call me in for an interview to assure herself of the correctness of my political convictions. It could have been a lot worse if Comrade Řeháková had gone into particulars, but

Comrade Řeháková was a good-natured person, good-natured
to the point of stupidity. She would limit herself to the questions: "Viola, you don't believe in God, do you? You believe
in the ideals of Communism, don't you?" I would say, No,
and of the two possible interpretations of this answer Comrade Řeháková chose a different one than I. Take it from me:
the kind, comradely ministrations of Comrade Řeháková (who
had known me since my childhood) did more to direct my
inherently materialistic soul toward the unfathomable heav-
enly heights than any careful study of the Bible could have.
I would leave the Agitation Center mumbling the Lord's
Prayer or a Hail Mary.

When I needed a letter of reference to apply to the
university, Comrade Řeháková wrote: "The comrade's pro-
Communist class-consciousness is evidenced by, *inter alia,*
the fact that the comrade herself does not believe in God,
whereas her grandmother does, and she makes efforts to convince her grandmother of the correctness of Marxist ideals."

I must say that I never made any effort to convince my
grandmother of the correctness of Marxist ideals, a fact about
which Comrade Řeháková (who was about fifty) maintained a
tolerant silence, though sometimes she would point out that
the old reactionary generation would soon pass away and we,
the young, would take our place at the helm of the world.
Comrade Řeháková had the brains of a chicken.

Nevertheless, Grandmother continued faithfully to attend church, making the sign of the cross and praying—the
rest of the time, when she wasn't standing in lines, she
watched television.

Yes, I'd have to say that was the queen bee in Grandmother's bonnet.

We lived together fairly peacefully in that three-bedroom
apartment in Prague for about a year; we had no relatives, or
at least we never saw them—and every evening Grandmother
would sit down on the bed in my room, talk and talk, cry, and

then talk some more, talk and sob—it went on and on like that, around and around, until I would finally manage to put her to bed and get her to sleep. The evenings became unbearable.

So I made up my mind to invest about three months' salary and buy her a television set.

Not out of the goodness of my heart, I might add. Just to get a little peace and quiet.

And as usual, like every charitable deed, whether well- or ill-intended, this one blew up in my face. Whenever I came home after that, as soon as I got to the front steps I was greeted by the resonating sounds of hilarity issuing from that box, and there would be Grandmother, following the action from her shabby armchair.

Grandmother would watch between eight and ten hours of television a day. She watched the news, the musical shows, the films and series, the ten-minute political bulletins, advice programs for amateur gardeners, the televised Russian-language courses (she didn't know a word of Russian), politicians' speeches, and even the intervals when there appeared on the screen a flowering cherry twig with the word INTERMISSION. She watched children's fairy tales and mystery thrillers, Westerns and Russian war movies, sports broadcasts and parades of flag-wavers on May Day. She watched everything without exception. Once I even caught her staring at a buzzing test pattern. In the course of years of TV watching, it had all become blended in her head into a perfect goulash; Grandmother often couldn't distinguish, for example, the different roles played by a single actor in several serials simultaneously. *The Woman behind the Counter*, *The Man at Town Hall*, or *The Hospital on the Edge of Town* would be mixed up in her aging brain with *The Thirty Cases of Major Zeman* or some historical program—and Grandmother would watch with stupefied amazement as the head surgeon dressed up in a suit of armor and ran the famous detective through with a rapier. On the other hand, Grand-mother would retrieve isolated episodes here and there from the fog of oblivion, and after the third or fourth rerun she would run joyously in to me to announce that she had known beforehand how it would end.

I didn't begrudge Grandmother her daily dose of drivel, but I also hated that damned box.

I hated its bluish glare, I hated the sounds that issued from it, making the whole apartment shake (because Grand-mother was, to top it all off, pretty much deaf), and I hated the whole system of brainwashing that chattering tube repre-sented.

I think television with two channels—on one a political speech, on the other a Russian film—must be the cheapest and most inhuman means to effectively make people stupid. The overwhelming majority of average families would gather night after night in front of the television like chicks under their mother's wings. And while people regularly nodded off in their political and civic training classes, while no one paid any attention to the posters and slogans anymore, and our radio waves were subject to contamination, since it was pos-sible to listen to *foreign* stations, people sat down in front of the television almost as if before an altar. Families returned ahead of time from weekend trips, dinners were cooked early so as not to miss *it*—people *voluntarily* sat down before the glowing screen to allow that pre-ground propaganda that pen-etrated every type of broadcast like lead seeping into the groundwater to be crammed into their heads day after day. The average person, although battered by everyday reality, still gradually becomes saturated with this positive thinking. The average person no longer objected that the enthusiasti-cally constructive socialist spirit as portrayed in films and series was completely ass-backward; on the contrary: he al-ready half believed it. The "historical" films about the Slovak national uprising and about the postwar years, about the February Revolution, or even the "newsreels from the crisis years" of the era of the 1968 invasion, turned reality inside out with deliberate cynicism; those at the top relied heavily on the fact that humanity forgets; that if there are no records, then there is no past.

How true Goebbels's statement, that a lie repeated a thousand times becomes the truth!

Our bright tomorrow resembled Orwell's world: in each room a droning screen radiates enthusiastic, constructive sounds. And people without memory walk, do calisthenics, behave, and make love just as the screen directs them. Perhaps Orwell didn't really predict anything, perhaps he was really the author of it all, perhaps *1984* was our rulers' model. (Very few average people had ever heard of Orwell.)

My addicted grandmother sat in front of the screen day after day, and the poisonous, infectious sounds from the box permeated the apartment.

I was afraid those sounds would drive me insane, that I would start to believe them, that I would lose the ability to see their stupidity. Although seeing that stupidity would certainly drive me insane, I was almost insane already out of fear that I might lose sight of the stupidity.

I wanted to live differently.

I wanted to do something, something different from the norm; I rejoiced in the gypsy fights that went on in Nusle . . . I lived non-generically, on my own, because anything was better than grayness.

That television in the apartment was proof to me that we were petit bourgeois.

In fits of rage (which, thank God, became rarer and rarer) I'd wanted a hundred times to throw it out the window, together with the screaming old woman.

Patrik, by the way, never let me forget that it had been my own idea to buy that box in the first place. (Mrs. Fišer, of course, had a TV as well. Color. With a crocheted doily on top.)

Our six-year-old black-and-white fossil was already on its last legs. It took five minutes to warm up, it croaked hoarsely, and the picture fluttered. I'd taught Grandmother how to give it an expert thwack on the side to steady it. I didn't want to call in the repairman, and Grandmother (luckily) didn't know how to use a telephone.

I watched the television passing away with amazing ambivalence. I looked forward to being rid of it. But I also knew that I'd have to buy a new one before long. Because Grandmother could no longer exist without that tube.

Yes, we all had our own drugs. Our own methods of survival.

Grandmother had the Church and that television.

Patrik had his camera, Kryl, and women.

And I had hitchhiking.

3

I was twenty-five and people said I looked eighteen. Probably because I never let big worries get to me.

Or because my face didn't show it right away when they did.

Long-haired, blond, with hair a shade too dark to be just the shining color that gets blondes kidnapped in films. It was true: I had luxurious, sparkling hair, and only a little sprinkling of straw-colored gray prevented it from being truly export quality. In spite of that, I refused to bleach it. I had a somewhat round but still fairly delicate face, with pale eyelashes that cried out for mascara, though I refused to buy any. There was nothing wrong with my nose, except for a few little black freckles that had haunted its sides since adolescence, which I refused to powder over. So I wasn't exactly a femme fatale, though on the whole I had nothing to be ashamed of. I was exactly that type of woman who can make whatever she wants of herself, who, depending on makeup and clothes, can be anything from a homely girl to homecoming queen. The type that fashionable women, indeed all kinds of women, were itching to do something with. That type that requires just a little effort in order to look—as my grandmother used to say—"a hundred percent more marketable."

Of course I adamantly refused to be marketable.

In any sense of the word.

4

Obviously, of all my friends (or better to say acquaintances, since Patrik was really the only person I considered a friend at the time)—of all my acquaintances, only a negligible percentage were willing to tolerate the obsession with hitchhiking with which, in their opinion, I was afflicted.

Particularly among my fellow students in psychology I was known as a peculiar, detached individualist who often appeared at lectures or training sessions in muddy climbing boots with a huge backpack. I was known as an individualist no one knew anything about: as impossible to reach at home as she was impossible to convince, for example, to come to a class party.

I was three or four years older than my classmates, because after graduation—while Grandmother and I were living together on our own—I had to, as the saying goes, work for a living.

An eighteen- or twenty-year-old living on an "orphan's allowance," as these paltry alms were called in government offices, stood no chance of going to school, even if she wanted to more than anything in the world.

An eighteen- or twenty-year-old provided for only by an orphan's allowance stood some chance of surviving, perhaps, but no chance whatsoever of maintaining a grandmother in addition. I worked, so they took away my orphan's allowance, and there was no hope of my ever wresting it back from them. I worked, and it took me a couple of years before I discovered a means of subsistence that kept me, the apartment, and Grandmother more than just barely afloat.

In any case, it was four years before I even dared try to get into the university.

My fellow students were in a different situation. Misfortune had spared their families, and their lives ran straight and regular, as if drawn with a ruler. Perhaps the difference in years distanced them from me, or maybe it was my experience of life, which (for better or for worse) lifted me above these adolescents. In our third year, those naïve, playful freshmen suddenly started developing personalities. They'd all been around and seen enough to understand where the feeding trough was. Those carefree companions became careerists and rivals, hating one another without so much as a shrug. The most "daring" anti-Communist "rabble-rousers" of the first years were in many cases already in the Mother Party, a fact which some kept scrupulously secret, while others justified it on the grounds that there was nothing else you could do if you wanted to make anything of your life. Unfortunately, they were right, if all you wanted was a career and a well-paying sinecure that wouldn't degenerate into work.

The same moronic simpletons, sons and daughters of Party functionaries who had gotten into school, thanks only to the influence of their fathers or bribes deposited in the proper hands, could now end their smarter classmates' careers with a well-placed rubber stamp.

Meanwhile, many of those I'd gotten along with perfectly in the first year, because they'd seemed relatively mature, had gotten themselves drafted into the Party and now thought only of their careers; from other formless cocoons grew good, solid, honest people. But there were depressingly few of them. And they usually ended up getting into trouble with the Socialist Union of Youth (of which we were all required to be voluntary members) at the weekly meetings, until they were finally expelled from the SUY, and as a result from school as well. Most of us simply fell out of touch with them, and few people were interested in risking unpleasantness by having any further contact with them.

Oh yeah, they just didn't know how to play the game, commented those who did know.

I played the game. I sailed along without getting too close either to the swampy inlets of toadyism or to the rapids the dissidents boldly tumbled down on their makeshift rafts. I guided my little dugout through the currents of that oily, troubled river of life; I smelled the filth and putrefaction that choked it, but it seemed to me that the slime and ooze could never penetrate my skin. I'd already thought a fair number of things through and I knew that I wasn't interested in a career. I'd decided to go to school because I wanted to know. In psychology I saw a way of penetrating to my inner core and to the cores of others, a way of getting to know the world and people's souls. In time, I learned that the overwhelming majority of information forced into my head was a motley collection of censored nonsense, a sort of thin broth boiled from the works of scholars who'd lived before us and predigested in the spirit of dialectical materialism.

Which was the only philosophy officially allowed and required in our motherland.

A philosophy that I had nothing against in principle, but which in Czechoslovakia was somehow turned against itself: the dialectic, which was supposed to teach independent thinking, became dogma, pumped into our brains without discussion.

I should have studied biology or mathematics, both of which did actually interest me. Perhaps mathematics was beyond good and evil. Perhaps mathematics couldn't be made socialist, the way our psychology was. Who knows, though? I became convinced that even cartography could be seen as Communist or imperialist. On our world maps, for example, the cylindrical projection was used, which made the more northerly Soviet Union seem bigger and somehow optically more powerful at the expense of the United States. The conical projection was not considered class-conscious, because it favored America. It was bedlam.

As it turned out, our socialist psychology unfortunately had more in common with philosophy than I could ever have imagined at the outset. We learned things that probably would have made a real psychologist's hair stand on end in horror. Freud's book on sexual psychology could be bought only in a special bookstore upon presentation of student identification. And his most basic error, as we learned, was the overestimation of the individual personality in comparison with human society. Jung and his dreams they would have preferred to keep from us entirely, but since that couldn't be done, we at least found out gradually what an absolutely false notion the poor old man had of reality.

We had our own socialist psychology, which apparently towered head and shoulders above world, or reactionary, psychology. Of course, we had to accept this on faith, since there were no sources for this malignantly imperialist psychology available to us: it was only the rare Western journal of psychology that could be found in the libraries. There wasn't enough hard currency for the purchase of books and periodicals from the West, we were told. And so (when working on our papers, at times on attractive topics, but with foregone conclusions) we struggled to crack the Cyrillic code of *Psikhologicheskii zhurnal* and piece together citations from Western authors as melted down into short (and ideologically correct) Russian abstracts. In general, a lot of Western books reached us in this form: printed on bad paper in the ever unpopular

Cyrillic. Books without pictures, their texts shortened and "corrected." Fortunately, between those Russian lines, which in and of themselves weren't all that clear to us despite many years of language drills, it was possible to grasp quite a lot. And their massive forewords commented on Western authors' positions, admittedly only to trim them down to size, and (with slightly contemptuous compassion for the misguided pseudo-scholars of the West) make it clear exactly where they had gone wrong vis-à-vis the correct, that is Soviet, views.

But I didn't intend to stray so far from my story. In any case, I felt at home neither in that apartment with my grandmother nor among my peers in the classroom. The celebrations after exams and pub crawls through Prague usually degenerated into meaningless drunkenness, and as a rule, watching my sophisticated colleagues stagger, puking, back to their dorms didn't really enhance my opinion of them. I kept in touch with very few people from school.

But I had my hitchhiking, which was everything to me.

5

Of course, I checked out all kinds of people from all walks of life and social circles. This interested me from a psychological standpoint (I persuaded myself). In reality, I was an adventurer with wanderlust—not stupid, perhaps, but somewhat irresponsible. I couldn't stand being very long in one place (perhaps that's why I was always out somewhere on the road and never at home with my grandmother): I couldn't stand any one job for very long, any one group of friends or any one guy.

So I was always passing through.

Through the republic.

Through the mountains.

Through friends and acquaintances.

And also through men.

6

I tried all kinds of things.

I wormed my way in among people of all qualities and types. I took advantage of the flexibility of my face—and of my behavior.

I tried the "artistic set." I knew a few people who were painters, writers, poets, or musicians, or at least thought they were. I knew the trendiest of café societies, with their intellectual conversations, and I knew those rap sessions over beer or rum in the slimiest dives in Prague.

I knew bands of hikers with guitars and weekend treks in jeans in search of the call of the wild.

I knew the environs of Prague's "dregs" and their bars, I knew the hotel call girls, the cabdrivers, and the girls who so blatantly twirled their handbags on Wenceslaus Square in the late-night hours.

I was familiar with the splenetic gatherings of "highly placed" journalists and the little café open only to "representatives of the press." (As a matter of fact, I knew about this through a certain particularly offensive suitor who was eager to sleep with me and unfortunately succeeded.)

I was familiar with the working sessions of environmental conservationists, those desperate and sorrowful meetings of green-hearted people, where such terrible things came to light that if a single undercover cop had turned up among us, we probably all would have ended up behind bars.

I was familiar with Christian circles, where young people sought crutches other than sex and booze. I knew the warmth of those groups; I knew their serenity and equanimity, the inner joy they brought to believers. I knew of an overflowing church, where every Tuesday evening young people attended Mass and the cops stood by the entrance writing down the names on their IDs. I knew a guy who looked like

Christ, played guitar like God, and sang like an angel, but who got arrested for unauthorized (and untaxed) public performances (admission was free, of course)—and he went to jail for those wonderful, pious, "treasonous" lyrics of his.

I knew more than enough of such things.

Not everything, of course.

But I knew enough to realize that none of those lives lived within me.

I had the ability to flit from one set to another, but could never stick with any single one.

I guess I was a loner.

A loner of an unfortunate type that couldn't stand being alone for very long.

A loner who constantly needed new faces around her.

New acquaintances. New meetings and farewells. New places and new roads. And—as you might expect—new loves.

New adventures, new marvels, and new disappointments.

In other words, I needed hitchhiking.

7

I lay on the front seat of the Liazka, letting the motor rock me to sleep, listening to the rain and dreaming. We were now descending the serpentine road that cut down the mountainside in waves toward Moravská Třebová. White beech trunks flashed by in the windows. I sat up again, just so I could savor them. The yellowish lights of the rig licked the tall, slender, silvery-gray trees, rigid and gloomy as dancers frozen in midstep. At that moment I couldn't stop looking at them (in fact, I had never been able to). It was strange: every time, absolutely every time I rode through here, I recalled a certain moment from my childhood. The little East German Trabant diligently negotiates the hairpin turns, the rain; Father drives, skillfully and with exaggerated caution; drops of water collide on the windows, the air smells moist, and two little girls in the back seat trace the raindrops with their fingers. The streaming drops web the view, and the girls gaze out at the world with eyes full of wonder. The younger one occasionally touches her mother's back, warm and fragrant. She needs to reassure herself, confirm by touch that Mother is here, that she will turn to her, that she will reach back her gigantic hand so both children can grasp her fingers, like shipwrecked sailors reaching for floating beams. And the girls hold on, gripping the hand, as if they already feel the need to fight against the unfair, vertical force of time that separates age from age, mother from child. The children protest the force they will come to feel, even though it hasn't yet touched them. The family is returning from an outing; and along the road, bathed in a light summer shower, stand the bleached, tremendously tall trunks of the beeches, radiating light into the countryside.

That memory returned to me again and again, every time I descended that hillside with those silver beeches on the way down toward Třebová from the highway rest stop. For a long time I'd searched for this whitest of all beech stands; for years it seemed that it must have been just an image from a dream I had no right to consider a part of reality. Then later, when I actually discovered that piece of countryside after all, it was as if someone had laid a bouquet of rainbows at my feet.

How often I recalled it! I looked forward to it. Sometimes the countryside, a single stretch of land or section of road, will take root in your consciousness more deeply than things you encounter every day.

Those white, straight, unchanging beeches served to remind me that I, too, had once had a childhood.

As a matter of fact, it's strange how quickly and ungratefully a person can forget. Year after year, the faces of people close to me dissolved in my memory, and I purposely wouldn't look at their photographs because I knew how quickly such snapshots could take hold. They become etched in the mind and bury living images—dissolve them into nothingness. And I couldn't allow them to.

Only those trees . . . the whitest beeches in the entire republic . . . could trigger the flow of memories in me. I knew a couple of stretches of earth with this power. Sweet hidden springs of memories. Not melancholy memories, by any means.

So I could actually even be happy.

I could ride along through the rain in a strange yet familiar truck and recall sweetly how I, too, had once been young.

The wipers tenderly washed away the salty tears from my heart. The rain diluted the bitterness of my thoughts—and I could feel as safe and protected as in my mother's arms, which no longer existed. I was able to curl up blissfully in the sound of the motor and become someone else again for the instant.

8

I lay my head down again and thought about the magic of the Night Road.

I felt the Magic of Night between my knees: how it slowly rose up the insides of my thighs to warm my lap.

I thought about the Magic of Night and my heart began secretly to pound.

The Magic of Night surged inside my bra, making my nipples rise, like the caress of someone's tender, eager hand.

It was interesting how closely connected memories of childhood were with adult appetites; I pictured (behind closed eyelids) the driver's smile and his eyes . . . The color of someone's eyes never meant anything to me, but his gaze always stuck in my mind—I could always recognize a person by his look.

The driver had a translucent blue gaze. Perhaps a little common, but understanding and serene. The kind I liked.

My hair, with its familiar silky texture, lay in readiness over the gearshift. Soft and supple hair, telegraph wires, antennae, electrical connections transmitting the Magic of Night from me to the driver's hands.

No, I didn't pick men up on the road, and I didn't try to get picked up. I didn't collect men and experiences in a deliberate way. Insinuation was against my nature—and so far nothing much could have been inferred from my eyes or body language. I always left the decision to my precious Serendipity until the very last instant. But for a long time my electric hair had served as a wordless agreement between me and anyone who understood.

We were now passing through Třebová, and we had to downshift on the cobblestones of the town square. I breathed the damp fragrance of rain deep into my lungs, and I already felt the driver's strong (and familiar) hand absorbing the electricity from those golden strands. I was drowsy, aroused, snug.

Because when that hand again made its way down to the gearshift (where it no longer had any legitimate business) and waded through my gilded thicket all the way to my forehead, it was clear that our truck would be stopping at the familiar shadowy rest stop just outside of Olomouc tonight.

9

It was nice.

Yes, that's the right word: nice.

Not unforgettable, but it had a charm of its own; after all, I'd learned long ago to reject the most ordinary experiences in advance. This embrace didn't remind me of anything that had gone before; it didn't fill me with those deep, intrusive memories, as so often happened in less skillful arms. On the contrary, everything from the past was washed away, took its normal place in my mind—and the lovemaking alone won its rightful place.

Even the rest stop (which I knew well from other nights and which he must have known just as well) belonged to us alone that night, including the lights of passing cars, including the sound of the rain, including the rocking motion imparted to us by each passing truck. The cab belonged to us alone, secluded, secure.

We said nothing.

We both belonged to the distance, to restlessness, road dust, and unexpected adventures—this was so implicitly obvious that we didn't need to speak about it.

The driver was one of those who understand.

We were both molecules of a great, almost completely stifled, age-old longing. A longing more powerful than love or lust, a voracious longing for the freedom, horizon, and azure of those mountains near the border. I'd learned which people carried this longing within them. He had it. And so, since we were parts of the same whole, it was pleasurable to connect for an instant, but that wasn't the most important thing.

It was important to keep driving, to go farther, to continue living, to take off somewhere into the womb of never-ending highways, roads, and footpaths that converged at the vanishing point of the infinite.

At that moment I had the infinite within me.

I felt that living, magnificent, absurd, and useful physical appendage; I savored its penetration and felt the savage heartbeat pulsing within it. I savored my body and gave it up to be savored; I pressed myself into those wonderful arms, familiar and strange, like a cradle.

Sure, I knew perfectly well that each of us had learned every one of those supple, intoxicating motions in which we were joined from someone else, but that made no difference to us at the time. It was controlled lovemaking, certainly not one of a kind, but still, for that moment, unique.

Nestled in those firm, tender arms, caressing and desiring me, I thought simply of nothing.

And this, precisely this, was the unrepeatability I was always searching for, that fundamental, perfect, pure ecstasy of soul and body.

10

I didn't succumb to the wedding madness that had afflicted my entire class.

In our third year, at a time when, as I've already said, personalities were taking shape, the overwhelming majority of my once fickle classmates began pursuing serious relationships.

My former colleagues from high school had become worthy mothers long ago: they'd all fallen into it together, before they'd even turned twenty, and—convinced that it was necessary to atone for their sins—they couldn't pluck up the courage to present themselves before the abortion committee. They got married as a sort of afterthought, at times to men they didn't know all that well, because pregnancy loomed a lot larger than any vision of conjugal life. Sometimes they regretted being tethered so soon to diapers and the kitchen range, but they never forgave anyone who failed to procreate. They elevated parenthood to some kind of hereditary duty, the fate of the normal individual, who was forced to bear it with head bowed in gray acquiescence.

My clever university compatriots, however, took a more premeditated approach to marriage, duly weighing all the pros and cons; they judiciously chose the least unsuitable groom and then—as I interpreted it—they persuaded themselves they had real feelings for him.

The whole class was gripped by panic: hurry, girls, get him! Get hitched before the state boards or you're a rotten egg!

I didn't succumb to the universal hunting spirit, even though I have to admit that there really was a grain of truth to the graduation theory.

The "few good men"—just like in a provincial village!—were picked over one by one, so that in the eyes of the average woman the only men past the age of twenty-five who remained unmarried were worthless paupers, inveterate Casanovas, mother's boys, and one or two who had managed to get divorced and who, of course, were already paying alimony for two or three kids.

In the big picture, our little world really was a village, a hamlet of two hundred people and without much of a selection, where the easiest (and safest) thing to do was to find yourself a partner from the next cottage over and apply the screws until that happy wedding day.

No one wanted to remain single, and people were looking for security; they didn't want to take any chances. A sparrow in your palm is better than a pigeon on the roof.

So in our third year even extremely pretty and desirable girls were starting to get jumpy and to search, evaluating boys as husbands and as progressives, sending out wedding announcements or quietly envying their luckier friends who had already taken the plunge and were out of the woods of insecurity.

The objects of envy became men and husbands, instead of strong emotions, fulfillment, or good relationships. It was important to enjoy yourself enough in your youth and still manage to snare Mr. Right before the transition from young beauty to old maid. In our third year all these potential old maids were saddling up in droves for the hunting season.

Believe me, I didn't share in this universal marital frenzy. It goes without saying that the dismal specter of an aging world picked clean of men, who in and of themselves are quite worthwhile, did sometimes pass before my eyes, but somehow I never really recognized it. If there existed a person I'd want to stay with until the end of time, I'd find him eventually. I could wait. And if no such person existed in the whole wide world (which seemed more likely to me), then I could easily live out my life and die single. I was sure of that.

I wasn't looking for any security.

In a world fenced in by barbed wire—a world of filth, sickness, and radioactivity, a world as tired and worn as a pair of jeans that haven't been washed for five years—the concept of security was absurdly subjective.

The security seekers were desperate escapists; they sought shelter from the hurricane under their bedsheets; at the sight of blood they closed their eyes and plunged their ostrich heads into the sands of their private wastelands. In the shadow of the mushroom cloud they scratched out little trenches in their gardens and brought their one-and-onlies home hand in hand, to have someone to lean on.

I wasn't looking for the security of anyone's embrace: to my taste, that was too high a price to pay in jealousy and captivity. I didn't need any of that. For me the most beautiful security was serendipity.

The serendipity that ruled everywhere.

The serendipity of the rainbow.

The magnificent, alluring, dangerous, and dependable Serendipity of the road.

Serendipity, whose only law was that she brought you the most iridescent adventures precisely when you expected them least and wanted them most.

The serendipity of the instant, who could give you anything, as long as you knew how to obey her.

And in this I saw the possibility of being truly happy.

While my peers sought shelter and pseudo-security, I was learning to live for the moment. That immediate instant that passes away but always leaves its imprint on the consciousness. That instant, profound but not heavy, without obligation. Magical in its lack of context.

You might object that too great a number of momentary memories causes life to splinter. To swerve off course. To lose its unity and direction. But that's exactly what we wanted. In the face of that prefabricated blueprint that sought to entrap us like little screws in a machine in a factory dedicated to the destruction of the world and the eradication of rainbows, Patrik and I armed ourselves with our philosophy of instants. Yes, from our childhood we had hunted those multicolored, uncontrolled, unexpected instants, sweet and bitter alike, and the more of these instants we caught, the more we wanted to catch and the better we got at it.

11

I lay in the truck on the cot (which was both strange and familiar) and experienced the instant.

The tiny cabin light shone above our heads (because sometimes you've got to give all the senses a chance, not just touch), and I wondered whether the shadows on the curtain that concealed us had revealed any of our intimacy: the hilly landscape of my heaving breasts as I lay on my back; his torso and his trembling head as he supported himself over me on one elbow, stroking my stomach with somewhat proprietary tenderness.

I sprawled out, domesticated, on the single cot, formed my lips into a half smile—and engaged all my senses, one after the other, so that the image of the day would sink in as deeply as possible.

I'd already checked out the situation, the dazzlingly white light illuminating the fluid on my raised hand, the shadows darkening into the background beyond my legs, and the almost unreal shifting colors of twilight.

And the face, with its pleasant (and now partly closed) eyes and overly large nose, whose elongated black shadow created a disturbing and harsh effect, artificially comical, like a circus clown. I touched the veins on his temple with my index finger, the moist dew of sweat caressed my fingertip, and beneath it I could feel the flow of blood. Touch. I closed my eyes, and with only red and yellow circles from the light penetrating my eyelids, I explored the skin of that strange familiar body with my free hand, and with my buttocks I registered the slightly sticky impression of the synthetic-fabric sleeping bag underneath me. It was hot, steaming hot. I cooled my shoulder on the iron wall behind me, gratefully remembering the people who made the Liazka, who couldn't upholster it, even with cheap vinyl. In a Volvo or Mercedes you had to open a window, but the Liazka was permeable to the night coolness. I could taste the difference in temperature between the sweaty supple body next to me and that sheet-metal panel. I inhaled.

The ever-present smell of dust. The overpowering, almost suffocating, deliciously animal concentration that requires at least two (but there were more!) physical scents. The smell of the worn blanket, and the distant smell of night, passed on to us through the window, opened a crack to the universe.

The smell of oil. Not unpleasant.

Whiffs of old, familiar smells, smells of the road, smells that cropped up in every cab of every truck on that Northern Road of ours. Common odors and odors all their own. Forgotten, but recalled upon in every subsequent encounter.

(I've never collected souvenirs. Gifts, rings, earrings.

But if I could, I'd save whiffs of beautiful nights in a little pouch on my chest, the way Indians keep the scents of the prairie.)

All the while, large and small raindrops had been drumming on the resonant metal roof. It was possible to hear each of the largest, less frequent drops as it burst on the metal, scattering a rosette of smaller drops. The roof answered the watery assault onomatopoetically, and the resulting performance was musical and balmy.

I listened to the car engines which appeared on the auditory horizon, changed pitch like an approaching bumblebee or helicopter, then whizzed by, rocking us gently before buzzing off into the distance.

The driver whispered compliments in his warm Central Slovak, and I smiled gently, like a beautiful woman who has just been well laid. And in fact, I had been well laid, and I wanted to let him know, but I wasn't sure yet what method I would choose.

I had saved the sense of taste for last, and I licked his chapped lips, the lips of a man, lips that had proved they could be attentive and tender to me. I caressed his cheek with my cheek; it was rough, and he sheepishly ran his hand through the stubble, making it rustle. I tasted the sweat on his throat and shoulder, and that completed my experience of the instant.

But on my left hand his seasoned, gorgeous sperm lay cooling and drying.

I spread it over my palm and played with it.

"You've got the most beautiful sperm I've ever seen in my life," I said. "Fragrant, smooth, pearly, and sparkling. Gorgeous sperm, a man's sperm."

He didn't believe me.

Of course, in a certain sense he was right not to believe me, since I had a reserve of such absolute confidences for everyone I met; I expected my nocturnal friends to divide every compliment by the coefficient of transience, the way I always did.

But he really was listening to me, letting it all pass through his head, and I (as I rambled on) realized that I was raising for him the colored arc of a new rainbow.

"You've got gorgeous sperm," I whispered, and in the light of the little lamp I revealed to him the magic of its translucent, milky sheen. I showed him those millions of invisible, vivacious little creatures. "Sperm is a source of both hope and fear. Some administer sperm as a life-giving elixir, because it contains life and is infected with life; some throw it away, rid themselves of it, wipe it off on a rag, despise it. Sperm is the bearer of life and death. Sperm is conception or contamination. Sperm is the union of animal juices; sperm is the seal of an eternal bond or complete nonsense. It's up to you how you look at it: sperm is everything. I love it . . ."

I didn't finish. Actually, I was interrupted. Because he took off on a journey down my body. And while he caressed and licked all those gorgeous, erogenous nooks he hadn't yet explored, I could concentrate only on his eager, grasping lips.

I watched.

He held my hips in his arms and it was wonderful to see those tanned and muscular veined hands on my skin. I watched. He was in no hurry.

I was in no hurry either; I felt safe in his warm, calloused hands.

And then, when he took me again, perhaps more tenderly than the first time, I knew that I had succeeded after all in awakening in him the rainbow that would unite us throughout the rainy night, until daybreak.

He held me in his arms like a little girl, like a doll, sheltering me from the world and its tragedies, and I felt like crying.

I came again and then again, until I was weak as a baby, and he smiled down at me and kept me safe.

Then, when the pleasure was too much, he suddenly rose up over me, and with his penis in both hands he delivered an arc of semen onto my body. It was a gift.

"There you are," he said softly and tenderly. I cried out.

And although there was a void in me after him, I kept crying out while he intently, carefully, spread that frothy, mysterious substance over my stomach, my breasts, my face. I could feel my skin growing taut and beautiful, and again I sensed those indescribable hot waves and shudderings that freed me from the pain of the world.

Always for an instant.

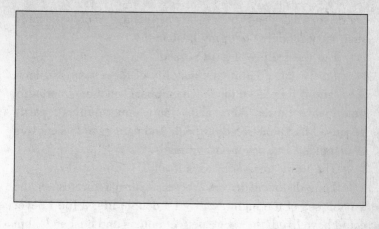

1

He let me off outside Poprad in the morning, and it was nice of him not to try to flatter an address out of me or arrange a rendezvous a month later at the fifth streetlight in Čadca or somewhere. Few of his colleagues, either before or after him, seemed to find parting so easy: most would begin wavering doubtfully about what might be the right thing to do, and I didn't much care for that.

A quick kiss, a door slam, and there I was outside in the deserted early-morning reality, and that suited me just fine. Only when the (familiar) ocher yellow semi had snorted off toward Prešov with one last hoot of its horn, only then did it strike me that neither one of us even knew the other's name or age; most likely he was married, but for that one night there had been no need to raise the issue.

I'd already decided a long time ago (however selfishly and simplistically) that it didn't matter if someone was married or not. It certainly made no difference to me, personally. I had more of a problem with their wives, with whether it was morally right for me to let their husbands sleep with me. The feeling of guilt was pretty unambiguous at first: I could imagine that I myself (in the wife's shoes) wouldn't have been too thrilled about a girl who spent her nights collecting and counting drivers like beads on a rosary of sins and could engage in such easy infidelity with my husband.

But the feeling of guilt passed.

Partly out of habit (the majority of these men had families, and if I'd placed too much emphasis on that, I certainly would have turned down many more opportunities), partly because I had penetrated the souls and natures of these lovers of distances and never-ending roads.

The word "distance" says it all.

Long-distance drivers, these nocturnal pirates on the asphalt sea of the highway, lived a double life, a life I never could have lived: they were perfect fathers and husbands, but they needed the road, too. Their families were their ports, the road was their ocean.

Whatever happened on the road belonged to the road; the truckers knew the rest stops, dives, and secret places; they knew girls who, like me (although with altogether simpler goals), cruised the republic; the truckers knew how not to drag their experiences from one life into the other.

Their adventures on the road became legends for their wives, the same way recollections of storms, reefs, and siren songs become legends for the wives of sailors. The wives seldom came along. The truckers would return home with the stamp of Never-Never Land, and only very rarely with the clap. The truckers knew how to live and how to keep their mouths shut, so the majority of them managed to combine a relatively happy marriage (quite an accomplishment) with the rich life of the sailor of asphalt waves, a life rich in just those kinds of events that rarely coincided with marriage.

I obediently accepted my role in these highway adventures and never transgressed the prescribed boundaries. It was pleasant for both parties—and after a short time I became completely at ease, stopped thinking about the other women, and followed the script.

*   *   *

So the night ended near Poprad, and in the distance the snowy Tatras played hide-and-seek with me from behind veils of mist. The sun rolled up over the horizon like a flaming orange billiard ball, and the colossal full moon—more silver than the sun—slipped slowly around the corner of visibility. It was a crisp, cold morning and the bitterness of the air penetrated to the bone; I shivered, but a fair store of cabin warmth remained inside my parka. I wiped the sleep from my eyes with my fists and felt them regaining that innocent transparency they always had after the best and least innocently spent nights.

Fresh puddles still stood on the road, but it hadn't rained for a long time—and innocent little Fialka hoisted her pack over her shoulder, preparing to head for the mountains, for her work. For her livelihood.

2

In a series of panting little coal trucks I finally made it to Tatranská Lomnica. The valleys were already thawed, but there was still skiing on the hillsides; precisely that waterlogged, burgeoning time of spring when I could go searching for my saffron.

Yes, today I was out for saffron. Year after year, from the very first bloom, I hunted all the flowers as they sprouted and blossomed in turn and used them to expand and fill my files.

My livelihood, my (private) business, and perhaps even my more or less undisputed "reputation" among the professional photographers who silently and vehemently despised me were based on the fact that my photo files of the natural world contained absolutely everything.

From the very first bloom of spring, year after year, harnessed with my old East German Pentacon, I headed into the mountains.

The camera and flash had been left to me by my parents, and I blew thousands every year on Agfachrome, the only decent color film you could get in the Czechoslovak Socialist Republic.

It was worth every penny.

I had already mastered the technical side of photography. My equipment wasn't the best, but it was good enough: I knew my little Pentacon and all its quirks. We were used to one another. Time after time I'd lugged my twenty pounds of camera equipment into the forests and mountains—and although I knew there was considerably better equipment weighing half as much in other countries, I didn't complain. I didn't complain when the shutter sometimes refused to close (ruining my best shots, of course); I didn't complain when the Pentacon got a little cold and the flash wouldn't go off, and on cold or windy days I'd warm it under my parka against my belly like an Eskimo child. I didn't even complain when the processing lab ruined the film; I sent the most important rolls to this one laboratory only in small batches—and I danced for joy whenever, after weeks of tense anticipation, I actually received the slides, intact and unspoiled. I would cut them up and insert them into their little frames and many a night I would project them on a sheet hung on the wall and derive intense pleasure from them. Photos taught me how to see: what a fantastic object, for example, a three-foot oak spangle is! I examined all the glimmerings and shadows; those gorgeously overgrown images of Mother Nature in my bedroom made the world beautiful.

For the last few years I'd limited myself almost exclusively to photomacrography. Of course, I'd dabbled in landscapes, wildlife photography, travel reportage, and portraits, too. But photography with a flash and extension tubes was my greatest weapon.

Exposure time and lighting were already a part of my

eye, as were the cropping and enlargement a shot would require. I knew how, with the help of a cardboard shadow box (which I dragged around on my back, naturally), to photograph into oncoming light and how to capture each natural object precisely and in the context which suited it best.

And what's most important, I knew how to see.

When, at the age of nineteen, I completely unexpectedly succeeded in breaking into professional circles, it seemed like a miracle to me. I simply brought my photos in to a certain editorial office—and lo and behold, they liked them! What for many requires pleading, bribes, or long years of struggling came to me with almost no effort at all. I was lucky, of course: at the time when I walked in, they needed some images of mushrooms, which I happened to have with me. Every year after that, the publishers would send me a list of photos they required, and every year I would bring them a whole armload.

The professionals didn't stand a chance. The list of photos would arrive in November, and they had to respond by January. That meant having the shots already in hand, which was beyond the powers of anyone without a genuine interest in nature.

What's more, those professional photographers, locked up in their perfect studios, never so much as batted an eye over the correspondence of their shots to reality.

If they were assigned the indigo-blue boletus, the pros would shoot it in a garden, in garish juxtaposition with rhododendron. The pros would plunk a swallowtail caterpillar down on a rose or blithely photograph dead butterflies or moths. True, they didn't fly away, but they didn't look too alive either.

At the age of nineteen, as if by the wave of a magic wand, I'd managed to capture a big chunk of the Czechoslovakian market—and I held on to it.

And since the market was not infinitely large, it didn't surprise me when the pros couldn't bring themselves to utter the name of this brazen, snot-nosed upstart.

It pleased me.

It pleased me even more when one of the selecting editors, one of the most important ones, one who had the power of veto, learned from me the incredulous question he then submitted to my rivals upon examining their oh-so-pretty photographs of pastel pseudo-realities: "And this shot was actually taken in natural surroundings?!"

3

Enveloped by the perfumed breeze from the mountains, I made my way up the hillside behind Lomnica. I had no interest in using the chair lift that day. I had a long trek ahead of me, since I'd decided to make the rounds of all my favorite saffron meadows; it would take all of today, and probably most of tomorrow, but I was looking forward to it.

I looked forward to my annual saffron quest.

Yes, the years rolled by, repeating themselves—and I went, according to the seasons, on snowdrop excursions; on spring and summer wild-snowflake treks; on orchid, iris, anemone, and rose expeditions; on occasional outings in search of whatever flowers I might find, or in search of botanical monstrosities.

I didn't just photograph.

I sought out deformed plants, rare and unheard-of concrescences of flowers and stalks, dandelions with two heads, tulips with eight petals, snowdrops with bizarre and mutilated blooms.

I judged my success or failure on the basis of these monstrosities.

Year after year, week after week, I headed out into the mountains and valleys, into the forests, farm tracts, hills and meadows, searching for mutated flora and gathering statistics about them.

In dozens, perhaps hundreds, of slides I documented odd colors and forms, abnormally structured blossoms, botanical dwarfs, and giants.

I knew dozens of nooks and secluded spots—and in a large body of statistics (the more I gathered, the more telling they became) I documented these diseased flowers.

Precisely because they were diseased.

4

We lived in an age of documentation.

We lived in an age when the meaning of life for many people lay in accumulating documentation about life in the present in order to pass it on to future generations or to smuggle it out to the West.

We lived in an age when photographers of events in the streets were led off in droves to the police station, where their film was ripped out of their cameras and they were asked to sign statements about their conduct. Patrik was not the only one who exhausted his youth in the effort to document.

"Dissident" photographers documented the same way dissident graphomaniacs wrote for the drawer and amateur musicians composed songs for which they could have been (and often were) locked up. And a few lucky semi-tolerated ones from among the ranks of the dissatisfied, who were allowed some limited public exposure, documented allegorically, transmitting their message to an audience who understood perfectly, who saw things just as clearly as they themselves did.

Yes, the semi-tolerated performances by songwriters or actors on the smallest (and most beloved) Prague stages were the officially sanctioned outlet valve on an overheated boiler, the escape valve designed to let off the pressurized steam which otherwise might have blown the entire pressure cooker to shreds. Within certain, very narrow limits it was possible to speak out, but the main things, the essential things that tormented us most, could only be documented.

Made as secretly understandable as possible.

Many households concealed piles of documents, most of them worthless, but nevertheless heroically safeguarded for the generations that (hopefully) would come after us.

Those who lived in the country buried their documents in their gardens beneath the roots of apple trees, the way pirates used to hide their plunder.

People stored forbidden books in their libraries in the dustjackets of children's books about Ferda the Ant, and albums by Kryl lurked among their musical classics.

Patrik kept everything in his sofabed, and many preserved their stores of dangerous materials right out in the open. There were probably anti-government documents to be found in almost every apartment.

I had some, too, of course.

But the most flagrant, the most damning of my documents lay innocently concealed in a cabinet among my photos. There was nothing forbidden in them, and even a surprise search of the apartment could have resulted in no trouble for me.

While many ferreted away records of dying illusions or dying people, I accumulated documents about our dying earth.

It was painful.

It grew more and more painful all the time.

5

I remember clearly how we used to gather four-leaf clovers a long time ago.

My sister, myself, Mother, and sometimes even my

television-crazed grandmother, before she became television-crazed. In a meadow, green and fragrant with summer, the attentive figures crawl on all fours and peer carefully into the clover.

It takes a while.

Half an hour or more.

Then one of the crouching figures jumps up with a four-leaf clover in hand: "I've got one! I've got one! A lucky clover!"

We pressed them, stuck them beneath the plastic covers of our tram passes, we would give them to one another lovingly, with a wish for happiness.

It was a naïve, delightfully playful, childish game.

My grandmother recited:

> *Four—your beau is at the door;*
> *five—the children soon arrive;*
> *six—then happiness comes quick;*
> *seven—pleasure, as in heaven;*
> *eight—for sorrow at the gate;*
> *nine—is for a marriage fine;*
> *ten—you'll meet a bitter end.*

Of course, we didn't believe that old nursery rhyme, but the symbol of the lucky four-leaf clover can't be erased from my mind. When Šárka had already started seeing boys and I still "had some time left," I hunted four-leaf clovers with redoubled passion: "Four—your beau is at the door."

But after the trip from which my parents and sister never returned, I was unable to hunt four-leaf clovers any longer: luck had not smiled on our family.

And I was aging, no longer thinking of four-leaf clovers or staining my knees in the clover patch. My good fortune was already elsewhere, if it existed anywhere on earth.

But those clovers came back to me, with a completely different meaning.

6

That clover patch had been a fallow field, and before that a cornfield, and before that a semi-steppe, an uncut meadow where anemones grew.

The meadow had once belonged to one of the nature preserves in the Bohemian Karst—and thanks to the anemones, it had been one of the preserve's feature attractions for us.

That was when I was still very young.

Every year we would drive out to Anemone Meadow in Father's little Trabant—and we were overjoyed by the shaggy blue beauties as they pushed up out of the earth, lifted their fuzzy buds, and bloomed with the slow majesty of the xerophytic flower.

We wondered at our anemones, watching the way they followed their stereotypical, unchanging, but never tiring cycle of life, how the curved deep-blue flowers rose upon becoming fertilized and how they filled the wind with dozens of ripening, almost weightless seeds, each borne by its own whitely feathered wing.

The seeds rarely germinated, they rarely landed on a hospitable piece of earth; there were no longer very many anemones here, and we had them all counted, so that we could assure ourselves that our little dears were still alive, that they would bloom again.

For Šárka and me this was like a religious ritual, the silent and magnificent celebration of spring.

Then the machines came.

They had no business entering the meadows. The preserve was not liquidated in one of the regular agrocultural paroxysms, like the campaign with the slogan "Not an arable acre nor a single grain shall be wasted!" But the cooperative farmers simply plowed the stony field under and planted it with corn, the Crop of Progress.

Voices were raised in protest from the ranks of the conservationists, but they were soon silenced: the little stone markers signifying the boundaries of the preserve went unnoticed by the cooperative farmers, and the land was already being farmed.

And so, instead of anemones, the field was filled with crops. The Crop of Progress, as I've said. Comrade Khrushchev once announced that of all crops corn had the greatest yield per hectare, and so it happened that the progressive thing to do was to plant it everywhere it would grow, and even where it wouldn't.

The fatted corn vegetated in all the usable river lowlands. Corn occupied every tract of moderately fertile land in Bohemia—and sickly, stunted stalks of this southern grain resolutely, if not too successfully, harrowed even the frost and gale winds of steep mountainsides in traditional potato country.

To make a long story short, corn was planted everywhere. In spite of this, no one ever saw an ear of corn, a loaf of cornbread, or a pinch of corn flour on sale anywhere—and the kernels for everyone's favorite popcorn, which was sold here and there in Prague, were said to be imported. At our northerly latitude (and easterly longitude!) corn, a biennial spring crop, was planted in the fall, and the next summer the scrawny, immature rows were already cut and chopped for livestock fodder. My beloved Lost Meadow suffered a similar fate.

(At the time we were already accustomed to calling my childhood field the Lost Meadow, and so I've always called it that—to this day with sadness.)

The cooperative farmers battled for three years.

For three years they heaped and piled rocks around the

perimeter; for three years they cleared that little layer of supposedly arable land below the gravel and above the mineral ores. For three years the tractor drivers abused their dulled plowshares (and, no doubt, the chairman of the Standard Farming Cooperative, too)—then they gave up.

The field—by now indisputably the property of the cooperative—had become a vacant lot. Weeds began to grow, and so it looked as if, through the natural processes of dozens of years, this lot might (perhaps) someday regain some semblance of its native vegetation.

We returned many times to look at it.

We returned to watch the regenerative power of nature; we appreciated her ability to heal the wounds we humans had inflicted on her.

But we quickly realized that something wasn't quite right with the lot. Where one expected a mix of all kinds of weeds and wildflowers, only a couple of species were growing. There were no dandelions or poppies, no quick-growing chrysanthemums, which in a year or two inevitably take over any patch of earth left vacant. On the contrary, the growth in the lot was limited to common weeds, which had entwined their long, inexterminable roots around every stone you lifted. Besides these weeds, the odd leaf of grass sprouted here and there—and that was all. Nothing in the lot flowered in the colors of the rainbow, no golden dandelions glowed in the distance, and there were no daisies with petals for me to count carefully (because I never tore them off) in order to learn the dubious truth of whether or not that certain pubescent someone, whom I can't even recall, loved me or loved me not.

It was strange.

What's more, around the field's perimeter all the sage had shriveled up, and along the border of the little forest that surrounded the lot the trees were beginning to wither and die.

This answered the question: to clear their newly won field the cooperative farmers had used a herbicide that selectively exterminated dicotyledonous plants, so that no weeds would grow among their corn. They'd probably dusted it on (perhaps more than once) by plane. That's why the poison had hit the field's perimeter and the edges of the forest. And if even the dandelions couldn't survive it, it must have been a formidable dose of some pretty damned merciless crap.

I shook with rage and impotence at the image of that terrible, nameless toxic substance seeping deeper and deeper into the earth, penetrating through the limestone into the groundwater and poisoning the streams and wells. The poison would be sucked into the minerals and water like lethal drugs into human veins. The pollution would accumulate and multiply, and earth, which speaks only by allusion and only to those who understand her, would endure all this and submissively waste away.

In time the herbicide in the Lost Meadow became somewhat diluted, and the lot sprouted with the normal, expected profusion of flora. Then the collective farms plowed it under again and planted it with clover for feed.

I went out walking in that succulent, healthy-looking clover. I crawled through it on all fours, and its brownish-green pigment stained my knees. I crouched down and I couldn't believe my eyes: in the whole field there wasn't a single three-leafed clover! In my Lost Meadow, wounded and poison-soaked, there grew clover with four and five leaves, with six, seven, and eight leaves, and eerie concrescences of stalks from which sprouted solitary mutant leaves.

I crawled through the meadow yard by yard and, in a vain, desperate, academic attempt to make a record of it, I wrote down the numbers and percentages of everything deformed.

These were no longer lucky four-leaf clovers.

From that time forward I documented monstrosities—and they terrified me.

7

I've never really been sure where natural variability ends and disease begins. Certain changes in the number of petals or stamens, the concrescence of flowers in certain plants can frequently, I am told, be caused by sudden changes in temperature.

By something which was here long before human interference.

It is possible that some of those mutants were truly natural. After all, while all things must have their order, they also have their exceptions—and not every diseased area stuck out as glaringly as my clover field. It was necessary to understand the patterns, and they weren't simple. The phenomena were statistical, like the occurrence of cancer among groups of people exposed to gamma radiation. The plants were sick, but I still couldn't tell exactly how sick they were. I longed for studies of the deformed sakura cherry trees in Hiroshima and Nagasaki, I longed for statistical data, which it seemed did not exist. Or was inaccessible. I needed to know—and just like every other time I needed to know something in Czechoslovakia, it looked as if I'd have to do all the research myself.

So I did.

There were deformed plants in saffron fields in the relatively clean areas of the Tatras, and very few people made the connection when I told them that in the Váh valley, in its meadows polluted by water from the pulp mill and choked with chemical runoff from the fields, there were much higher percentages of these deformities.

Few people believed it when I told them that the wild snowflakes on the banks of filthy streams in the valleys were more diseased and altered than those in the mountain meadows.

People just didn't believe it.

Or didn't want to believe it; it was more comforting not to think about it. Even the conservationists concerned themselves only with the plants closest to extinction.

And after all, flowers were still growing.

8

I was terrified.

And this was perhaps the only fear I'd ever known, fear for Mother Nature. People are like little puppies, they bite their own mother's ears in cruel and childish ignorance. But the bitch whines and snaps at her offspring. Perhaps Mother Nature was complaining, too, but we refused to hear her.

We failed to protect her.

And I didn't want to protect myself, either: my desire for perfect contact reached the point where I wanted to taste the poison: I didn't protect myself and was pointlessly, fruitlessly proud of it. This was actually foolishness, a pose, because I refused to think about what might happen later, when . . .

I inhaled the filthy, ash- and fume-contaminated pseudo-air that fell to the earth from factory smokestacks.

I traveled to Kolín to cover myself in soot and to sample the nauseating stench of the oil pools seeping into the pavement around a certain chemical plant outside the city.

I wept over the small skeletons of birds who had mistaken the surface of these asphalt puddles for drinking water.

I went hunting around the rubbish heaps near Kladno, because they were radioactive. I convinced myself I was studying the way the dandelions and first blades of grass took root in this dead wasteland. But in reality I went there for the invisible particles that carried death. I didn't want to protect myself from them, either.

I went swimming in the Vltava downriver of Krumlov, not to show off, as some people I knew supposed when I dissolved my bathing suit and skin in the foam and nauseating stench of sulphurous lye from the paper factory. I needed to make contact, to redeem with my own body all mankind's evil. I longed to atone for my own complicity by sacrificing myself.

I could feel the filth and stink and poisonous gases seeping into me; every cell was becoming saturated with the essence of death, and the blood flowing in my veins was becoming contaminated.

I wanted to contaminate myself, because contamination was like contact, and it gratified me that deep within me, in spite of all that pollution and contamination, some pure inner essence (which grew purer all the time) remained unchanged.

Both Patrik and I had this essence.

And the only thing that could actually hurt us was when we found the iridescent essence within ourselves to be a little grayer and less inspired than we might have wished.

9

I wandered through the springtime Tatras in the Age of Documentation and strained all my senses to make contact with the mountains' delicate wonders.

Perhaps only transient things, like rainbows, could seem beautiful to me.

I searched for my saffron meadows; I counted, photographed, and documented. Although upon deeper reflection there was absolutely nothing to be glad about, in some selfish personal sense I felt utterly free, happy, and at peace.

1

Spring was passing, just like any other year—and just like any other year I headed out of town down those familiar roads to hunt snowdrops and wild snowflakes, anemones and orchids—and just like any other year I accumulated botanical documentation in hundreds of photos on my shelves and personal documentation in the tactile cells of my skin. As in any other year, life zigged and zagged according to the adventures my friend Serendipity laid at my feet. Like any other year I gathered the fleeting and magnificent experiences in my arms and accepted the small thrills and dangers excitedly or calmly, for they formed an inseparable part of the Iridescent Extraordinary.

Life continued along its path, a path which could not be called conventional, yet which proceeded so automatically that without my eccentricities, without my quest for contamination and rainbows or without hitchhiking, I probably couldn't have existed.

I didn't even notice that I was also getting older.

2

Most of my classmates already had had their wings clipped and were building nests.

Almost everyone "had someone," while I wanted everyone and no one; I gave myself to Serendipity and took what she gave, and I couldn't imagine myself with someone else's rope around my neck.

Of course, a few times I had tried going out with a guy and even living with one. Maybe I never found the right one, maybe I didn't know how to fall in love for real and let down my guard, but in any case, it had never worked out quite right.

I forgave my short-term lovers: they quietly entered their names on my skin and none of them ever asked anything of me afterward. I never had to be jealous about the past or future, because there wasn't any; I never had to confess to these serendipitous men, never had to adapt—and all those ticklish moments, except for sex, were reduced to hellos and goodbyes. It was easy that way.

As I've said, I had tried to take things beyond that, but aside from boredom, sadness, and difficulties, there wasn't anything more in it for me. I had been selfish: I had wanted to possess them hook, line, and sinker, but (out of calculated self-interest) I had never been able to surrender myself completely. I had been jealous, and I had always wanted to know things, which in fact annoyed me later on, when I realized how petty and small those pangs of acquisitiveness were. Sometimes I had been jealous of the future, afraid that I would lose him (many times it had been someone I'd already broken up with in my soul); and I had been jealous of the past, also, under the stubborn and painful impression that perhaps the women before me had found his soul more sensitive and his heart less hardened than it had become.

I found attempts to make me more settled and more rational repressive, and no matter how strong my feelings for a man, I had always felt uneasy about the blank spaces left behind by the chance occurrences and contacts that slipped between my fingers while I attempted to be faithful.

I'd already known for some time that the simplest and most exciting thing would be to live without obligations, and so I lived without them.

To live without obligations, at least without artificial ones, that was Patrik's and my credo.

Still, I don't think we were bad people; we didn't consider ourselves to be the kind of unreliable good-for-nothings most people thought we were.

We wanted to see things.

We wanted to live.

And whenever we could, to help, or at least to document.

We were simply cynical and naïve hunters of the rainbow.

3

It was Tuesday again, the day almost defined by my weekly visit to Patrik, and I lay stretched out on the bed in his cubbyhole, listening reverently to Kryl.

Lately it had begun to seem to me that Mrs. Fišer was welcoming me even more vociferously than usual, and I tried with annoyance to think about what I might have done to incur this new (and even greater) wrath.

But there were more important things on the day's agenda.

Patrik still couldn't get an erection, and although nervous Patrik knew very well how to handle himself in front of his parents, I had a suspicion that Mrs. Fišer had finally guessed that something was up (or not up), thanks to the pedagogical-maternal instinct she undeniably possessed.

It seemed as if that self-assured fourteen-year-old had proved all too fateful for Patrik: since that incident (it had been about three months already) Patrik hadn't even attempted to test his member on anyone else. Besides that, other things were going wrong with him, and they had him running from examination to blood test to examination. Meanwhile, it was beginning to seem to him that all those sealed hospital envelopes and file folders (stapled shut, since the patient never had the right to know what was actually wrong with him) must have contained something highly unpleasant.

Patrik kept going to work and fiddling around with his bare hands among the stinking slime-clogged pipes, among the excrement-filled bowels of the buildings, and using a philosophy of life remarkably similar to mine, this intimate contact with human feces put him in some pleasantly disgusted moods.

Patrik continued to be a good plumber, even though he'd stopped putting the moves on women at every occupational opportunity; and if his boss wanted to send him to fix a blown washer on the faucet in one of the apartments whose plumbing he already knew more than intimately, he now preferred to trade with a colleague and replace the main waste pipe, because this job was in the basement. There were no women in the basement.

Patrik was simply refusing to tempt fate, which was unlike him.

In some kind of vestigial attack of puberty (or so it seemed to me), he merely dragged about ten pounds of porno magazines up to the apartment and carefully cached them in the sofabed. I don't know how much they cost him. Probably a lot. I allowed myself only to remind him that he could have gotten up to three years for that, which didn't make any difference, of course, since if they came to search the apartment he would wind up in jail anyway. Patrik claimed that in his old age he needed magazines to find the kind of inspiration no garden-variety woman had to offer. But these frantic attempts to muster a hard-on seemed pathological to me. He'd never shown any bent for such things before.

Patrik's physical and mental condition still didn't seem critical to me. Of course, I was making a big mistake, because I was comparing his soul to that of an average person and Patrik had never been average in any way. It hit me only later how egocentric I was being, how psychologically naïve I was in thinking Patrik's condition was just the result of his wounded sense of pride accompanying the collapse of his self-image as macho Casanova of Humanity. In reality, Patrik had never been a macho Casanova, and I had rashly (and hostilely) classified him among them simply because my spiritual vision was incapable of accurately imagining what it would be like to be impotent.

I was simply a woman—and a bad psychologist on top of that—a fact I was proving all too well week after week after week.

At the time, of course, I didn't realize it.

4

Patrik brewed some strong tea and brought it to me in his cubbyhole, because I preferred not to show myself in Mrs. Fišer's kitchen.

"You're beautiful, Fial," he said.

I dipped my spoon into the cup, and when I removed it, I watched it steam. The steam began only a little distance from the spoon, and the translucent, iridescent corona fascinated me. I let the first hot drop trickle onto my tongue and savored its deep tan color. Patrik was a master at making tea!

"I'm not beautiful," I said. "I'm getting old and pretty matronly. Not to mention that most women my age at least use a little makeup, but I find it completely and totally disgusting."

Patrik looked at me calmly and watched as I blew on another spoonful of black tea, poured it down my throat, and savored the heat flowing pleasantly toward my stomach.

"Sometimes I even think that I should do something about my appearance, but I'm way too lazy."

"You're beautiful to me," Patrik said, slipping a little closer to me on the couch.

I moved away.

Pointedly.

There seemed to be a plot thickening here, and at the moment all I wanted was some static scenery. What the hell was wrong with Patrik, anyway?

"I mean it, you're beautiful," he repeated, and obediently reseated himself at the other end of the couch. His eyes examined me with such an incomparable mixture of cold objectivity and enthusiastic connoisseurship that I almost burst out laughing.

"You say that like you want to get me in the sack!"

Patrik turned away. He crouched on his heels and carefully scrutinized the craters on the illuminated side of the moon. I didn't like this pose of his.

"Maybe I do," he said after a while, as if changing the subject. "Maybe I've wanted to for a long time, and I don't know who wouldn't, because you're a damn beautiful woman, and you've got a brain, too." (To have a brain—this was the highest compliment a woman could earn from Patrik.) "I wouldn't mind sleeping with you at all," he continued. "And if I haven't tried up to now, it's only because you'd probably ditch me. You'd do it with me, then ditch me, which is your fundamental philosophy of life. And I applaud you for it."

I couldn't quite believe my ears.

Patrik. For years we had argued and cried on each other's shoulder for our lost ideals and lost loves; Patrik, with whom I'd shared a tent for so many nights, the same Patrik who had always carefully avoided any contact with my body (not out of shame, but to maintain professional distance); my old friend Patrik was now explaining to me with insane arrogance that he would like to jump my bones and that I would *let* him!

That pissed me off.

That pissed me off, and I jumped up and grabbed him by the throat. I laughed into his eyes and shook him. "You miserable shit! You dimestore Don Juan! I! I'd let you, would I!?"

"Ce-ertainly," he croaked as his head slipped and bounced against the wall. "No doubt about it. Y-ou let two out of every three guys sleep with you, if you haven't been pulling my leg."

I let him go.

"Well, well, then," I said with exaggerated fury put on to mask my genuine fury. (Is it really possible that I sleep with two out of every three men?)

"Now I've seen everything. You tell him everything, you give him advice about women, you trust him with your friendship. Then he turns around and says, Two out of every three! If you'd at least said, With every other idiot, then I might have forgiven you, but two out of every three . . . !"

"That's the way it is, Fialinka. Probably more like four out of five."

Patrik lightly grabbed the hand I was about to use to strangle him. "Don't try to kill me again. I think it's great. Sleep with anyone you want. I told you, you have a brain. You can do whatever you want to, and you'll still never be a bimbo. You know damned well those guys you sleep with aren't worth your little finger. And then you're so nice to them, you don't even let them know it. I was only pointing out, when you started strangling me, that"—he swallowed anxiously and re-aligned his Adam's apple with his thumb—"I was only pointing out that, as usual, you look very, very nice today."

"Well, thank you *very, very much* for the compliment, Sir Lancelot. What about some flowers, too, then."

"But of course!"

Patrik jumped off the divan, opened the door a crack, and carefully squeezed through. Then stole on tiptoe into the living room and returned with three flowers from his mother's *Saintpaulia*: "Violets for my Violet!"

I sniffed them.

Patrik bowed and sat down across from me. He examined me again with a frightened and pretty unattractive half smile. "You're strange. You have such open features. You're beautiful, but even if you weren't, probably no one would notice it. You have a terribly rare face, so sincere and open. Nevertheless, it's clear that you're just a bitch," he added in a tone of shallow philosophical contemplation. "But now let us speak as psychologist and patient, if you will permit, Doctor. Could you—pardon me—strictly as a *scientist,* you understand—elucidate for me the manner in which you administer oral sex to your lovers? Could you—once again, as a *specialist*—discuss whether you have ever experienced the hardening of the male organ in your mouth and, if so, how this came about? Would you be so kind as to share with me—most assuredly in strictly academic terms—the technical details of how you are able to achieve this? And finally, might I ask you, a *specialist,* in the most precise sense of that word, the *clinical physician* who successfully treats four out of every five lustful souls, if you would not be willing to apply your expertise to my own small problem?

"To my own *truly small* problem, if you understand my meaning without further elucidation. And I must believe that you of all people most certainly do."

And Patrik, my longtime friend, my platonic companion, who had never in his life allowed himself the least physical intimacy with me, unzipped his fly and revealed to me his boxer shorts, crimson as a toreador's cape.

5

Patrik!

Do you still remember how we used to understand one another better than either of us has ever understood anyone else?

Do you recall, Patrik, how we never concealed the smallest word or experience from each other, we, the two eccentric loners no one else knew anything about?

Do you remember, Patrik?

How we nearly froze to death more than once out there in the mountains of the East, in the few socialist mountain ranges open to us, trailblazing every inch with the soles of our sneakers?

Do you recall how we wrote STOP ACID RAIN in English on our T-shirts and walked around Wenceslaus Square until they picked us up? Then at the station they asked us what this "ah-tsit rah-yeen" was and why we were protesting it. They didn't believe those old-wives' tales about acid falling out of the heavens. I had purposely not worn a bra, and the comrades scrutinized my T-shirt in great detail—and you, Patrik, got beaten up for trying to defend me.

Do you remember? Patrik!

6

Patrik was diagnosed with multiple sclerosis, and many things lost all meaning.

1

I had never realized the shockingly superhuman self-sacrifice one could sink into in the process of caring for someone.

There had never been any reason for it to occur to me: Grandmother had always been healthy, and one of the few things about her I really liked was that she wasn't a hypochondriac.

And the rest of my family?

In spite of everything that happened, perhaps fate was not so unkind to them after all. The same goes for me. No one was ever crippled. No one ever needed constant care or moaned and groaned. The circumstances of the accident remained a mystery, and—in spite of the fact that I had been a legal adult almost a month—no one ever showed me any photographs or offered any explanations. A solitary Trabant crashed in one of the districts near Hradec Králové: the driver lost control of the wheel, to put it in the usual parlance of such accidents—and there was no need for the ambulance someone had called. At the autopsy it was supposedly proved that the driver had been under the influence, but I knew very well that Father never drank. Father didn't drink because since he'd been a young man the slightest amount of liquor or wine made him ill. Not to mention the fact that from the time he lost his job at the university Father had always wanted to look fate straight in the eye. He despised drinking and summer houses and every other form of escape: he always tried to erase even the smallest traces of escapism from himself, from Mother, from Šárka, and from me.

I was eighteen at the time, and I hadn't seen the site of the accident yet. I was old enough to take care of the wrecker's bill and arrange and pay for the funerals. I didn't have the strength to go out to the crash site for several weeks. I was busy enough with inheritance taxes and the impersonal faces of the executors of the estate, who poked their noses around in the apartment, looking in all the cabinets and closets, and demanded that I estimate how much I could get if I sold all the clothes and other personal property left by the deceased, including the furniture and Father's books.

I only went to look at the place a few weeks later; it wasn't a road we often traveled, and I had to search out the stretch of curve on a map. They said the driver, under the influence of alcohol, had lost control of the wheel and crashed. Father was buried with the label of drunken murderer of his wife and daughter.

A woman from the village told a different story. She was obviously one of those vestigial holdouts, one of the last of those talkative but hospitable and decent women who even today invite travelers in for coffee and curd cake—and who, loitering on the weekends in the gardens of their gingerbread houses, keep an eye out for passersby and snare anyone who so much as nods at them in the clutches of their endless volubility.

She was an expansive, perspiring gossip, with the type of Old Czech hands that required wiping on her apron every minute or so. And over the tops of the fragrant rosebushes along her fence she told me the Story.

"Have you come a long way?"

"I'm from Prague."

I walked on.

But it was too late—the backlash inspired by this statement forced me against a fence post.

"From Prague," she said. "Yes, from Prague, from the big city. It is a long time since I have been in Prague. But everyone who comes by here, everyone, I tell you, is from Prague, can you imagine . . . ? So, from Prague, you say . . . Those three people at the end of March, they were Praguers also, you know. You haven't heard about their misfortune up there in Prague? No? No, of course not, they don't write about that sort of thing anywhere at all, isn't that right? But it gets around by word of mouth: you know that yourself. So they make out like it's an automobile accident, they say the driver was drunk, you know—just imagine, a tank runs over a Trabant, three people killed—and they say it's an accident, an *accident*! As if a milk barrel had fallen off a truck. When that airplane crashed over there, two hundred or more people died, and that catastrophe, that national disaster, that massacre—they call that an *accident*, too. You're still young, you still don't know . . . and they say those people had another daughter, you know . . . What will happen to her, nobody knows. Perhaps she's still little . . . If she's got no relatives they've stuck her in the children's home for sure, people say, yes, they'll make quite a mess out of her there . . . But you never know for sure, people say all sorts of things . . . They say she wasn't even at the funeral . . . Just imagine, that turn over there, you see the building right on it? You see that hole in the wall, where they fixed it? No? There, where the plaster's peeling off, that white spot on the gray wall . . . here by the road everything white turns gray, but look . . . that's where the tank crushed that little Trabant . . . like an eggshell. How could those poor people have lived through that . . . Růža said, she lives there, she said the whole building shook down to the foundations, there was such a crash the windows shook, you know; they thought maybe it was an earthquake, that the fault must go right through their living room, right from the easy chair to the television, the picture on the wall moved . . . So they run outside and there they see the little Trabant . . . flat as a pancake. And do you know how it happened? Oh yes, there was nothing about it in the newspapers, and nobody here wants to open their mouth, but you know that tank of theirs, an armored transport, really, is what they call those big ugly green-and-gray monsters; anyway, they say it barely tilted a little to one side . . . Just match that little plastic Trabant against that steel armor. So the Russian, they say, took the turn much too wide, never mind the white line, he was way over on the left side—and that poor driver in the car, how could he get out of the way?! And those Russians, they didn't even stop, and when the first people got here from the village, all they saw was that red star disappearing into the distance . . . The neighbors say there was some kind of big wig in it, so they weren't allowed to stop for anything . . . and that soldier, the one who was driving it, they say he got a few days' house arrest, *house arrest*, for murdering three people . . .

"But listen, I don't even know why I'm telling you all this, you can't have heard anything about it, things don't get around there in Prague the way they do in our little village, you know; there's no place to go, nothing to do, the pub is way over in Boušov, five kilometers from here. So we just go on and on . . . we talk about things, drink a little beer, well, you know how it is . . . and then, God knows what truth there is in all of it. I don't believe anyone anymore, you know, if you only heard half the things those people say . . . but that thing . . . Oh yes, there was a little bulletin about it in the paper, maybe you saw it . . . I always read that blotter, a person finds things out that way . . . J.F. killed his girl-friend, D.Č., they write it just like that, and always with the age, so you know whether to feel sorry for the person or not . . . Yes, people today die very young . . .

"But listen . . . what's the matter? No, wait, you're pale as death . . . Did you know those people or something . . . No, no, you couldn't have known them . . . Listen, you know what, come have a little coffee, at least . . . come on in . . . Come in, at least for some coffee . . . and tell me what's wrong . . ."

2

I was lying on the cot in the cabin of someone's semi, someone's rolled-up sweater beneath my head, someone's body breathing warmth alongside me, the residual crust of contact covering my body like layers of onionskin.

That someone next to me breathed peacefully and steadily, but I never slept at such moments. I was twenty-five, and the layers of contact formed a rind, like mock armor plate or oak bark, dividing me from him.

From suppleness.

From love.

From the world.

Perhaps if I could throw off that rind, peel myself like an onion, the same way I strip off my clothes in preparation for touching . . . Perhaps I could strip down to the core, to the heart, to the blood . . . maybe nothing would remain of me . . .

I lay on my back in the rig and peeled away the layers one by one. Imaginary layers. Imaginary armor.

I peeled away the layers of contact and men's hands.

Lovemaking. Contacts. Loves and half-loves.

Contacts. First kisses and first loves . . .

The deeper I plunged into myself, the further into the past I dared to go, the more sensitive those layers became.

Until at last I was snuggled in my mother's arms, in her hands, in her belly, back before I'd ever tasted mother's milk;

protected by the inner wall of the womb, I was completely untouched.

I was hot, aching, growing, and barely even conceived.

I was defenseless, vulnerable, safe, and pure.

3

For years I had borne the sources of my moods in my body; by proper control of my thoughts it was easy to choose among these tactile memories, to invoke the very ones I wished to recall.

I drew the freshest sensations directly from the tiny hairs on my skin.

The pleasures radiating from my clitoris and nipples, pleasures which seemed unique every time—but which also repeated themselves over and over, and through repetition erased themselves, faded.

From the layers of contact it was almost always possible to choose the most desirable ones.

And when I really wanted to, I could grope my way down through the substrata of my skin to my mother's hands.

My mother's hands, which no longer existed.

In the right mood, with the right degree of concentration, I could grope deeper and deeper beneath my skin. But the deeper I went, the more lonely my pleasures became; the more cables, wires, and connections there were running toward the core, toward the great dense knot of sadness.

Toward my . . . *soul?*

Was it my soul? That white dove that is supposed to shake itself from the breast and wing its way into the heavens after we die if we have been worthy?

I didn't know.

Oh, I knew quite a bit, of course. From the dissection room I knew all those small bloody nerve bundles and connective tissues that spilled out of chest cavities when you cut them open. I knew the functions of the nervous system and could have named all the paths and branchings of the individual nerves "blindfolded, drunk, and on my deathbed," as my anatomy professor so floridly demanded of us.

In spite of that, I didn't know if the soul existed.

But there was definitely something like a soul—a mass, a white dove, a quasi-soul—in the center of Patrik's breast. This much I knew, and it was tormenting him.

We'd never spoken of souls or quasi-souls before—but now, suddenly, we couldn't avoid it.

Patrik was dying.

4

Patrik was dying more of sadness and longing and resentment than of the actual disease that certainly would leave him a few more years of life.

When he tried to sleep alone on the sofabed in his cubbyhole, without sheets, covered by a single blanket, his terrible dreams plagued him.

Patrik pounded his head against the wall (prefabricated and resonant) in his sleep—and Mrs. Fišer (still in the dark) reproached him every morning about how terribly he had again disturbed her.

Patrik had never planned to live to ninety. Subconsciously he'd reckoned that at thirty-five or forty he would collide with something somewhere—and that would be it.

It wasn't the simple fact that his disease was terminal that caused Patrik pain.

The disease was an insult to Patrik: he'd always wanted to die like a man.

Falling off a cliff. On a difficult climb, high up, with no rope and no companion and—to be frank—without the slightest trace of dexterity.

Freezing to death in the mountains. But not in any old mountains: it had to be some dangerous wilderness range, where three years later some wandering pilgrim would find only a camera and a desiccated skeleton, licked smooth and white by ants and silver foxes.

Getting beaten to death by police batons and kicked to pieces by their boots during one of the many interrogations he was forced to endure.

Getting run over by a government limousine. Even this death, if not heroic, would at least have been documentational.

Poisoning by tap water.

Radiation sickness.

Cancer of any kind, as long as its cause was entirely clear and it testified to the failure of "the safeguarding of living conditions in the socialist state." Unpleasant, painful, slow, but, after all, documentational. Patrik would have liked to become a document, like a deformed flower.

Patrik was open to all sorts of possibilities.

But this disease—prolonged, terrible, and stupefying— this most inhumane of diseases—whose cause, moreover, was mostly genetic, as far as could be discerned from learned books—this meant the loss of all his hopes.

There still remained two ways to die which—despite a certain triviality—Patrik didn't reject outright: drowning in a vat of Moravian wine or dying lasciviously *in the act*.

When he had pulled his boxers back up, Patrik said, with a forced laugh sounding more like a sob, "Well, there you are, Fialinka, there you are. Nothing left now but that vat of wine!"

5

Still, Patrik had other worries besides reflections on his fate.

Less metaphysical concerns.

The search for a wheelchair, for example.

6

The illness progressed rapidly from the very start, although its effects were not particularly apparent on Patrik. After a few weeks he'd pulled himself together enough to return to his usual philosophical view, that everything was bullshit—and that one photographer more or less in the world wouldn't make any difference. But he had to stop working because he was no longer physically up to plumbing, and even though running (or crawling) from doctor to doctor took up a lot of his time, he still had far too much of it left on his hands for thinking.

Mrs. Fišer found out about it before long, of course, and although the true essence of the disease was to her—a simple woman—completely mysterious, she understood that Patrik was going to die of it.

Patrik's desire for liberation acquired unprecedented urgency, because Mrs. Fišer behaved as if every hour were Patrik's last. Comrade Teacher and Mother's hen brain failed to grasp that her maternal pressure could make her dear son's life infinitely more miserable than the mere pressure of imminent death.

Mrs. Fišer just couldn't cope with the idea. She stopped sentencing him to household chores. Her educational efforts ceased.

After a tearful two-hour scene Mrs. Fišer convinced her son that now—with him being so sick—he couldn't possibly lock himself in his room anymore. And that enormous, beautiful, rusty lock, which I'd brought Patrik from Romania, was confiscated.

She called him from school, running off in the middle of class to do so—every half hour she had to assure herself that everything was all right with Patrik and that he didn't need anything. She already saw Patrik—who was still pretty damned alive—as her poor, unhappy, perfectly obedient child at rest in an elegant, tiny white coffin.

She went at the task of burying Patrik with such abundant tears, such funereal eyes and—ultimately—with such readiness, that I began to suspect secretly that deep down in the oozing caverns of her soul there was nothing she could have wanted more than this, that she found it wistfully beautiful to cry over her dying son; that she felt her undeserving and disobedient son, who was incapable of petit-bourgeois decency, was atoning with his death for all the wrongs he had done his long-suffering mother over the years; that she saw him, after all this time, finally becoming that helpless, unresisting little bundle in his mother's arms . . .

No, I don't mean Mrs. Fišer any harm.

Mrs. Fišer simply behaved toward Patrik as toward a sick person, without distinguishing the type of illness. She hounded Patrik to rest and look after his health, just as she had—when he was little—wound a scarf around his neck at the slightest sign of a hoarse throat, then bundled him off to bed to be hopelessly bored.

Yes, that's the way it was: Mrs. Fišer had her little invalid at home, her runny-nosed, coughing, sick, weak little child, and it was her maternal duty to feed him, care for him, gently chide him, and nurse him back to health.

Patrik—in his own words—was disintegrating from the inside out, like a fallen pear among the debris—meanwhile, an agitated Mrs. Fišer tenderly and repeatedly felt the temperature of his forehead with that perspiring and loving, unbearably maternal palm.

7

A wheelchair. I needed to get my hands on a wheelchair.

Outwardly a symbol of helplessness and dependence,

but in reality—once you get used to the notion—the ideal means of retaining independence for as long as possible.

Patrik knew that. While he was crawling around to all sorts of examinations and tests, Patrik would sometimes ask one of the doctors when, in his opinion, he would need a wheelchair.

Basically, the answers fell into two categories.

There were inane, evasive (though apparently sometimes well-meant) assurances that his illness would never progress that far, that his legs wouldn't even be affected, that Patrik really wasn't all that ill—and even if he had been—well, let me assure you, today's medical science is making enormous strides . . .

And there were the (slightly, too) sensible promises of the comically gruff neurologists that he wouldn't live to see the complete disintegration of his already wobbly limbs anyway, so why worry about that now . . . The illness could have a whole slew of other symptoms—so he should be happy for the present that he wasn't wetting himself.

For Patrik—although he didn't see the humor in them—these cynical observations were more agreeable. He probably found the insensitive, crude professionalism of medical personnel inured to everything to be a sizable improvement over his mother's tearful approach.

Then Patrik came across a man who could provide his practical question with a practical answer.

He was an orthopedist, but in many ways seemed more like a general practitioner. He had Patrik bend over and thoroughly palpated his spine. Then he scrutinized the series of test results, doing calculations in his head for a moment, and said, "Winter. Winter, I would say. Perhaps as early as the end of fall, perhaps not until spring . . . It depends, Mr. Fišer, on a number of factors, which must all be taken into consideration. And, of course, it depends on you yourself— and how well you fight. In the meantime . . . when it comes to that . . . practice staying on crutches as long as you can. Because when you exercise your legs, you are also exercising your head, remember that . . . Plan on winter. Yes, winter."

The doctor got up. He walked over to a cabinet filled with all sorts of papers and smiled sadly at Patrik, who had been unable to tear his eyes from the doctor's heavy gait. "Yes, Mr. Fišer, I have a limp. Since I was a boy. A prosthetic hip joint, and not the most successful operation, either. You see, that's why I became an orthopedist. Not a bad one either, even if I say so myself. Our limitations, Mr. Fišer, determine our lives and our . . . successes . . . more than anything else. Think about that."

For Patrik this old gentleman was a symbol of medical wisdom. The clean but wrinkled white smock; the old-fashioned fountain pen in his breast pocket; the slow, but not lazy, that sort of . . . personalized manner of speech—the way Patrik had always imagined the general practitioners of ages gone by. Even when the doctor put his glasses down on his desk, somehow differently, in an old-fashioned way, the very sound, that click, reminded Patrik of those white-haired and trustworthy old gentlemen whom he'd never met, those men who were born to be doctors. Experience and bedside manner had been squeezed out of hospitals and health-care offices by science and technology, represented by a single electrocardiogram and a miserably outfitted laboratory in which a few poorly made-up, poorly paid, and, more often than not, poorly mannered girls slaved away under a flood of specimens for analytic tests they simply couldn't get the hang of. The charming older doctors had for the most part been replaced by young idiots, barely hatched from the university—and that was thanks only to the good graces of friends in high places, who had not even matured into the full glory of their hearse driver's cynicism, although it was already clearly visible in their every movement. Anyone older who still remained in a doctor's chair was probably some sort of fanatical Party hack. The wise gray hairs of the old doctors had apparently given way to the premature bald spots of the younger ones. From dissolute living, Patrik said: sponging off bribes, getting drunk on the alcohol their patients had given them, and squandering all their masculine energy on the prettier nurses.

I avoided doctors scrupulously, so I couldn't really judge whether Patrik was right. But I was willing to bet he was. So it made him all the happier to finally meet that old orthopedist. It didn't seem as if many people were capable of imparting strength to a patient with an incurable illness, and this strength shone forth from the orthopedist. Patrik valued it highly.

The old gentleman took a few forms from the cabinet and carefully filled them in with blue ink from his old-fashioned fountain pen. He showed Patrik where to sign and said, "This is an application for a wheelchair for you. I'm going to send it right away. Don't be alarmed, I haven't lied, there's plenty of time until winter. But the process takes quite a long time, you'll see for yourself. I'll do everything in my power to speed it up."

Then he fell silent and watched unsmilingly as Patrik left the office.

The doctor hadn't lied.

Sometime later Patrik was informed that as an officially certified invalid with a protracted terminal illness he indeed had the right to be provided with a wheelchair. That, yes, our socialist fatherland would make it possible for him to wheel his behind around in a piece of equipment that would cost our socialist fatherland as much as twenty thousand crowns. That, in fact, he would obtain a modern, imported wheelchair, for which our socialist fatherland would have to pay in hard currency. That this wheelchair would be absolutely new, never used by anyone else. And that the approximate waiting period for an invalid in his category was five to ten years.

8

Toward the end of summer a bruise-covered Patrik had mastered the art of hobbling on crutches.

The sound of Patrik's awkwardly falling body and the banging of his crutches against the prefabricated panels of the floor did not please the neighbors who lived on the two or three floors below, but when Mrs. Fišer tearfully explained to them about her dying son they gave up complaining. To Patrik's favorite pastimes was added clumping down the building's stairs, which was accompanied by concussive shocks that echoed through the entire apartment block. Patrik claimed that he was exercising his arm and shoulder muscles, but I think a more important goal was the raising of hell. A hell to which no one in the building dared object. For the first few days the neighbors would slink out of their apartments, but upon seeing that the cause of this terrible racket was a man on crutches, they always returned shamefaced to fume in the safety of their own homes. And Patrik just kept pounding his crutches into the concrete, bitterly ecstatic about his unenviable cripple's immunity. Only Mrs. Fišer sometimes came after him, to bring him home half by force.

"Patya! Patrik, my little boy! You must rest, you must look after your health, do you hear? You must look after your health; after all, you're sick! After all, you're so terribly sick!"

9

Protected by his cripple's immunity, as he liked to call it, Patrik was deteriorating quite rapidly, from the inside out. Like a fallen pear. He was hurting inside, I know now, but before his despairing mother and his friends, before everyone whom Mrs. Fišer informed of her son's condition and who—

more or less out of obligation—felt sorry for him, he reveled in his invalid status and displayed a darkly humorous, almost affectionate attitude toward his illness.

Yes, during that half year he had inwardly, intentionally degenerated through the ranks: from Great Wanderer to Hobbler to Stick Figure to Crutch Hanger, where he lingered awhile—and in this way he hoped, by the end of fall or the beginning of winter, to work his way down the ladder to High Commander of the Rolling Butt Sling.

It looked as if he would succeed.

Like one who has been bedridden for a long time and is relearning to walk, first on crutches, then with the help of a cane, Patrik was relearning how *not to walk*, and he was making progress beyond all expectations. He was degenerating. He was degenerating intentionally, despite efforts by myself and others to pull him out of it at least a little. By the end of fall or the beginning of winter he would need that wheelchair.

But there would be no wheelchair.

For Patrik, who never thought ahead, the phrase "five or ten years" represented an entirely incomprehensible concept.

As it did, come to think of it, for me as well.

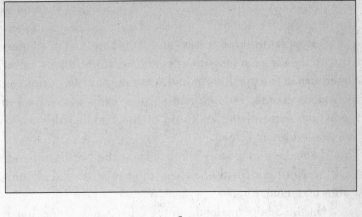

1

The Northern Road was not the only truck route across the republic. But only one other route was well traveled: the Southern Road.

Whenever I left Prague and headed for Slovakia, I had a choice—and it goes without saying I knew both ways, though most times I'd taken the Northern Road. This mountainous road felt somehow safer, more familiar, homier, even though I had to spend over an hour on a creeping tram just to get to the edge of the city where the Hradec Králové road begins. If I took the Southern Road, seven minutes' walk got me from my apartment to a spot where there was pretty decent hitching. On top of that, this second route was faster, at least as far as Bratislava. All you had to do was catch the right ride on the highway.

I ricocheted from town to town all across the north with the drivers, slowed down with them through populated areas, hit the brakes for the familiar—and ancient—potholes; I climbed the hills in third gear and carefully approached the dangerous turns. I waited at the railroad crossings on the Northern Road with the cursing drivers until the barricade was finally lifted. We'd worried together about the transit cops, who could fine you for anything, and I learned the best ways to get out of these jams. I flew from side to side around the turns and was jolted all over the shabby roadway surfaces.

I stopped with the drivers at pubs where, out of solidarity with the socialist long-distance truckers, who almost never dared drink, I sipped those foul, carcinogenic soft drinks in poisonous greens, yellows, and purples; pubs where I got to know my share of the staff and of the huddled drivers by name, and a few in bed.

To make a long story short, I knew the Northern Road, and the Northern Road knew me; the two of us had an amicable understanding.

On the Southern Road, on the other hand, it was tough to know anything or anyone well.

The Southern Road belonged to the Intertruckers.

Intertruckers who came in inexhaustible sorts, shapes, and colors. (The sorts, shapes, and colors of their rigs, lights, faces, and whatever else.)

Czechoslovakia, enviably and profitably situated in the heart of Europe, formed an outpost just beyond the Good Germans of the East, a defensive outpost for the lands and ideas of the East (the political agitators had pounded this into our skulls)—this, our dear socialist Czechoslovakia, was at the same time the preferred link between the West and the Middle East, between Scandinavia and the south, between trade companies scattered all over Europe. The republic was an outstanding trade route, and over the years the transport construction department had adapted to this increase in auto transit. And this highway, this celebrated southern highway—the first in Czechoslovakia, stretching from Prague to Bratislava and beyond, and augmented by a very respectable road reaching all the way from Prague to the West German border—seemed to testify to that.

Plzeň, Prague, Brno, Bratislava—that was the route of this dangerous Southern Road.

All along it thundered rigs of every foreign tongue and

currency. These were not the good old rattletraps from our own Liaz factory, with drivers behind the wheel who feared every run-in with the cops like the Devil fears the cross. On the Southern Road, in rigs of foreign make—like an apocalypse of mighty engines—the dauntless riders of the West roared dauntlessly across the republic. In rigs which didn't rattle but smoothly surged across the badly joined prefabricated segments of the socialist expressway, keeping to the fast lane and blowing past the puttering private cars, whose drivers never dared go much faster than the 110-kilometer speed limit. The limit for commercial vehicles was 70, which meant that on the Northern Road almost no one, except a few nocturnal maniacs with a death wish, dared go faster than 80; meanwhile, on the Southern Road, 130 or 140 wasn't rare at all—and this turned the private drivers pale with envy. What's more, after dark the drivers sometimes didn't even bother to stop for cops waving their flyswatter-like paddles at them to pull over; at those speeds the police couldn't make out the plates, and they weren't about to give chase—even if they'd tried, the offending Intertruck, crowned in its litany of lights, would be long gone, already lost among dozens of other Intertrucks. For the truckers, the Southern Road was candy.

I usually stuck to riding in trucks on the Northern Road, but that was just a matter of personal preference. True, I'd been happy enough to accept rides in cars from time to time— for a change of pace—but the trucks were more comfortable, and I'd always had more to talk about with truckers. You only had to know the rest areas, hangouts, and routes a bit in order to make it from Prague to, say, Humenné in Slovakia in a night and a morning: the drivers all knew each other and were buddies; they transferred the hitchhikers from one to another at the major interchanges.

But on the Southern Road, commercial trucks were almost the only way to go. At any rate, it would've been tough

any other way, since private cars didn't like to stop for you—
and even when they did, they were never going very far and
getting stuck standing somewhere out in the middle of the
freeway wouldn't have been too pleasant. The first ones to
stop for you out there would probably be the police. The most
fine-happy, nosy, and suspicious police in Czechoslovakia.

But that's another story.

The modern-day fairy tale of imperialist trucks in a small
socialist land.

2

My earliest hitching roots went back to the time when semis
still rolled merrily right through the center of Prague, puffing
poisonous diesel fumes into pedestrians' faces and slowly
undermining the foundations of dwellings and historic buildings with continual heavy concussions.

Then they put an end to that. They built the so-called
perimeter circle around Prague; traffic arriving from all directions was supposed to be routed onto it by means of arrows—and discouraged from passing through the city center
by all kinds of threats and prohibitions.

By careful study of the city's main departure and approach routes, I discovered that this fortified perimeter was
constructed primarily of the aforementioned arrows and
threatening road signs, rather than anything resembling good
solid pavement. The more timid and poorly informed Intertruckers, together with their Western suspension systems,
careened in and out of the potholes and slogged tediously
through the never-drying bogs around the periphery of
Prague, poking through the desolate construction sites of freeway junctions abandoned a decade earlier. The cleverer ones
chose the straight line through Prague—with one or two packs
of Marlboros displayed prominently on the dashboard.

These Marlboros had become a silent pact between the police and the Western drivers, a pact you slipped wordlessly into the cop's palm.

3

The cops' favorite hunting ground for semis was just outside the inner city at the Klement Gottwald Bridge in Nusle— which linked the Brno expressway with downtown Prague— and of course, the purpose of this was not to preserve the historic landmarks of Prague. The police had to keep all heavy traffic off the bridge, because the bridge, not even ten years old, might not have survived the weight. Since my youngest days, the Gottwald Bridge had been hailed as one of the great Monuments to Socialism, an achievement erected by the sweat of our workers' brows for the good of workers everywhere—and so on. The not-so-towering, reinforced-concrete structure spanned the Nusle Valley from Pankrác to Vinohrady—and through its bowels ran the metro, affectionately known as the "Mole."

From the bridge you could get a pretty good view of the smog-infested Nusle Valley: the filthy, dilapidated, but still friendly-looking prewar tenements rose up like toys right below you when you leaned out over its low, not very reassuring railing. On the most cheerful days, in a pleasant breeze, when the wind blew some of the fixed screen of smog away from the city, you could see far down the Vltava, gray and sluggish in its channel—and in the other direction as far as Strašnice, where the black ribbon of smoke from the crematorium chimney lofted the remains of the departed into the heavens.

On the ninth of May, when the fireworks cascaded over Prague in honor of the Liberation, there was an unforgettable view from the bridge of the illuminated Vyšehrad Castle: all you had to do was squint your eyes to be transported into the heroic past of Prague, of which—as far as I could tell—nothing remained.

Anyway, the bridge offered one of the best views in all of Prague—and what made it truly unique was that by walking along it you could change the scenery of houses sprouting below, with their chimneys smoking up into your face. It measured a bit over a kilometer, and in the first years after its construction any Praguer would have been happy to take his whole family there for a nice stroll. Of course, that was before the highway route through central Prague had been finished, when the traffic whistling by was not quite so unnerving.

But the hypnotic view into the depths could also seduce one into free fall, and over the years many dozens of suicides were said to have ended their lives covered in white sheets on the black asphalt of those little Nusle streets. Of course, they didn't write about that in the papers, just as they didn't write about the gang of teens who voluntarily assisted people who didn't want to go over the low railing. Eventually, they say, the police caught them (all they had to do was close both ends of the bridge, so there was no way out but down), but not before the youths succeeded in tossing off an undercover cop who'd been sent onto the bridge as a decoy . . .

The accounts, some perhaps fabricated, of what went on on the bridge flowed from mouth to mouth faster than a rushing mountain torrent, and even radio waves (if anyone had talked about these things on the air) could never have carried the tales more quickly than people's mouths.

The bridge became one of the few relatively new monuments to prove itself worthy of stories as terrifying as the ones connected with the old fairy-tale castles.

Whatever the truth might have been, the number of outings to the bridge fell off significantly, and soon not a living soul could be spotted along its railing. People even preferred not to linger directly under the bridge, and when they did, they turned their timid eyes upward, for fear that someone might jump that very instant: one story told how a certain man who hurled himself off the bridge into nonexistence landed smack on the head of a completely unsuspecting elderly lady pensioner, who was instantly killed. The man himself, it seems, only broke some small bone in his wrist. But justice was served in this case, when they gave the desperate man three years in minimum security—for "negligence."

Of course, not only suicides fell from the bridge.

After only three or four years, the entire structure of socialist reinforced concrete (cured no doubt with the sweat of the workers) had begun to crack and crumble ominously.

At first there was just a fine white dust that made the eyes smart a little and left a delicate blanket over the zone below the bridge, giving it a slightly lighter shade than the surrounding areas.

Then chips of concrete started breaking loose.

The possibility of the entire bridge collapsing was allegedly negligible; even if the hanging walkways, the roadway, and all the supporting concrete columns were to collapse, the wire cage through which the metro ran would supposedly remain suspended over the Nusle Valley.

This information, too, was passed along through the grapevine, but I had a feeling it was another one of those rumors sent down into circulation by the big shots. It was impossible to write about it in the papers, and people wouldn't have believed them anyway. All they had to do was inoculate a couple of known gossips with this "reliable underground information" and this trustworthy news item would reach the majority of Prague's ears in no time.

Eventually a protective cage was built over Křesomyslova Street to prevent pieces of this Monument to Socialism from raining down on the pedestrians' heads. The bridge wasn't doing too well. It shook nightmarishly every time the

Mole passed through its innards (its builders apparently hadn't overly burdened themselves with resonance calculations), and even from a distance the gaping holes in its design were no longer apparent only to the expert eye.

The Czechoslovakian engineers (at least those who had any direct input) had no idea what to do to fix it. The Swedes offered a special concrete-injection method—and they promised that after their intervention they could guarantee the functioning of the bridge for another hundred years.

However, for this service they wanted twelve million Swedish crowns.

In hard currency!

This caused shock and confusion in the circles responsible for the release of such funds—and there followed an indignant rejection of those imperialist exploiters who dared think they had progressed further than the socialist construction industry.

So the bridge, abandoned to the four winds, vibrations, smog, flying ash, and exhaust, merrily crumbled on over the Nusle Valley, helping the workers along on their path into nonexistence—and littering chunks and splinters of its cruelly suffering reinforced-concrete body upon their heads.

4

Considering the strict prohibition of all heavy vehicles on the Nusle bridge, the unbroken stream of multiple-ton trucks rolling across it was truly remarkable. For the majority of Intertruckers the cost of this simplest and fastest of all routes through Prague (which included a tour of some notable historical sights along the way) remained that single pack of Marlboros.

The police flyswatter, for the Czech trucker a symbol of Big Trouble, had been reduced on the Southern Road into the mark of the humble parasite begging for a few crumbs from the rich man's table or, more accurately, a warning sign for an upcoming tollbooth.

Instead of actual tollbooths along the Prague—Bratislava freeway, there were squad cars, and these collectors made up their own tolls. Usually Marlboros.

One pack for crossing the bridge.

For speeding—two, three, maybe four.

For a cute little hitchhiker, easily a whole carton. Not for the hitchhiker. For the cop. The hitchhiker would get some pretty-smelling soap, hard currency, makeup—and at times almost anything she asked for.

Because on the Southern Road the hitcher was a different story, written with a special pen.

Actually, by many pens.

By the countless exotic ballpoints of countless foreign truckers.

5

At first glance you didn't notice much of anything, really.

These girls didn't need to make a special effort to stand out from the common crowd of bystanders milling around somewhere at the Můstek or museum end of Wenceslaus Square.

They didn't need to walk the square, treading that fine line, with their eyes made up to suggest everything to every potential customer but absolutely nothing to the cops, including the ones in plainclothes.

No need to fear that a satisfied customer would run off without paying, much less that a girl would misjudge a client and, after the deed was done, find herself, to her horror and disgust, in the arms of an undercover cop.

No need to worry about the competition, or to fight for one's place in the sun. There were always plenty of semis available.

No need to look extra-special either—they couldn't make out anything from a distance anyway, and they were horny—what's more (thank God), different nationalities had different tastes.

And languages? There was no point in learning a hundred of them just to speak every dialect of every foreign tongue that cruised the republic on eighteen wheels: the endless variety of languages between Prague and Bratislava could always be distilled down to a half-mute, half-deaf Babel Tower of hand gestures.

Let's just say that any girl who felt like moonlighting on the Southern Road didn't have to twirl her handbag. All she had to do was strike a pose by the shoulder of the road and raise her right thumb toward the sky.

6

We lived in darkness.

We lived in the darkness behind the Iron Curtain, a darkness illuminated only by the dying red twilight of five-pointed stars.

We lived in a prison cell of death, decay, and enforced ignorance; we lived in a cage enclosed by electrified barbed wire.

However, the heavy leaden door was open just a crack onto the West, enough to allow a few rays of sunlight to penetrate.

Or were these just the neon signs of decadent, glittering bars overflowing with the lascivious Unknown?

In either case, it was light: it was impossible to squeeze through that crack in the doorway. You couldn't even see much through it, because it so dazzled the eyes.

Czechoslovakia was a border country.

And even someone who at some point finally managed to break out, thanks to the kindly permission of the big shots—

someone who finally got the chance to look straight into the eyes of the Hydra of Imperialism for a few enchanted seconds—even he could not trust his eyes 100 percent.

The eye accustomed to permanent gray requires time to adjust, and time was the one thing those timid socialist tourists were never granted.

We all stretched toward that light; like sickly yellowed plants we bent our stalks toward the narrow open crack—and with the last remains of our chlorophyll, we desperately absorbed whatever light we could.

And, of course, we had no idea whether that light penetrating from the West was really rays of sunlight or just the unhealthy flickering of fluorescent tubes that weakened the eyesight.

7

The Iron Curtain did, however, admit trucks. They squeezed in, drove through—like panting mobile avatars of the Unknown—and after carelessly churning up the fetid surface of the Known, they disappeared again into the distance.

The Southern Road was full of whirlpools, movement and danger, like the wake behind a fleet of ships. Full of sharks that formed an escort for the ships; sharks that, in place of dorsal fins, thrust their flashing blue sirens above the surface as a warning.

The trailers and cabs on the Southern Road were not all identical like our own good old Liazkas. Each one represented an independent, slightly enigmatic, and entirely distinct world. Each cab had its own specific odor, which was more characteristic of the cab itself than of the driver. Each semi had its own particular, alien pattern of lights. And although the variety of trailers was far from infinite, it wasn't easy for someone accustomed to monochromatic grayness to tell them all apart.

And still there was one thing all the cabs had in common, the most important thing of all for the girls who habitually traveled this route.

Each cab was a warehouse of imported merchandise. Merchandise any of these girls would have died for. Merchandise you couldn't get in the hard-currency shops even for half your monthly salary.

From Plzeň to Bratislava roared eighteen-wheeled traveling drugstores, candy shops, and bakeries, leather stores and perfume shops, boutiques, pharmacies, and foreign currency banks. Music stores with records and tapes of Western and outlawed groups. Stores with watches, tape players, cosmetics, fashion accessories, and expensive, unobtainable brands of cigarettes. Bars full of liquors with intoxicating scents and flavors, things you'd never even heard of before.

Consequently, a clever girl who knew the price of admission could provide herself with almost anything on the Southern Road.

8

Of course, *I* was different.

Just as I was different in almost every other respect. I didn't count myself a member of that widespread, diverse population of highway whores who barely knew one another but were somehow still remarkably homogeneous.

Like everything else in Czechoslovakia, they, too, had their stereotypical, immutable gray foundation. They used makeup. Almost everyone used makeup, for among the girls and women it was commonly believed at the time that every female who cared even the least bit about her appearance should plaster half her cosmetic supply on her face first thing every morning, replenish it in the course of the day, then let it fall off overnight, since they didn't sell makeup removers and no one ever thought about it anyway. As a result, from

the age of fifteen all those creams, powders, and paints became ingrained in the complexion, which never again saw the
light of day. Accumulations of powdered and oil-based eye
shadow saturated their eyelids and formed a dark filling in the
tiny wrinkles of the skin structure which would probably
never come off. Women claimed that without makeup they
felt "naked"—and it was a fact: once you started, you had to
hide your damaged epidermis under makeup forever. If you
cared about your appearance, that is.

The girls who traveled the Southern Road, just like the
ones who'd spent their lives as call girls in hotels or hunting
foreigners in the center of Prague, could easily be recognized
in the common crowd of domestic hookers by the quality of
their cosmetics.

True, not always by the quality of its application, but in
the end you could distinguish at first glance its touch of class
from the plebeian coating of expensive but poor quality
makeup that any respectable citizen could respectably purchase in Czech stores.

(I remember an experience I had when I visited Moscow
a few years ago: I was riding the bus, surrounded by faces
which I could barely tell apart, faces even more alienated
than the ones you encountered in Prague. I looked around,
trying to get a grip on their features—and suddenly, as if
leveled by a bolt of lightning, I saw it. A revelation. Those
faces were all made up identically! Young and old, smooth
and wrinkled, gloomy and somewhat happy, ugly faces and
faces bearing some trace of beauty. Ultramarine blue shadow,
applied with the finger on the lids, so that their eyes would
have some color. Eyelashes without contrast; most likely the
government-run department store had no mascara. The same
shade of powder on every face, whether tanned or sickly
yellow. And the lipstick, yes: the color of a fading rose or the
lips of a drowned woman, pasted on in a rich, almost crum-
bling layer that extended well beyond the natural boundaries

of the mouth. On top of it all, the bus was bursting at the seams with the stench of intrusive Russian perfume mingled with the sweat of rarely washed bodies.

I got off the bus. I preferred wandering on foot across half of Moscow to waiting for another busload of those otherworldly girls and women. Girls and women made up precisely according to the selection of available goods in Moscow's department stores.

No Western trade routes passed through the Soviet Union.)

9

Let me return to those girls who so loved to roam the highways.

They used makeup (while cosmetics had never touched my face) and always made themselves a little too much at home in a cab as soon as they got in: the arrogant self-confidence of the customer who knows she has the price of admission.

It made me happy to think that when *I* set off on the Southern Road, I was in a different category, distinct from that mass of desirable, available, but too cheaply sold bodies. It made me happy to think that I could ride the same routes as those girls and yet remain separate. My own woman.

Of course, not everyone understood that—and there were a few rest areas along the Southern Road where I'd argued, or even fought, with some guy who didn't get the picture and tried to approach me with the sleazy solicitations of the businessman confident of his merchandise, his little bars of soap and his perfumes.

But in the end there were always enough who could see and tell the difference, or who at least acted as if they could, and I was happy to believe them.

I had a few amorous adventures on the Southern Road in my collection, and I wanted to believe they were unique.

For both parties.

Of course, you can't rule out the possibility that there was something missing in *my* understanding of the spirit of the Southern Road. I refused to admit that.

10

I was taking the Southern Road to Brno to visit a girl friend. A nice young Swede had picked me up, and that improved my mood a little, because I liked Swedes: they had class. The unpretentious, friendly class of Northern peoples I always found refreshing.

I got out on the outskirts of Brno, and we exchanged addresses.

It was nice to hold a piece of paper with a Stockholm address in my hand (what if I made it there someday?). Stockholm, where they say the green and azure water constantly resounds with the ringing of ice floes. A translucent, pure image of the North.

It was clear to me that we would probably never write; nothing "happened," as the saying goes, at any of the rest stops between Prague and Brno—why should it have?—but we really got along well. This person, whose last name I couldn't even pronounce, was headed for Baghdad—and he promised to call me when he passed through Prague on his way back north.

I warned him that I probably wouldn't be home and that he wouldn't be able to communicate with my grandmother, but that didn't really matter, since God only knew what might happen in the meantime. I never set my heart on those hastily sealed semi-friendships that were fresh and strong one day but could dissolve into boredom by the next. Although, who could tell . . .

I had no list of relatives and acquaintances in the West; none of my close friends had emigrated, and my Czech relatives (with whom I never kept in touch anyway) had all proved to be perfect homebodies. No "uncle in America" or "two aunties in Germany." Not a soul.

Of course, the maintenance of a small army of grandfathers, grandmothers, aunts, and uncles around the capitalist globe had become something of an essential fashion accessory for anyone who wanted to keep up with the times. And the melancholy letters about how much they were missed frequently augured the coming of Christmas. The letters could for the most part only be filled with wistful pining, because no one dared describe to their aunts and uncles abroad the horrendous and worsening chaos in the republic. The censor functioned silently but inscrutably—and you never knew what you might get screwed for. And so the experts learned to communicate between the lines, to furtively impart to their aunts and uncles much of the mire the country was sinking into at an ever quickening rate.

Be that as it may, this pining acquired its most urgent form just before Christmas, birthdays, and similar events. ("Just imagine, Vera, that no matter how hard I look I just can't seem to find a decent tape player anywhere—and Franta so wants one for Christmas! Even if I could find one, it would cost two months' salary. Oh, and did you realize I turn twenty-nine on the seventeenth? Time flies, a body gets older, and what is there left in this stupid monotonous life but the children, who just keep growing, it's enough to drive you crazy trying to find clothes for them. Marcelka is now 98 centimeters tall, has a 43-centimeter waist, and wears a size 2½ shoe.")

The aunts and uncles then proved themselves either evil and stupid (for they didn't always want to understand these requests) or good—but ultimately still quite stupid, because they showered their lucky relatives with badly chosen gifts that no one really needed.

It wasn't easy for these aunts and uncles.

I had no one like that, but material possessions attracted me very little and I wouldn't have wanted to feel indebted to anyone, even if they were in another country. Over the years I'd worked my way toward a kind of minimalist philosophy of reclusive root-feeding, figuring that the main thing was a person's soul, and perhaps feelings of physical pleasure as well, which could be developed easily enough according to methods tried and true since the dawn of time.

I was *different* and I took great stock in that. Illumined by my philosophy of the Soul, so to speak, I walked the streets of Prague in holy jeans, with hair below my shoulders and a knapsack on my back. I refused to buy decent, fashionable clothes or shoes or handbags.

It was a pose, of course.

An incomplete attempt at existential living. Actually, none of my clothes ever quite reached the extreme of genuine rebelliousness, and they were always acceptable, though never modern.

I did not argue with anyone about this attitude of mine: if you didn't like it, you didn't have to look at it. And everyone I knew had gotten used to it long ago.

But there were a few Western things I longed for almost to the point of tears.

Cameras and film. The indispensable tools of documentation. Agfachrome, which I always managed to get my hands on somewhere, cost me 50 percent extra in bribe money paid to the saleswomen so they would save me some under the counter. I lived in constant terror that one day they would stop importing it into Czechoslovakia altogether and I would never be able to take a decent picture again.

The other things were books. Books, magazines, newspapers, *information*. But the essential ones, the ones I needed most, couldn't be mailed in. They didn't have to be "anti-Communist" at all. It was enough that they didn't have the socialist stamp of approval. So these informative books and documents would have to be smuggled in by someone. Someone bold, someone who would be willing to risk it. Or else someone with immunity, someone the Communists couldn't harm.

A Western truck driver, for example.

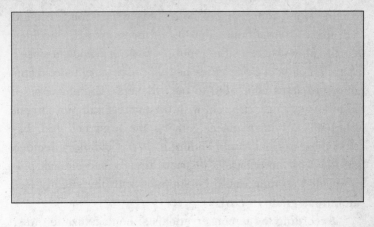

1

The next day, my pack on my shoulders as always, I headed off through the gentle, sunny summer morning for one of the highway feeder roads. The sun's rays rose slowly from behind the low hills in the east, rubbing against my legs like a kitten, and condensing my shadow. The silver mist above the horizon gradually gave birth to the slopes and peaks—and the little houses and cottages amid the spacious fields; but not the Brno skyline, which lay out of sight below me, marked only by a balloon of heavy fog. Microscopic droplets of moisture colliding in the polluted atmosphere above the industrial zone.

The difference between cities and villages still exists, I said to myself.

The great agglomerations of humanity are still differentiated by the dome of smog, and you can still find pure little hamlets, spring water, and little beards of lichen in the Šumava mountains.

And there was still a blue sky.

About six months earlier, the authorities had gotten it into their heads that, in conjunction with the policy of conservation of the means necessary for the support of life in the socialist state, there should be a "homogenization." I heard from the conservationists that it had been officially decided that the atmosphere in the republic was not homogeneous— the inhabitants of large cities had an unfair surplus of respiratory problems compared to the villagers. Therefore, as of the following year, the coal with the highest sulphur content would be burned in places hitherto the least polluted, because these regions could endure it. It was officially decided that the Most and Ostrava districts already had enough pollution, and so they would be supplied with the slightly less sulphurous grade of coal.

According to the conservationists, homogenization was, of course, outright lunacy: the last of the lichen would die— and there would be no place to go to escape the city.

Homogenized sky, homogenized milk, homogenized homes. Worldviews ground to a pulp, mixed together and poured into the same gray mold, which, of course, was not to be tampered with. I looked up at the sky. It was still blue. So far.

2

I trudged toward the feeder road near the Brno city limit; there were no sidewalks or paths, just a lot of mud, dried to a crust and cracked by the summer heat, and fresh asphalt roadways laid between embankments that still weren't fully grown over.

I crouched down and picked up a clump of dry clay in my hand. I smeared it around: living, fertile, reddish-brown earth, from which here and there grew dandelions and a few stalks of wormwood. My hand was stained with clay—and now I was walking through the wormwood, through a thicket of wormwood in the roadside ditch: fine yellowy pollen rose up from the herbs, still moist with morning dew, and drifted off in clouds to coat everything.

Including me.

I rubbed a couple of wormwood leaves between my fingers—and the blast of scent was so overpowering I had to sit down for a moment. Everything made me dizzy that morning, the great virtue of fragrant mornings.

There was no traffic whatsoever on the highway; I don't know why they built such a network of highways when few Brnians ever traveled in that direction.

The scent of wormwood was as enticing as ever: it invited you to do something great, something uncommon . . . it invited you to go somewhere far away, somewhere where you could sit by a ditch and sniff wormwood again.

Or at least to do something you don't usually do, something unexpected, something scandalous—to experience something every passerby doesn't experience.

I climbed up the still barren reddish clay of the embankment—and I stretched out on that moist, barely dried, pleasantly cool morning earth.

I put my pack down next to me and plunged my whole body into the clay: my heels, my thighs, my buttocks, the crown of my head, like a mummy.

I knew I would have clay in my hair and on the back of my neck and T-shirt, that I would press my elbows into the deepest, stickiest layer of mud, that they would be as brown as a farmer's. I knew—and I didn't care.

I sniffed the still inviting southern scent of wormwood on my fingertips and I sniffed the rising scent of the soil below me. I felt free and airborne.

I was contaminating myself.

This time in a more positive sense.

3

My selective urban deafness allowed me to choose from the surrounding sounds only those which I found appealing.

So I was not bothered by the drone of military planes on drill or by the distant motors of semis roaring down the highway; I listened to the buzzing of a fly over me, the rustling of the breeze among the wormwood stalks, and the deep bubbling of the spring by the highway: a bubbling so deep it seemed as if it came directly from inside me.

From all those odors, I picked out the scents of earth and wormwood. And the colors of the instant were soil-brown, wormwood-pollen-yellow, and the uninterrupted blue of the sky.

I felt perfect.

I fell asleep.

4

I'd been trying for some time to get that wheelchair for Patrik.

I asked my friends if anyone knew where I could get one, and I placed a want ad in *People's Democracy*, but no one responded.

I pasted posters on fences around town announcing that I wanted to buy any kind of wheelchair. But the only result was a series of prank calls from jokers who'd never seen a wheelchair in their lives—and Grandmother began avoiding the telephone like the plague.

In spite of the fact that my posters quite clearly specified that I wanted to *buy* a wheelchair, a few desperate people called me thinking I wanted to sell one, and a whole slew of bedridden invalids promised me dizzying sums and wept on the telephone over their hopeless situations.

It began to dawn on me how infinitely lucky I was to have two healthy legs.

I searched out several paralyzed and legless invalids in the area (Christ, how few of them there were on the street all of a sudden) and worked up the courage to ask them or their relatives what they would do with that wheelchair if somehow . . . when . . . he . . . somehow . . . gets better . . . or . . . you know . . . I mean, simply, when they were done with it.

It was extremely awkward.

To walk up to an invalid on the street and say, "You know, sir, I've got this friend, and he's a cripple, just like you, so what do you say, would you be so kind as to pass that wheelchair of yours on to me when you, excuse my frankness, kick the bucket?"

It was extremely awkward.

Of course, I don't mean to imply that I walked the streets of Prague chasing down invalids just to guess how much longer they had to go. I'd always been well behaved, helping the blind cross the street, helping the elderly up the stairs with their groceries or bringing them coal from the cellar. I never participated in any of those idiotic school campaigns like Let's Help Our Elderly Comrades, but I always did plenty for anyone in need. I'm not bragging about this; I never bragged to anyone about it. The effusive gratitude of sincerely touched grandmothers embarrassed me—and I always disappeared as quickly as possible after my "good deeds." No, goodness had nothing to do with this behavior: I had no real concern for these people, and I wasn't trying to show off: Oh, look what a caring person I am. I simply couldn't stand to watch that helpless fumbling, that is all.

Now I was beginning to see invalids and cripples—and especially the poor devils confined to wheelchairs—in a completely different light.

Among professional invalids there was no spirit of solidarity. Solidarity ended at about the level of a broken leg. Those who would be back on their feet before long could afford to help one another. But true invalids, invalids for life, knew perfectly well that skating on the thin ice of socialist health care was safest when done alone.

At first I thought they were just bitter. Gloomy and taciturn.

Then I came to understand that these were the symptoms of the struggle for survival in a brutal wilderness.

Nusle, filled with more aging and infirm people than any other neighborhood in Prague, was a particularly savage wilderness.

The District People's Health Care Center, to which all the ill applied, was supplied with medicine in strictly limited quantities. As a result, the more people needed a certain medicine, the harsher the struggle to get it. The more infirm there were in a certain district, the more overworked that district's doctors were and the longer the waiting list. Rivalries sprang up among all the elderly men and women who occasionally required a doctor's care. Everyone scrimped and saved their measly pensions in order to buy liquor and coffee beans for their doctor, just to stay on his good side.

The big shots had succeeded in channeling people's justifiable fury over miserable health care into personal feuds and silent duels. For years Grandmother had been bringing me the gossip from the street about who had "had it" and who was "out of the woods"—and for years I'd failed to understand that gleam in her eyes when she passed on one of the more unhappy news flashes. It wasn't until now that it dawned on me: to me the news sounded bad, or—I admit—for the most part uninteresting. But for Grandmother each corpse was a small but heartening victory in the pensioners' struggle for survival.

But I was willing to think in those terms only once I saw that Patrik had a solid chance of becoming a professional invalid.

And I didn't believe he would make it.

But I was looking for that wheelchair for him anyway. Once, in a fit of charitable feeling—when I still had no idea what it meant to be a pensioner—I knocked back two shots of rum and ventured out to find a very far-gone old-timer with one leg who'd been feeding the birds in Jezerka Park for years. He fed the tits and sparrows quite faithfully, and the pigeons, when he thought no one was looking, since it was strictly forbidden to feed pigeons in Prague.

I said I'd really love to know where he got that marvelous wheelchair of his.

I said I had a friend, a young man who couldn't walk. I said my friend could really use a wheelchair like that . . .

The old-timer looked at me with watery, vacant eyes shot through with bloody capillaries. He didn't respond for a long time. Then he spat saliva mixed with half-chewed bits of bread crust at me and wheeled toward me so suddenly that he knocked my legs out from under me.

Next he chased me along the park paths in his motorized chair, shouting, "We'll see who they bury first . . . me or you, you impudent slut!"

The old-timer had sensed my hidden message and was fighting for his life in his own way.

Not too long after that, it began to seem to me that an unusual number of pensioners turned their eyes away when I passed; that far too much randomly fired spittle was landing precisely near my feet. Then my television-crazed grandmother brought home the news that word was out I was making the rounds of pensioners, advising them to die soon and make room for the new generation.

It seemed I was on the wrong track.

I visited the Handicapped Production Cooperative and exchanged a few words with the kindly old chairman. The chairman didn't look handicapped at all. He ran nimbly from office to office, a ruddy, balding old guy—working hard to give me the impression that he was keeping his invalids' noses to the grindstone (in a most socialist manner). He seemed too secure.

The good chairman kindly informed me that they had no wheelchairs, never received any, never produced any, and never would produce any; however, if my afflicted friend was still good with his hands and not blind, he would be happy to see to Patrik's employment at the plant. How about tying bristles onto broom handles?

I wrote to my acquaintances in East Germany, asking them if it was by any chance easier to get wheelchairs there—and I was informed that it was easy to get wheelchairs but illegal to export them.

My passport had been revoked for the time being, so I couldn't even try to risk it, and to ask someone to slip a wheelchair under his shirt and smuggle it across the border, that would have been naïve, bordering on abusive.

5

Yes, on top of everything else, I didn't have a passport.

They'd taken it from me on the Hungarian border the year before, when I was on my way back from Bulgaria. I was issued a temporary identity card for the trip from the border town of Komárno to Prague (of course, as prescribed by the regulations, I'd left my Citizen's Identification Booklet at home before going abroad), and I was told to save any discussion of my travel documents for my appointment, six weeks later, at the Department of Passports and Visas.

The comrades did not specify why my passport had been revoked, but I suspected it was on account of my mouth.

I'd been traveling from Bulgaria with an Intertrucker—and I forgot to get out in time. When hitchhiking across borders you always had to get out about a kilometer before Customs and walk the rest of the way. If a girl got caught with an Intertrucker, there was an interrogation almost as a rule.

And so, sweating away in a tiny, dusty, poorly ventilated

cubicle on the border, between two comrades, one of whom (according to the established script) was amiable, the other more severe, I unexpectedly lost my passport and I didn't even know how.

I stated my full first and last names for the comrades about three times: I recited where I went to school; I thanked them for asking and added that, like my mandatory summer of student service camp, I had already completed my exams—and pointed out that I hadn't done anything wrong and so, for God's sake, they could let me go on my way.

"Do you frequently hitchhike to Bulgaria?" asked the good cop.

"Where else can I go, comrade, when you won't let me travel to the West?"

"He means hitchhiking! How often do you do it?" barked the bad cop.

"Oh, every so often, comrade. The train fare went up about 30 percent last year, so I hitchhike."

The nice one wrote something down on his pad—and both of them looked at my T-shirt.

Oh yes, my shirt allowed my nipples to show through a little—and in the last few minutes they had somehow become erect, though certainly not out of arousal. Maybe out of anger.

"What languages do you speak?" asked the nice one.

"Languages? A few. Let's see: Czech, a little Slovak; my Russian is quite goo—"

"Languages!" the stern one howled at me. "We're not asking you about Russian. Foreign lan-gua-ges!"

"Is Russian not a language where you come from, comrade? I really do speak Russian well. I passed the state exa—"

The bad cop's leg moved toward mine under the table. I recoiled as if I'd touched a snake. True, I had shorts on . . . and I liked it when people on the road turned to look or whistled. In fact, I didn't know why on such a sultry summer day I shouldn't be allowed . . . I certainly hoped they weren't planning to require students to wear nun's habits during summer vacation.

The bad cop made a notation on his pad: "English, German. You have . . . courses in English at the university, don't you? —*Shprekn doych?*"

"*Sprechen Sie Deutsch*, comrade," I sighed.

"Aha. So English, German. Do you speak French?"

I shook my head in exaggerated remorse. "No, unfortunately. I'm sorry to say that beautiful tongue is Greek to me. I studied Greek a bit, but without results. *Parlez-vous français?*"

"So that's it for languages," said the nice one in a weasel voice, turning the page.

"And the state exam in Russian, comrade. Don't forget to make a note of that. The state exam in Russian."

The stern one kicked me under the table again. Or perhaps he was just trying to . . . make friends?

The good cop ignored me.

6

I was giving them the old "comrade" once or twice every sentence as a rule, and that probably got on their nerves. After half an hour they started calling me "Miss," which was never a good sign.

The cops used Miss with a special undertone with girls they later took down to "sleep over" at the station, or in herds in great big police delivery vans to collecting stations somewhere outside Prague.

I was playing with fire the whole time. And I knew that, of course, but I couldn't help myself.

I usually couldn't help myself in my run-ins with the State Police. In such cases it was enough to respectfully answer their questions for a few minutes, say, Yes, comrades, I'm hitchhiking from Bulgaria because I lost my return ticket (best to say it was lost, under no circumstances stolen) . . . I'm hitchhiking, scared out of my wits; I've never dared hitchhike so far before, but now . . . what else could I do . . . ?

Show a little remorse.

A little humility.

Or maybe that wouldn't have been enough. But it certainly would have helped to wear a heavier T-shirt. A less clingy one. And long pants.

Or to sprinkle some preventative ashes on my head, so the comrades wouldn't suspect me of anything.

Or not to go to Bulgaria.

Or not to hitchhike.

Or . . .

Ah yes, now we've arrived at it: what it was that upset me most about the police apparatus—and why, in those uncomfortable situations, I became a bit of a wise-ass, streetsmart, wary as a fox: a decidedly suspicious character.

All those *random* document checks, *random* customs searches, *random* identification checks on the street, or *random* extractions from trucks for the purposes of *random* verification—all these forms of loathsome bullying had only one function: to threaten you.

No, miss, of course it is not illegal to hitchhike, miss, but, you understand, we already have a fair number of reports on you from all around the republic . . . Are you absolutely sure that you *really are* a student, miss? Would you be so kind as to show us your Identification Booklet one more time, *just to be certain*, just to double-check?

Of course it was not illegal to hitchhike, but it wasn't advisable; you weren't supposed to—and the comrades always pointed out to you that all those reports about you were sent to the Center. That the interview transcripts, in multiple copies, were accumulating somewhere in a file folder with your name on it—and someday, when there were just too many of them, then, citizen, then . . .

I imagined the Center as a monstrous spider's lair, resounding with chaotic impulses arriving along sticky filaments. The filaments of a spider's web that bound you the more tightly the more you struggled. The more you buzzed, little fly. Tiny little fly.

Day after day, year after year, it became clearer and clearer that we were nothing but serial numbers.

Precisely catalogued, mass-produced screws in the machinery of a single, enormous, filthy factory for the defiling of the sky and the homogenization of rainbows.

We were screws in the machinery, positioned according to our levels of tested reliability wherever the engineers felt they could afford to place us. Stupid and reliable screws were used for construction. And unstable, rebellious screws, screws that jiggled and slipped, were used where they posed the least threat.

I felt the burning of the dozens of X-ray eyes the comrades used to examine every inch of my rebellious steel soul. I hated it. And as I refused more and more to be a good little screw, the factory engineers paid more and more attention to me.

In light of all this, it was a miracle they hadn't kicked me out of school yet.

7

Patrik (although he was like me in this respect, his only advantage being that he wasn't suspected of any form of prostitution) said I was a fool. He was convinced that, when dealing with the police, not being an idiot meant acting like one.

"You can't let a cop know you're smarter than him," he

philosophized. "The pig's got to think you're weaker. That you're afraid of him, scared shitless."

"Yes, teacher," I peeped like a model pupil.

"You've got to be meek. Play the submissive role, as you psychologists call it. And the main thing is to answer every stupid question the morons ask."

"Miss, did you sleep with the driver who gave you a ride from Sofia?" I said.

"Well, then, of course, you say . . ."

Patrik thought about it. It was clear that he himself rarely had to answer questions from the Higher Organs about whom he'd slept with.

"Miss," I added, "what did he give you in exchange? A bar of soap, some Bulgarian rose perfume . . . Or perhaps he took you out for a steak dinner, miss? So, now tell me, miss, did you sleep with him?"

"You've got two options—they're both about equally embarrassing; one of them is a bit more unexpected. They expect that everyone will answer no."

"I wouldn't answer them."

"Because you're an idiot. They expect you to say no. And at the same time they're a hundred percent sure that you've screwed the guy at least seven times. You can say to them, Jesus Christ, I beg you, the whole trip I'm praying nothing will happen to me and you ask me that kind of question. My boyfriend would kill me if I did anything like that. Jesus!"

"Hm. I see, I invoke the Lord Jesus, and they say, 'So you are religious, miss, I see, yes, and what church do you attend?' "

Patrik laughed. "Bullshit! You know how many times I've been at the station and heard the cops yelling 'Jesus Christ' and 'For God's sake, why are you lying to us, comrade?' And in Slovakia the cops are religious like you wouldn't believe."

"Whatever you do, don't say, 'Why, comrades, how could you think such a thing. Really, that driver was so awfully nice to me, he took me out to dinner three times and forced me to take God knows what all from him—just look at all these things he made me take.

"He even gave me money for my boobs," I added—and I made as if to take my T-shirt off—"have a look!"

Patrik laughed. "That might just fly, Fialinka. But that's enough out of you, wise-ass. You basically have two options. Act like an intelligent bitch or like a nice, decent, intelligent girl."

"I'll take the nice girl."

"Well," said Patrik, sizing me up and looking unconvinced, "that option somehow, Fialinka, also doesn't quite . . . but okay: a nice, intelligent, independent girl. When asked the question Did you sleep with him? she takes offense, but meekly, meekly! She soberly explains that the other party seemed to display some sort of improper desires, but she rebuffed these advances with a reproachful wave of her virginal right hand. Just in time."

"And the nice girl raises her reproachful right hand and, with a few well-placed blows, knocks all the comrades, the typewriter, the desk, and the cabinets to the ground; then she grabs one of their pistols, leaps from the fourth-floor window into the Danube, and shoots her way across the border into Austria. Thank you very much."

"That would be overdoing it, Fialka," Patrik reprimanded in a professorial tone. "That is a perfect example of your excessive self-expression, Miss Jourová. Next time try to avoid casualties, please."

"Fine. What next?"

"It's simple—once you've managed to play the role of the nice, reproachful girl successfully, you're more or less home free. That's pretty convincing: a girl is left stuck in a tight spot in Bulgaria and she fights her way heroically from

Sofia to Komárno, all the time the picture of moral goodness, then finally falls into the comrades' arms at the Czechoslovakian border post and breaks down in tears of joy."

"Then she tells them all to go to hell."

"I keep telling you, he that is his own counsel has a fool for a client. But, for you, Fialka, there's still one chance left. Confess to the comrades tha—"

"Confess what, may I ask?"

"Well, confess that you slept with the driver!"

"Look, Patrik. First of all, I've got nothing to confess to the comrades, since going to bed with someone, I believe, has not yet been declared an anti-Communist act. And second, I didn't sleep with the guy."

"I don't believe you."

"See that . . . you're just like the cop. Goddamn it, just because I've got shorts on and he can see my legs—which, by the way, is only so I can get a tan and so I don't die of heat prostration in long pants—just because of that, it means I must have slept with him! I could have slept with him, of course, and maybe I have slept with people under similar circumstances, but it pisses me off when every guy thinks I'm ready to sleep with him. It really pisses me off."

"Don't get excited, comrade. Don't get excited. That only proves that you haven't got a clear conscience," Patrik said, rubbing his hands in the unmistakably typical gesture of a stupid, self-satisfied cop who's caught you red-handed. Patrik had observed this gesture in the dozens of police stations he'd passed through, just as I had over the years, he as a photographer and I as a simple hitchhiker. I was a loose screw that needed to be tightened. And Patrik was a rotten, treacherous screw that needed to be eliminated.

I knew the price Patrik had paid (sometimes in blood) for these confused words of wisdom he was now passing on to me. I knew Patrik had been through a great deal more than I in police custody—and that the questions he'd been asked had come a little closer to the bone, so to speak. A fist to the head. A boot in the gut. I, who had only once, long ago, been the recipient of a few blows (and I had cried over them while still at the station, which I'm ashamed of to this day), I, for the most part, only had to endure insinuations touching upon whom I'd slept with and where.

"It makes no difference, Fialka, whether you did something with the guy or not," my friend continued. "The main thing is that you pacify them. Don't say, the way I'm sure you would, Why, yes, comrades, I slept with him. But that's none of your business. No. First, you blush. Do you know how? I doubt it, knowing you. Watch!"

Patrik fell silent. He inhaled deeply, forced the air up into his face, and waited with half-bowed head until his cheeks darkened. Then he slowly let the air out, inclined his head to one side—and with a precisely blended mixture of guilt and submissiveness looked up at me in bashful anxiety. When I laughed, he said, "I worked on that for a long time, Fialka. You learn it, too. You never know when blushing might come in pretty damn handy. I think it saved me a lot of trouble last August."

8

For as long as I could remember, Patrik had always spent the second half of August in Prague.

Afterward he would relate his adventures to me.

To put it plainly, nothing at all ever happened.

No one on the radio announced the approach of the Second Communist Liberation of our beloved nation. No one decorated their windows or hung out flags for the twenty-first of August. The anniversary of the Warsaw Pact invasion in 1968 was one nobody celebrated.

Here and there someone gave a lonely sigh; or people counted on their fingers the number of days and years the liberators had stayed. Among especially good friends, or in especially drunken company, dozens, hundreds of jokes made the rounds, the kind that could have lost you your job or put you behind bars.

The daily press was especially selective at that time of year. The organs of censorship, and self-censorship, which under normal circumstances passed on information in a very narrow stream, now restricted it to a bare trickle.

The radio announcers tirelessly informed the community about the progress of the socialist harvest, singing the praises of ardent farming cooperatives in the southern lowland regions, where the crop was already safely siloed, and cursing the somnolent loafers in the cold and mountainous regions, where the harvest hadn't even begun.

All was quiet in Prague.

Oh yes, quite a few dared to listen to that foreign radio propaganda (jammed especially meticulously at that time of year), and many remembered the sad anniversary as sentimentally and dimly as we recall our lost youth or someone who died long ago: yes, yes, it's ten years already, twelve, fifteen—well, how time just flies and flies!

In the Western press, there supposedly appeared a little blurb here and there about the anniversary of the invasion of Czechoslovakia, a country somewhere in Europe, but how was any of us to get hold of a Western newspaper? And in the couple of years I'd known English well enough to listen to the BBC, it had become obvious to me that the tragedy of the Czech people had less and less meaning all the time: the great unknown Western world was becoming deafer and deafer to our cries for help.

(Help? Was anyone still crying for help?)

Those who listened to the Czech-language broadcasts on Voice of America and Radio Free Europe were under the naïve impression that we were still of great concern to the rest of the world, but they were mistaken.

There were too many of us, too many suffering nations, great and small. And there was no reason to expect our Western comforters to spend decades bending over each little nation like a kindly nurse in a private hospital. No, our sensation-seeking and troubled globe was more like a bustling military field hospital, where the wounded lay on the floor while the overworked nurses had enough attention and morphine only for the patients closest to death.

A silly metaphor, of course. But all sorts of things occurred to you when you wandered around the blistering August streets of the Old Town, plodded the pavement depopulated by summer recess, seeing all the signs in the shop windows declaring CLOSED FOR VACATION and engulfed by the smog that hung over the melting asphalt, motionless except for ripples of heat. The images radiated from the brick walls; from the Vltava, still so cold you couldn't swim in it; from the burning sidewalks and their ornamental cornerstones. Whoever could leave Prague did. Even the lazy pigeons cooed exhaustedly, copulating listlessly, lazily lounging around on the statues of giants and absentmindedly shitting on their heads.

During the critical August period, the police presence increased just enough to be noticeable, and for a short time it was amusing to pick out undercover cops in the crowds of normal citizens. There were plenty of them.

Nevertheless, you saw no soldiers with tommy guns standing watch on every corner, no beggars lounging with outstretched hats near the churches (in any case, the cops would have chased them out of there pretty quickly), no naked and hungry children running around Prague in packs, crying.

In other words, there was nothing in Prague for Western reporters to photograph; that is, if there had been any in the city in the first place.

Sometimes it occurred to me what bad luck it was that the greatest event to come to pass in our country had not been sufficiently appalling. The personal tragedy of the Czech people had been unable to survive for very long on the front pages of the Western press.

It hadn't been brutal enough.

It hadn't been photogenic.

God knows how many years ago the occupation tanks rumbled through Prague—and then the soldiers, officers, and whole Russian families settled almost innocuously in small peaceful towns in Bohemia and Moravia and Slovakia.

Innocuously?

In Bohemia there took place a gradual, inconspicuous sovietization process at levels that are difficult to pin down—but went ever deeper and deeper. Russian tanks. Russian barracks. Russian towns. Russian schools. Russian perfume. Russian books and magazines. Russian babushkas. Russian fairy tales, and Russian vodka. And the surreptitious permeation of the typically Russian way of thinking. Or what's worse, the Soviet way of thinking.

The Young Pioneer Scouts were rewarded with trips on the friendship train to Moscow, and the Great October Revolution was probably a bigger holiday in the satellite countries than in the Soviet Union itself. Ours could be defined as the perfect occupation: perfect, because the average person no longer even realized it was happening. It was the occupation of human souls.

Of course, the fewer soldiers with tommy guns stood in the street, and the quieter and sleepier Prague was during those August days, the greater the threat of foreboding for those who could still see. The war had already been lost.

In Afghanistan the Mujahadeen rebellion was raging and people were dying by the thousands. Defending themselves. Photogenically. Women and children were starving. The occupation forces were interrogating children—and the politicians left them to burn to death covered by napalm. By the hundreds.

Meanwhile, the first (and only) flare-up of rebellion in Prague had taken place in 1969, five months after the invasion. A young man named Jan Palach, younger than I am today, set himself on fire somewhere on Wenceslaus Square (that was even before they routed traffic through it)—and people said, A crackpot, an adolescent stunt; so he burned to death—what did it prove? What about his parents, what about them? And then, later on: God knows what really happened; I heard he had cancer, have you heard that? And he wanted to go out with a bang, to go up in flames, not just to die like an average citizen, with an IV tube in his arm and full of morphine . . . But I am right, aren't I—it's better to stay alive?

And the further into the past all that receded, and the older these speakers became, the more people there were who were convinced that the most worthy goal in life was to stay alive.

To succeed in surviving until your appointed death.

9

Now and then it really bothered me how quickly I was aging, how quickly and irreversibly the years of my youth had elapsed—and how unfairly and imperceptibly the years continued to slip away. But sometimes I felt I had been born too late.

In 1968 I was a young girl, so young I couldn't remember anything. Patrik had been nine at the time. I had been even younger—and we both cursed Fate for not making us a little older, even by just a few miserable years! At eleven, twelve, thirteen years a child can at least perceive events, even if he can't understand them: understanding comes with age.

I don't know, perhaps my childhood up to the age of seven or eight was muffled in that impenetrable veil Freud writes about. I had been wrapped in a blanket of unconsciousness; I had seen the world through the weave of a knitted scarf: separate, distant . . .

I couldn't remember a thing from that fateful year. Or anything that preceded or followed it; everything, every single thing I knew about it, had been read or heard from someone else.

Me! The one who never trusted anyone's impressions but my own, as a matter of principle.

Patrik was the same way. We listened breathlessly to the recollections of witnesses only a couple of years older than we. We leafed through the yellowed pages of dusty issues of *Young World* magazine; somewhere in the attic, wrapped and bound in a chest, they had been saved for us, thanks to the Era of Documentation.

We gulped down the barely censored texts in issues of *World Literature* from the early sixties, magazines which our parents had kept hidden behind the bookshelves (I remember their corrupting influence on my early adolescence). We fought over every little scrap of paper, opinion, or fact, and extracted a confession from anyone who was the slightest bit willing to talk.

And the result of all this was that we fell boundlessly and hopelessly in love with the Prague of the sixties, a Prague we had never known, although we had actually lived in it!

We had been right in the middle of it, and we knew nothing about it! We cursed and raged at Fate. We cursed ourselves for not being more precocious children; we raged in our hearts at our parents for being too careful and not conceiving us a couple of years earlier. Just a couple of years!

We knew the Soviet tank shells embedded in Prague's stucco walls—those shells about which our teachers were instructed to say that they were the remnants of World War II, if the topic came up.

We went on excursions to touch them: those chunks of steel which fit snugly into your palm—and they were silky smooth from the hundreds of hands that had touched them before. Probably without realizing what they were, but perhaps . . .

On hot August days they grew warm in the sun and radiated heat.

The heat!

We searched for the heat of August in people's faces and—Lord!—how little of it there was left already. Those hands, somehow joined by their common contact with that same heated piece of metal—those hands would never again join to do something about it.

To *do* something.

Prague was always tranquil in those hot days of August. Those who remained in the city quietly went to work and quietly swore about the conditions in the city. Mobs of tourists, mainly from East Germany, whose citizens weren't permitted to travel anywhere except Czechoslovakia without a visa, flooded Prague with their boisterous German. Pensioners stood in lines for goods, and doctors complained to one another of life's hardships and took the tram to the Vltava to feed the gulls.

The nightlife seethed a bit more furiously in the great city, for Prague teemed with all sorts of other foreigners in addition to the East Germans. And young women, girls, even middle-aged ladies, issued forth into the streets to hunt hard-currency men, their ambitions graded on a scale: make a few marks—have a good time—marry to advantage.

And the students? They were forced to toil away picking hops somewhere in the countryside, or else they were studying for their last exams. The student protests had died down long ago. The students all kept their noses to their own little grindstones and out of trouble. Patrik and I used to talk about how strange it was, the way those youngsters had managed to *become sensible*: all but a damned few of the ones who wanted to study even a little past high school had stopped screwing around a long time ago. Even the Omnipotent Sorceress of Puberty had lost her influence. They all had it planted in their heads from childhood that just one little screwup could block the path to success forever.

Or rather, the path to what people in Czechoslovakia had been taught to call success.

People escaped into individualism.

To their families, their little certainties, their cottages in the country, or their carefully chosen handful of friends and pseudo-friends.

And—when I think about it in these terms—the path Patrik and I had chosen was individualistic in exactly the same way.

10

Individualism . . . We all felt exceptional to some extent.

Perhaps not unusually intelligent or gifted, perhaps not infused with any special ability or strength that made us somehow better than everyone else. We were simply different—and from many experiences we knew very well how few people understood us.

There was an enormous number of us exceptional people. Hundreds of independent individualists, people understood by no one, standing in lines in front of stores and stepping on each other's feet in trams. Among the crowds of lonely seekers for understanding we wandered through Prague without a word to anyone. If we did, after all, enter into conversation with someone, the conversation was brief and passing, or it lingered so long at the level of superficiality that each party concluded that the other was one of those people who understood nothing. There were no magical moments of agreement or glittering instants of friendship. The Praguers wandered through their city day after day, shielded by little bubbles of opinions they shared with no one. Hitchhikers wandered the republic—and only by terrible accident might you discover that this other person sitting beside you shared your destination. Lonely microscopic personalities wandering across an overpopulated globe.

We lived separated by our silence, tedium, and anxieties.

And if—even just once in your life—you actually met someone, someone with whom you never ran out of things to talk about, that was an absolute personal miracle, pure and simple.

11

Whatever efforts and strivings remained somewhat beyond individualism in Czechoslovakia belonged to the realms of Tenacious Preservation and Documentation.

Tenacious Preservation—or, more precisely, attempts at it—was the territory of the protectors of wildlife and of historic monuments. I knew some groups of conservationists whose work consisted of pulling rusty cans out of streams and explaining to park visitors why they shouldn't pick the flowers. Of course, they could do nothing about the factories spewing tons of ash into the atmosphere and barrels of waste into the rivers. One of Patrik's and my close acquaintances worked to preserve the old Jewish cemeteries (though himself a pure Aryan), and on his hands and knees he had mapped the entire underground tunnel system beneath the Old Town, into whose fantastic and inaccessible depths he would take us if we begged him pathetically enough.

Documentation was the polar opposite of Tenacious

Preservation—and its manifestations were far more pronounced. To document meant more or less to give up all efforts at correction, in the belief that correction was impossible. The fundamental principle of documentation was to collect materials that were damning—and therefore illegal.

Self-appointed archivists saved up clippings from the newspapers, news items and editorials, especially the most blatant propagandistic absurdities—and also anything that hinted at the greater freedom and less restrictive censorship of the past.

Singers and unofficial writers documented: they saved their observations and opinions for themselves, for their friends, and perhaps for the future, should it prove to be any brighter.

The more naïve ones kept diaries, and even ordinary everyday people started family albums.

But photographers like Patrik gave their lives to documentation.

Perhaps to an unhealthy extent.

12

There's no other profession that requires you to be more deft, alert, and perceptive than street photography. There's no other profession that requires you to be in more places at once, to be simultaneously squatting on the ground and hanging from a nearby roof; there's no other profession that requires you to make so many different decisions so quickly: the angle, the aperture size, the shutter speed, the correct instant to release the shutter.

There's no other profession where more chances slip away from you, and where you're more aware of it.

Street photographer is not a calling, a hobby, or a way to make money.

It is a way of life.

Patrik was addicted to it.

To photograph, to photograph with passion, meant not living in the present but tirelessly hoarding it for the future, before finally relishing what you have captured of the past. I steered clear of that. Oh sure, I had my photographic equipment and I traveled to document those diseased, monstrous flowers of mine. I even made my living that way. But that was just an unhurried, patient act of gathering. Patrik was a lunatic reporter who hung from roofs to get shots of the streets below.

I'm not a reporter by nature, and I know all too well the price paid by those rabid hunters of the instantaneous. Life, the whole world, was for them reduced to a series of moments, an exhibition of snapshots. Instead of eyes, they had their camera lenses. They strode around with broad swinging steps, permanently tilted to one side, even when they had no equipment bag on their shoulder to pull them in that direction. The troublemakers, like Patrik, wore flowing overcoats in winter and in summer, so they could always hide their cameras.

The majority of these self-appointed reporters shot only in black-and-white, because decent color film was difficult to find and expensive—and these bathroom developers had never even dreamed of a genuine color darkroom. Consequently, another characteristic trait of theirs was an exceptional sensitivity to light and shade, coupled with a loss of sensitivity to color. Black-and-white photographers instantly translated every color of the spectrum into the corresponding shade of gray—or perhaps they never saw colors to begin with.

But this didn't mean they weren't searching for rainbows.

All the photographer's other senses were forced to submit to the single, dominant, most perfect of all senses: their vision. Nevertheless, their senses of smell, touch, or even taste were not impoverished: by means of some mysterious process, described in no psychology text I know of, the photographer's own subconscious mind was able to provide the other, missing senses for each photograph—but only later, when there was time to savor it in peace. Even other people's photographs spoke to street photographers in this way: old photos from newspapers, books, or family albums spoke to them in far more dimensions than we simple humans could perceive: each photograph instantly invoked the entire gamut of senses for them: to see a photograph was to smell, touch, and taste it. Perhaps because they couldn't even process these secondary sense perceptions except by means of visual images.

Certainly, other artists also perceived the world through the prisms of their incipient masterpieces: sculptors by the shape and texture into which they would transform the stone, painters by color and visual imagination. Every conversation was recorded in the writer's mind as a future dialogue, and life's adventures and problems instantly became narratives. But these artists always had plenty of time to put it down on paper or sketch it—their only struggle was to maintain the inspiration long enough. The photographer was always losing his subject. Every day of his life he lost his most magnificent pictures: he ground his teeth for not clicking the shutter in time; he raged at himself for screwing up the exposure; he banged his head on the railing when, having framed a certain fantastic shot in a bustling crowd, he snapped some ignoramus's uninvited butt instead.

Every technically imperfect shot was a loss for the street photographer. He fumed at his own inability to be in more than one place at a time. He cursed his lousy reflexes. He swore at anyone who trespassed on his field of vision. He railed against the sun, the darkness and shadows.

That, precisely that, is a portrait of Patrik.

13

And one particular though very commonly occurring species of street photographer was the so-called treasonous photographer. Hunted. Harassed.

Taking good photographs was more than a question of being in the right place at the right time with the right exposure setting. It was not just a matter of disappearing before the moldy old man you just photographed picking through the trash had time to yell at you.

Photographers of Prague's street life had to conceal themselves from the sharp eyes of the guardians of order, in uniform and out, who could appear without warning from passageways and cars that came out of nowhere. Dragging you into some corner, they say, "Okay, comrade, let's see your Identification Booklet. What have you been photographing, comrade? Let me see your camera for a moment . . ."

People whose recording efforts might have been entirely apolitical at the outset soon became known as notorious criminals in the police stations of Prague, and they got used to having their faces slapped during the monotonous interrogations.

For those with no record of photographic hooliganism in their files, there was nothing illegal about strolling around Prague on a sunny day, wearing a calm and satisfied expression and photographing Young Pioneers or the pantile roofs of Malá Strana. But as soon as you got caught focusing your insolent lens on something forbidden, it was checkmate.

The incriminating subject might be a drunk reeling out of the Two Cats.

A line of expressionless human faces winding like a

serpent from the butcher's shop in the foreground all the way back to the Lenin Museum.

A citizen casually spitting in front of a wall-sized propaganda poster.

The better you knew Prague, the more situations appropriate for documentation you could find. All you had to do was go for a walk, keep your eyes open—and you were guaranteed no end of material good enough to land you in prison.

But it rarely came to that. The police usually limited themselves to pulling your film out of your camera and to those unpleasant interrogations. To lock the photographer up would have been too blatant—and why make waves in the swamp of sovietization when it was festering so beautifully?

The big shots knew all too well that they really had nothing to fear. After all, could any of these potentially dangerous subjects do any real harm to the republic? Within Czechoslovakia, for us, such photographs were meaningful—but did they say anything to anyone abroad without explanation? The world needed to see something painful, something terrifyingly photogenic: something that made everything go dark before their eyes and spoiled their appetites. In order to be affected, the world had to see open wounds—and all we had to offer were bruises, scrapes, little cracks, just the gently riffled duckweed on the surface.

A blurred nighttime photograph: police club a long-haired hippie shielding his face with his hands.

A drunk and broken-looking pensioner wistfully caresses an empty bottle of Homeland Rum in his frozen fingers. His bed is at the base of a building, on a newspaper on which you can make out *Red Right* and a few sickles, hammers, and stars. The pensioner is being buried alive, little by little, under an unexpectedly early first snow—and just below the half-unzipped fly of his ancient, urine-soaked trousers a headline about the Great October Revolution festivities disappears beneath his body. It must be November.

An ugly gypsy girl with doleful eyes offers herself to passersby from a tenement entryway. A dirty, uncombed little gypsy girl who raises her skirt and petticoats with her left hand and extends the right for alms.

Patrik roamed Prague in frenzied ecstasy. Deaf, dumb, and blind, he saw everything.

The preparations for the celebration of the February Workers' Victory of 1948 on the Old Town Square in Prague. A worker climbing a ladder attaches a red slogan across the outside walls of palaces and historic buildings. And one of the enormous spikes the worker hammers in to hold the banner up blinds the Madonna who has gazed outward from the plaster façade for centuries. The slain Madonna bearing the red flag . . .

Patrik photographed the dandelions growing from the broken roofs of cathedrals and the pigeons who shat on all those statues, tribunals, propaganda posters, and banners considerably more openly than the populace did.

Patrik traveled with me to the border to photograph little country churches. To photograph the peeling paint and cracked frescoes with inscriptions in Gothic script. To photograph the moss taking hold in the eaves of God's tabernacles, the bright green aspens and birches growing through the rafters, the whole church itself leaning to one side and dying an agonizing death, a slow death . . . before the eyes of the villagers, who were forbidden to make repairs. No, the Communists didn't level these little churches. They simply made it illegal to repair them—so the churches had been decaying for ages. People got used to their passing: not erased by bulldozers, not devoured by flames, they just passed away, faded out of reality as furtively and inconspicuously as that ancient spirit of religious solidarity . . . The tooth of time was eating away at them, neighbors, just the ineluctable tooth of time . . .

Just as it gnawed away at those country churches, the tooth of time was gnawing away at mankind's ideals and sense of solidarity (it was forbidden to repair them, too). For Patrik and me, the dangerous, decaying rafters of those churches near the border of our republic symbolized the decay of the entire country. Everything was falling apart on us. Rarely razed by bulldozers. Almost never consumed in flames. We just rotted away beneath the green (or red) surface of duck-weed in a morass populated by drowsing ducks; our decay was foul, reeking, and entirely unphotogenic.

14

But our tiny, homogenized republic was damned non-homogeneous in places: from the abundant ideological cracks left by the Communist pavers, the weeds sprouted as wildly as did the inexplicably fresh tufts of grass from the cobbled streets of Prague. The truth-seekers and rainbow-seekers walked with their eyes either cast downward or raised toward the heavens. But these were neither the downward gazes of humility nor the elevated attention to Communist ideals re-quired by the state. These were evil days for seekers of truth and seekers of rainbows, because any rebellious, truth-loving element in the peaceful little mire was in danger. Those photos Patrik collected, those photos of cracks and rafters and warped wood (like the warped veneer of a badly pitched wine barrel)— those photos were unlikely to do any damage. Photographers could hardly do any damage with their amateurish documen-tation. But a camera hidden beneath the coat had became the distinctive plumage of a certain breed of truth-seeker.

And seekers of truth could not be allowed to multiply in our quiet, rotting, fraudulent republic.

15

I lay in the dank, moist ditch outside Brno—and it was still morning. I felt the coolness of the soil beneath my thighs and shoulder blades as it seeped through the fabric of my clothes; I turned my head to the side and exposed my face to the long sunbeams which inched toward me with the unfolding of morning. I squinted obliquely at the sun, through the thick black primeval forest of my lashes. Around each little lash, where it diffused the light into translucent gray lace, an embryonic rainbow emerged. I felt like purring.

I stretched out my leg and lightly kicked a tuft of wormwood. As each fragrant stalk fluttered, it gave off another yellowish cloud of pollen, which settled on my sneakers. I sucked in the air. And each grain of pollen, each small messenger of life and growth glittered as it flew through the slanting sunlight, then continued on its mission. A long mission, and most likely unsuccessful: how many grains of pollen are there in the world and how many of them succeed in fertilizing a blossom . . . transmitting their essences, their I's? Each of those grains had its own I, though they swarmed as chaotically and soullessly as humans . . . In the slanting sunlight outside Brno, each grain of pollen became my private star—and I could not resist: I was once again looking for parables in everything. Patrik always claimed that I was as addicted to parables as I was to hitchhiking, hopelessly addicted. He said I should write the Hitchhiker's Bible, who else but me . . . ? Chapter One, Verse 1: In the beginning there was darkness upon the face of the earth and no one stopped for anyone. And God said: Let there be truck drivers! And they were begotten of the mud of sins, and they grew fruitful and multiplied, thanks to the earnest efforts of the hips and crotches of the women of the highway . . . Hitchhikers by the side of the highway are the most religious of people. They pray for mercy—the driver's; the ritual of prayer consists in the raising of the right thumb (the left thumb in barbarous lands) and the lowering and lifting of the outstretched hand . . . Are these not divine offices? In that slanting morning sun, as you travel from the east, your shadow will take the form of an elongated, distorted cross . . .

Patrik laughed at my diseased penchant for comparing everything to everything else. Comparativitis, he called it, a leveling disease—and you are a hopeless comparatic, Fialinka. There you go parabolizing again, he would have said to me at that moment. The parable of the pollen grains: you are dust, and to dust you shall return; and even if you are somebody's star—just look, you naïve fool, into the deep nighttime sky: indeed, you are but one of thousands, millions of holes in the torn canopy of the heavens. Just look—and fly, earnest one, just fly; all the same, you will never reach your fresh and willing stigma.

16

Patrik told me how he had arrived at his theory of blushing.

One hot August day he was photographing one of our favorite subjects, those tank shells imbedded in the stucco, which the perspective of the street magnified beautifully, downright treasonously, against the background of an impressive red banner shining a couple of buildings down: in enormous letters, it proclaimed into the streets: USSR = PEACE.

He got caught. Snared by a cop—in plainclothes, of course. The very fact that the policeman recognized the connection between the tank shell and the banner took Patrik by surprise. The undercover cop was extraordinarily civil, chatting almost amicably, but Patrik, always on his guard, understood very well that this was intended to make him slip up, unwittingly confess his treasonous (artistic) design . . . And suddenly, out of nowhere, he started to blush. It came almost naturally, almost entirely from genuine embarrassment and uncertainty. Patrik inclined his head to one side . . . "And that blush, Fial, that blush made it impossible for him to pretend to carry on his nice little chat with me—and he also couldn't accuse me of refusing to respond to police questioning. Every time he said anything, I just bent my head to one side and blushed . . . Finally he got fed up, he just got completely fed up . . . Learn how to blush, Fialinka! It's worth it . . ."

Then Patrik started to teach me how to blush. With the severity of a theatrical director he monitored the color of my cheeks, to make sure it was sufficiently bashful, and sadly appraised the inclination of my head. "You're a shitty actress," he scolded.

17

I lay next to the road—and only the sensations I desired had permission to approach me. But a hostile, disturbing sound invaded my pleasant and harmonious space, and began to come nearer along the highway feeder road. At first it sounded like the buzzing of a bumblebee somewhere in the distance, but then this bumblebee began growing and getting closer, until its buzz became the unmistakable sound of a motor.

The sound did not go whizzing by me—the car stopped, and I lazily prepared to open at least one eye: it was probably some kindhearted guy who wanted to give me a ride and would ask me envious questions about my vacation; I'd have to explain that I was sunbathing at the moment and wasn't interested.

I raised an eyelid.

Two cops stood next to the ditch. Each one had the sun in his hair and one flat shoe half imbedded in the clay; they looked at me with a suspicious expression that struck me as kind of cute. I smiled, at both of them.

(The main thing is not to resist. Don't be insolent, just pretend you're an adorable, ditzy idiot, Fialinka . . .)

One of them said, "What are you doing here? Where are

you from? Were you headed somewhere for vacation? Alone?
Let's have a look at your Citizen's Identification Booklet; yes,
a routine check . . ."

He said it diffidently, abstractly—it really was kind of
cute the way the practiced, subtly threatening tone that saturated the voice of every law officer was shrouded by his
charming Brno accent . . . Let's have a look—he said it as if
there were syllables in L written at least a fourth part higher
on the scale: *Let's have a look* . . . Oh, Brno.

(Be careful, Fialinka, blush; most important, don't be a
wise-ass, for God's sake, don't be a wise-ass.)

"Comrades"—it just slipped out—"I just *adore* the way
you Brnians talk. Say something else for me. Let's have a
look at my ID . . . *Let's have a look* . . . It's so refreshing,
comrades, I just can't get over that Brno accent, I just can't
. . . Let's have a l—"

18

They released me from the police station in the center of town
about three hours later. It was recommended that I head
straight home and not even think of hitchhiking on the highway—the comrades would be keeping an eye on me. I was
told that my behavior was extremely suspicious and that the
comrades in Prague would be checking up on my studies. So
I shouldn't be surprised when they called . . . Do you understand, comrade *student*?

I took the tram (without buying a ticket, of course) that
ran most directly out to the Southern Road. A tight-lipped,
severe, not very pretty smile of determination was ripening on
my lips. A sneer.

My mind was made up. I was on my way to look for that
wheelchair for Patrik.

1

The sun had been at its zenith a long time already when my tram finally jolted up to the end of the line. I worked my way over to the prohibited highway through the honeycombed mire of dried and cracked puddles. I ran down from the overgrown embankment and took a look around. No cops in sight. And as soon as the promisingly Western silhouette of an Intertruck appeared on the horizon, I thrust out my chest and stuck out my arm. Not the usual supplicant gesture of humble, honorable hitchhikers everywhere. I stretched it out seductively and imperiously, like a girl who had the price of admission.

The rig began to slow down almost immediately, and the screech of brakes in that cloud of swirling dust on the shoulder added to my self-confidence. I didn't sprint the few meters to the cab as usual. I picked my pack up out of the ditch deliberately and approached with the slow step of a queen of the highway. I caught sight of a face reflected in the side mirror. The driver backed up right to my feet, jumped out, and ran around to open the door for me.

And since I'd noticed a little D next to the truck's license plate, I cleared my throat and said: *"Fahrst du nach Pressburg?"*

I didn't add *bitte* or anything like that—I chose the

informal *du* over *Sie* without even being at all sure how old he was.

It made no difference anyway.

He smiled (pleased I spoke German), nodded, and, when I added a regal *danke* after he lifted my pack up into the cab, he observed cheerfully, *"Aber du sprichst Deutsch sehr gut!"*

And that was the beginning of the long period, maybe too long, when I decided to become what almost every cop already assumed I was.

I had decided to get Patrik that wheelchair.

2

After twenty kilometers of small talk I was pleasantly surprised at my long-untested German. I smoked Marlboros (somehow convinced that without a cigarette clasped between my delicately outstretched fingers—even though they were still smeared with dirt—the impression wouldn't be complete) and, with a few successfully composed complex sentences, brought the conversation around to the difficulty of life in a socialist state. Kurt (we'd long ago exchanged names) steered with the barest touch of his left hand and, with his face turned toward me, nodded attentively. He was taking the bait. I don't know if he was listening, probably not, but he still kept saying how much he admired my German: God knows how few of these highway girls knew anything more than *bunsen,* the German word for fuck. He doesn't look unsympathetic, and I could do worse for my first time, I thought to myself. I babbled on cheerfully—and contemplated what would probably happen. This was not like an adventure that comes to you. This was not the work of my old friend Serendipity. I still wasn't used to my role—and I knew that I was going to have to take matters into my own hands.

Kurt asked, "Are you hungry? Do you want to eat with me? *Willst du essen?*"

"Sure," I said. "*Warum nicht? Ich will fressen,*" I added, replacing the verb "to eat" with the verb "to feed" (like an animal).

Kurt burst out laughing and leaned over to clap me on the shoulder. His hand slipped down to my breast.

"*Aber du sprichst Deutsch sehr* sehr *gut. Wo hast du alles gelernt?*"

"Right here," I lied, and pointed over my shoulder to the well-appointed little Intertruck sleeper. "*Hier . . . hier habe ich* alles *gelernt.*"

Kurt was already sitting almost next to me on the seat and weighing my tits on his palm. "*Du bist so fantastisch! Ist das möglich?*"

Everything is *möglich,* I thought for a second, everything is possible, you horny, half-assed imperialist bastard. But right now you're going to have to wait, old boy, because first we're going to discuss the terms.

I rolled that word "terms" around on my tongue and suddenly felt myself endowed with a power and strength I'd never known before. I was a girl who had the price of admission.

3

At the time I spoke German quite well and I'd studied English the only way a citizen of landlocked Czechoslovakia could: with the help of dubious textbooks, scholarly journal articles, and a few Agatha Christie novels. Patrik had started to study Spanish, and I was dabbling in French. In comparison to the average Czechoslovakian citizen we were practically linguistics professors.

I don't say that to brag. Learning those languages was no noble achievement. It was more like a revolt against the gradual Russification of our nation: that other Slavic language (which is not at all ugly, by the way, although lots of people hated it) had been hammered into our heads so painstakingly at every stage of our lives that it called for compensation.

And so these two stubborn, rebellious kids, these two disobedient screws, Patrik and I, filled our heads with imperialistic languages—which, though not prohibited, were not exactly encouraged either. Suspicious languages.

I learned most of my pet languages just by hanging out in Prague's tiny pubs and restaurants (I remember how, years ago, when I was still a baby, I acted as interpreter at the U Pinkasů Pub when some Canadian hockey players were in town for a championship game), through chance meetings with people looking for directions or adventures in Prague— and on the Southern Road, too.

I'd always stood out on the Southern Road, because a lot of drivers (from Germany, Austria, England, plus the more educated ones from other countries) could actually *communicate* with me without their hands getting tired. Which must have been a nice change for them, since the majority of highway girls had only the vaguest clue about German, English, or any other language, if they had any clue at all. As far as grammar went, they were absolute virgins.

I used languages as bridges over the abyss between the West and us, as hypodermic needles to shoot myself up with magical drugs. It was beautiful when some kind of understanding (even if it was short-lived) was created between myself and a foreign visitor on the basis of language; an understanding which, for them, perhaps, was just pleasant but for me was unusually educational and practical. Intoxicating.

Sometimes it struck me that—whether I met them hanging around Prague or one of them gave me a lift on the road—with a lot of Westerners I could reach a better and deeper understanding than with most of my average fellow citizens. If I could just polish my languages some more, penetrate more deeply into those languages, I could finally reach some understanding of the world.

So I buried myself non-stop in totally unreliable text-books and whatever I could get my hands on in English and German. With a heart full of enthusiasm, desperate for un-derstanding, that ocean of understanding, I ground away at those languages—and I set myself up to hear from my lazy friends, who had no awareness of the shores of perception, how worthless it all was, how I'd never get to see the outside anyway, and how I'd be better off just going out with them for a beer. By night I hunched over the books; on buses, trams, the metro, or during a deadly lecture in school I would imag-ine what I would say and to whom, how I would explain certain things . . . in English, in German . . . and every meeting, every single meeting with anyone at all from those Lands of Make Believe was a holiday for me.

Even then, as that Western eighteen-wheeler sailed me smoothly down the uneven freeway from Brno to Bratislava, even then it occurred to me that the payoff from the linguistic investment I'd made might just turn out to be fantastic, ab-solutely fantastic in an entirely different sphere . . . All I had to do was change my approach to hitching on the Southern Road the tiniest bit.

And I was already changing it.

4

At a rest area Kurt got out and went around to the food pantry he had on the side of his cab. He returned with bread, a hunk of cheese, and a big salami such as I'd never seen in my life: like Hungarian salamis, only more tender . . . and the smell, God, how good it smelled! My stomach started rumbling.

Then Kurt showed me how to lift my seat and haul out from under it a huge storage chest of drinks in cans; I almost went blind gazing at all the different brands and types of juices, colas, beers, and soft drinks. I reached for one completely at random and opened it, careful not to aim it at myself. When it popped and a couple of drops sprinkled on the floor, Kurt gave me a congratulatory smile, almost like the one you give a good doggy when he offers you his paw. Oh God, how gifted I am! I can even open a soda can!

"I'd like to take you somewhere for lunch," he said apologetically, "but I don't know of any decent restaurant around here. And besides . . . in Czechoslovakia, actually anywhere in your Eastern Europe . . . well, I really don't like to eat at any of the places. I like to bring everything with me . . . Otherwise, I get sick, and I can't afford that, you see?"

He said it as if apologizing, but at the same time it didn't occur to him that he was speaking with someone who practically never saw anything but the local food . . . It never made me sick, I was used to it . . . It suddenly hit me that he saw Czechoslovakia as something like a pigsty—even though I, poor little piglet, was cute enough, he wasn't about to stick his snout into the slop that sustained me from day to day. It could make him sick.

The Southern Road, by the way, unlike the Northern Road, was definitely not lined with homey, warm and smoky, cozily bespattered taverns. On the Northern Road you could have a plate of gristly goulash for a fiver or soup for two crowns—and that's what we ate up there. The Southern Road, on the other hand, was lined with a bunch of so-called first-class restaurants, where trying to eat for less than fifty crowns was considered to be in bad taste, and the waiters, all spoiled by hard-currency tips, would give the cold shoulder from on high to any piddling Czech who happened to stray in there. In short, the places on the Southern Road were specially designed for the filthy-rich drivers of Western semis.

Kurt unwrapped the enticing yellowish-brown loaf of imperialist bread and a packet of margarine. He sliced the salami and cheese on a paper tablecloth stretched out across the space between us—and meanwhile I spread margarine on some slices of bread. Perfect teamwork . . . I didn't hesitate for a second that day: I was hungry—And good manners? Ha! Why pretend, girl? After all, is this guy really worth being proper? Is anybody really worth all those contrived social lies?

I started stuffing myself with salami and cheese. I was dimly aware that this was the best salami and cheese I'd tasted in my life—and the bread with margarine was substantially better than if it had been smeared with socialist "Fresh Butter of the Highest Sort." I was pigging out without mercy, and Kurt, taking only an occasional bite, looked at me agreeably and hospitably, as if he were feeding his favorite dog. He injected, *"Gut?"*

I nodded with my mouth full and bit off another piece of bread. I suddenly found myself in the middle of a dream. Or—if I had any inclination toward acting—I would say I found myself in the middle of a theater piece. I'd plunged headlong into one of the leading roles, without a clue as to how the whole drama (or was it a comedy?) began or ended. I hadn't learned my lines, I wasn't thinking in advance about what to say the next second, and there was no time to recall what I'd said a minute ago. I was standing in the middle of the unfamiliar stage—and yet it was as if sometime long ago I'd played this role a hundred thousand times before. I didn't know what I was supposed to say, what would happen or what the male lead would say to me. But a prompter (not one who poked her head out occasionally from a booth below the stage, but one that was fixed somewhere in my head and was speaking to me directly), an unfailing prompter always assigned me just the right line or gesture at just the right moment to fit my part. I could see everything from the inside and the outside at the same time, evaluating my dramatic performance as I went and finding it satisfactory. As for the rest, the director and the audience were irrelevant. The main thing was that I was completely satisfied with my role, that I was comfortable in it: it seemed to me that it had been tailored especially for my body, that the author of the play had written it for me and nobody else but me, for this second Fialinka, for a worse and more cynical I. I knew that I would never have wanted this to be my everyday existence—but I had always known that such a person lived somewhere within me, and it was intoxicating to be able to act out my second I . . .

Who am I now and who had I really been before? I had *always* been playing a part, I, the notorious seeker of truth. I had lied. I had deceived with my body . . . Was I deceiving any more now than I had before? I adapted to Kurt, my fellow player; I made myself the way he wanted me to be: supple, just the slightest bit unlike the others, not stupid, but not overly clever either, with a superficial, suggestive wit . . . a promising girl, who's easy to get to know.

I stuffed myself with bread and margarine, greedily sucked at my fingers, still stained with Brno clay (my entire back and the back of my pants were caked with clay, but that made no difference at all at the time)—and the precise, perfect prompter in my head kept telling me what to do next. The prompter determined what I was to say, how to act, what faces to make, how to move my hands, my body. She decided what I was to think about. *How* I was to think.

(You're a shitty actress, Fial, Patrik used to say to me. You don't know how to transform yourself, and if someone ticks you off, you insult him right to his face. If only you could just pretend a little for the pigs. Just the tiniest bit . . .)

And now I could feel within myself dozens, hundreds, maybe thousands of potentially possible lives, from which I'd chosen just one at some point long ago (and God only knows if it had even been I who'd chosen it). It was embarrassing: at some point I had developed into a complete personality, fully balanced according to all the psychiatric norms. But those ten thousand voices were arguing, fighting, and voicing their opinions inside my skull, and it was making my head spin. And those hundreds of complete, plausible, legitimate lives—each of which wanted to be lived—were locked in a battle for their rights. I was feeding on West German bread and perfect, moist salami, more delicately seasoned than any I'd ever tasted—and I allowed one of those other lives to grow and dominate. I gave it permission to be lived.

No, this was no longer just a prompter. A little sadly, I closed my eyes (from the outside it looked like a blissful fluttering of the eyelids from tasting that salami) and plunged headfirst into metamorphosis.

5

After a good lunch, one needs a rest, observed Kurt. He drew the curtains closed, and the atmosphere in the cab, heated by the summer sun, suddenly became erotically sultry. The curtains were red and turned my little German's cheeks pink. The remains of lunch had long been carefully cleared away. After rolling them up in the paper tablecloth, this great lover of order had chucked the whole mess out the window and instructed me to do the same with the juice and beer cans. (A guy who had until then been sitting idly nearby in his little Škoda MB had immediately shot out to scoop up this rare prize.) A few last crumbs that had slipped out of the paper were now itching me under my back as this person pulled me over next to him and started sounding the depths with his hot, impatient hands. Actually, he wasn't really doing much sounding. He was quite sure of himself.

I let him fondle my breasts a little—just through my T-shirt—and then I pulled away and got right to the point: *"Ich brauche Geld."*

(This time the prompter in my head seemed to have made a small mistake—even though Kurt had probably heard those words a million times, my tone didn't quite fit the image of the average highway hooker. I said it too significantly, with too much urgency: I was going to have to make a lot of money—as much as possible in hard currency—in order to get Patrik that wheelchair.)

Kurt was a little taken aback. Just the tiniest bit. Then he reached into the glove compartment. He opened it a crack, just enough to stick his hand in (I wasn't supposed to see everything he had in there, I realized), and groped around. He pulled out a large bottle of shampoo. *"Willst du das? Willst du?"* He turned the fine container around in his hands, like a shopkeeper displaying his merchandise. Look, little girl, how shiny! Now, how 'bout a feel of those titties? The shampoo really did glimmer beautifully; it was tempting stuff: even from where I was sitting I could smell its sweet apple scent. "You have such beautiful, wonderful hair, Vila . . . This will be a little something just for you . . . Just a sort of small gift. Out of friendship. Would you like it?"

I shook my head—and I suddenly felt pretty awkward. I couldn't explain my desire to him at all, why I needed cash. There was no time to go through the whole story about Patrik. He wouldn't have listened—and if he had, he still wouldn't have believed it. Any long-distance trucker could tell you that every single Czechoslovakian girl had, as a rule, all kinds of relatives and at least two dozen best friends, all on their deathbeds with terminal diseases.

I didn't feel like going into that whole story. He simply wasn't worth it.

(Oh yes, if we had met under different circumstances, I would have run up to your truck . . . refused your cigarettes . . . I would have used the formal *Sie* with you, at least at the beginning . . . and we might even have talked for real. Actually communicated. But I had already decided that my words were not going to communicate anything: I would use them only to weave a web, in which I had to catch at least a few West German marks. Perhaps we could even have gotten along, Kurt, you don't look stupid. But you have been chosen, selected for this beginning, and you can't change a thing about it now. Neither of us can. It's impossible.)

"*Ich brauche Geld,*" I said. With shocking offhandedness (shocking to me), I pulled a Marlboro out of his pack—and without making even the slightest move to light it for myself, I waited for him to lean toward me with the lighter flame.

"Do you understand?" I said through the cloud of smoke. "I don't need your damn shampoo. If you want it . . . if you really want it . . . then I need cash."

With no less shocking offhandedness, I undid the button of my jeans and the fly unzipped by itself. (The majority of zippers of Czechoslovakian manufacture immediately leaped at such opportunities to unzip themselves—Patrik always claimed that this was one of the methods by which Czechoslovakian manufacturing enterprises contributed to the campaign to encourage population growth.) I undid the jeans sort of casually. They peeled away from my hips a little.

"*Wieviel?*" he whispered. He was getting to the point.

(It occurred to me later that this must have been monotonous for him, to say the same words to various girls. Veefeel?—this much some of them must have understood. Veefeel? Veefeel?)

He didn't look as if he wanted to pay very much, even though at the moment, by all appearances, he was longing to make love to me. Christ, why put it so delicately—I mean, he wanted to fuck, it was clear from certain physical signs. Impressively obvious physical signs, I couldn't help thinking, and the not-for-profit part of my physical instinct had already begun looking forward to it, more or less. The commercial part asked, "How much can you give me?" And it repeated, "I really need cash, get it, I need cash."

* * *

This was a sport, a game, I was gradually realizing. Kurt was definitely not poor, and even though he probably picked up some girl on every trip he made through Czechoslovakia and had to pay for it, I was sure he could afford to hand me a couple of hundred marks. It was a sport: pick up as many girls as possible in the East and then outdo all the other drivers bragging about who nailed what girl for how little. Supposedly, the consensus among Western Intertruckers was that "Czech whores are good whores, the cheapest whores on earth"—and except for a few insignificant cases, the truckers tried not to spoil them . . . it was a sport. I remember this one Dutchman, a pretty nice guy, who once gave me a lift on the same route I was riding that day, but under completely different circumstances: he gave Fialinka Number One a lift, while today a newborn second Fialka rode that highway. He told me how he and his friend once made a bet on who could score a Czech highway girl for the lowest price. I had one for five marks, the Dutchman said modestly. You couldn't get breakfast for that in the Netherlands. But my friend, he outdid me. He bargained this one girl down to one mark, *one mark*, can you imagine, howled the Dutchman, and she wasn't all that bad. True, she gave him the clap . . .

I'd always laughed at those prices, determined more by location and nationality than by the quality and appearance of the girl. And sometimes I was ashamed for my countrymen— still, it'd simply never occurred to me just how damn personally those highway prices could affect *me*. *"Verstehst du mich?"* I repeated. *"Ich* brauche *Geld."*

And poor, dear Kurt (in different circumstances I certainly could have gotten along with him and, God knows, maybe even have made love to him on an entirely different philosophical basis), this Kurt stared at the strip of tummy below my T-shirt, sighed, and said, *"Fünfzig Mark? Ist das okay?"*

I thought it over, then nodded.

6

The red curtains were made for lovemaking (that is, if this particular act didn't call for a change of terminology); the conditions were almost brothel-like. The sun, already substantially lower in the sky, shone straight into the cabin and illuminated it perfectly. Redly. Shamefully. Maybe red actually is the only color for this, I said to myself, and I noticed the shadow of the fabric pattern on that other face; maybe only red light will do, because suddenly there was not a trace of shame in that cab.

I'd never done anything like that in the cab of a truck during the day before; not that I needed darkness for such acts, quite the contrary; but that clear summer day outside somehow didn't seem right. Actually, I just didn't feel like it—even the other one, the buyer, didn't show any special enthusiasm. Any real desire. He was simply buying himself a whore and he'd just closed the deal with her . . .

He quickly kissed me: tongue thrashing in my mouth, a kiss supposedly passionate but in reality commercial and lukewarm. I guess he figured it was his duty.

He hurriedly checked the swaying folds of the curtains, to make sure no prying eye could look in. *"Gut,"* he said, satisfied.

Then he pulled down his shorts.

7

The prompter in my head, that precise, intrusive, internal voice, never let go of my hand. I knew exactly what to do, even though I'd never slept with anyone under these circumstances before: it had always started with my consciousness becoming pleasantly, mistily bedewed by someone I liked, so that the pleasurable feelings were always clear and unambiguous. But today I didn't even know whether I liked Kurt or not—and it made no difference at all. I had always wanted to be warmly intoxicated with perfectly mellowed (though perhaps only transient) desire; I would let myself dissolve into pleasant reverie—and the truckers who caught on were then allowed to come after me. Come into me. Pay a tender, longed-for, intimate visit. Always for a limited time.

But now—now I saw everything with perfect and loathsome sobriety. Without ardor. Without desire. I examined the shameful lighting in our little cab without shame: everything had perfectly clear, absolutely sharp outlines; gone was that undulating, dewy translucence I needed so badly during my Nights of Distances, my Nights of Instants. I was stone sober and wide awake: I was an actor on the stage of my own private theater, and the role was translated by my lips and movements with perfect precision. It became the way I could seductively (like a typical easy woman) slip out of even that clay-caked T-shirt. It became the bowing of the head I used to inconspicuously avoid direct eye contact; the precise and realistic movements of body, hands, lips. I knew exactly what to do, although I had never behaved this way before. And he didn't get it. How could he have guessed I had a prompter directing me from inside my defenseless-looking head? He surrendered himself to my hands and lips without the least sign of surprise. I did exactly what he anticipated. I did exactly what he expected and wanted, and if anything especially turned him on, it was that he didn't have to ask for anything. He was not so experienced that I couldn't surprise him. I was functioning. I didn't try to assess him, to figure out whether I liked him at all. I paid attention only to myself—concertedly, critically. I did everything I could think of doing—and although I'd never studied what was most pleasing to (average) men, my intuition helped me. I kissed him deeply, a kiss no less clinging than the one he had given me before—then I let him sigh blissfully. Or semi-blissfully. It was an experienced and wet kiss, well calculated—but still just a sort of half-kiss. Everything was halves and semis . . . Our semi-rapport. Our semi-commercial exchange. The half-light. Semi-desire. And we were half-human. We were marionettes, waving our hands, moving, living according to the puppet master's nimble fingers . . . And when that large, actually very large, and hard piece of flesh (*Fleisch*, it occurred to me, *Fleisch*) plunged into me, I realized that even this time I would feel pleasure. Semi-pleasure. I was making my acting debut on the stage of the Southern Road—and the sun had shifted slightly in the sky, so that the shameful lighting colored my rival's face. (Yes, he was my rival, my opposite number in a business deal: my rival, though not my enemy.) Perhaps all my old sins and loves returned to me and aroused me as I conscientiously, attentively (and no doubt artfully), rode him like a hobbyhorse, rocking and plunging. Men like it when they don't have to exert themselves too much, reasoned the prompter in my head. And I was willing to provide good service for good money. I rocked and plunged, more vigorously and deeper, to the point where it hurt—and through the filter of perfectly sober thought I felt my eyes becoming moist and saw the same voluptuous moisture in my rival's eyes and my thighs quivering with the first tendrils of pleasure that were beginning to spread from my crotch, after all . . . After all . . . ? No, there was no after all about it; this was the approach of a powerful, compact, nearly painful orgasm, its potent, absolutely unfeigned spasms gripping my rival like a velvet vise. I bit his shoulder and neck to stifle the moans and the scream that struggled to leave my throat. We weren't the only ones parked at that rest area. I gripped him again and again in the velvet vise and looked with my misty but perfectly sober eyes directly into his; I observed how his face twisted, how he cried out and groaned and pulled me toward him, his nails digging into my buttocks, one hand on each, spreading them. He pulled me toward him and his face twisted with the animal grimace of genuine ecstasy; the quivering spread to my thighs and groin and down my legs . . . I knew the convulsion would come soon—and it would be a painful one—but payment had been made. I held on, and when I felt the hot liquid streaming into me like a firehose into a burning house, I calmly realized how perfectly my prompter had everything planned: these were my safest days of the month . . . Soon the convulsions stopped in my thighs, replaced only by a trembling exhaustion, and my rival, or sexual partner, was still quivering, too. He was overcome. And lying next to him afterward, tired, trembling, my prompter did not forget to speak up and show me precisely how to place my hand on his heaving shaggy chest so that it would seem intimate without applying too much pressure—though, of course, this meant nothing at all. I was still trying to catch my breath in the sultry atmosphere of the shamefully lit cab. That was good, solid lovemaking, it occurred to me.

A good fuck.

8

Kurt was obviously headed for Komárno, through Hungary and onward toward the Middle East, so I let myself off near Dunajská Streda, just southeast of Bratislava. I didn't bother to explain why I wanted to get out just there. I didn't bother to explain why I was hitchhiking in the first place. Kurt imagined that he knew why: he unequivocally classified me among those destinationless highway girls who hitched to earn a little extra money on the side. He had no reason to doubt it: I had behaved like one of them. And for him to search for some kind of depth in me—well, who could expect that of a long-distance Intertrucker. And why should he?

Still, my first raid on the Intertruckers had turned out well. I'd actually gotten the promised and well-deserved fifty marks—and more. He'd peeled off another fifty and smacked it into my hand. Then he dug out some of the contents of his glove compartment (prepared especially, no doubt, for permissive female hitchhikers) and dropped it all helter-skelter into my hands: some bottles of shampoo (the beautiful, sparkling, apple-scented kind), bars of soap (also scented), and expensive and unheard-of kinds of makeup. At first I wanted to refuse all this, but then I said to myself, What the hell, why not play your part out to the end? I said, *"Danke,"* and threw it all into my pack. Offhandedly. As if I'd done it a million times before.

On top of all that, I got an address, a pad to write my phone number on—and an unbearable flood of chatter. How great you are—we've got to get together again . . . I'll call you on the return trip . . . and you'll be home, won't you, promise me that.

Kurt went on and on, and so I said I probably wouldn't be home—and with a twisted smile I pointed at the asphalt. "I'll probably be here, *glaube ich*." Kurt smiled, half hurt, half understanding. I'll call anyway. Promise me you'll be home, promise me . . .

I slammed the door behind me.

9

It was a miserable performance, a bad way out, and not the best spot for it either. A double handful of useless gifts rattled around in my backpack—and there I was trudging through the late August afternoon inferno in the Žitný Ostrov district below Bratislava, the most fertile area in Slovakia. It was not the usual goodbye: instead of morning, it was afternoon; instead of spending the night together, it had been part of the day . . . and he didn't even want to fuck me twice. I was used to the brightness (or gloom) of morning after a long night's lovemaking, not the withering tail end of the day after screwing through the afternoon. It was unusual. Stupid. I didn't like the time of day. I didn't like the way he said goodbye. I didn't like the German language. I didn't like him. And I didn't like those gifts. I didn't even like the hundred marks. I didn't like myself.

(Yes, just an instant before I'd had my prompter in my head and everything had been all right. For an actor on stage there can be no "afterward." But now—as soon as I stepped backstage—there was no prompter to help me anymore. I was just me again. Me, the old me, satisfied and unhappy, without friends, without love, without prompter.)

10

I headed down the dusty trail away from Dunajská Streda; next to the limed white cottages with thatched roofs, peaches ripened on trees I had last seen in bloom. In the reddish-yellow approach of the summer evening everything smelled of the heat that promised nighttime coolness and morning dew, renewal. Just the thought gave me goose bumps: I felt dirty and slimy, like an old salamander crawling out of its den—there was nothing more beautiful than the fresh droplets of morning dew, and I wanted to wait for it here, somewhere near the Danube. As long as I didn't get caught. It was obvious I had no business here, and I didn't think even my Liberation-celebration documents would save me here. The Danube, about twelve kilometers away, constituted a national border.

I floated along through the dust in the direction of Gab-čikovo, to have another look—a quarter year later—at the place where I had searched for and documented deformed summer snowflakes in what was left of a meadow-filled forest. There wouldn't be any snowflakes there anymore, I was perfectly aware. And it wasn't just because of the season: about twelve kilometers ahead of me stood the foundations of the

Gabčikovo Dam construction site: an insane complex which, according to the conservationists, would flood half of Žitný Ostrov and liquidate the few woodlands and meadows that remained. A complex which, for some reason incomprehensible to me, had to be finished as quickly as possible.

My pack was digging into my back and my legs hurt, probably not from walking: the day's experience had exhausted my muscles, my whole body—and even my mind. My sneakers were chafing, and the sweat on my forehead and under my nose had dried into an unpleasant oily film. A feeling of dirtiness. I must stink, I realized. In the descending dusk of summer nightfall I was dying for some water. For cleansing, for purification.

And when, after an unbearably long time, I finally got beyond the foundations of the dam (conservationists in Czechoslovakia opposed it, and their counterparts in Hungary had organized a protest march, but of course it did no good, and the meadows and forests in the Žitný Ostrov district were doomed thanks to this latest Monument to Socialism)—when I finally stopped by the broad, lazy current of the Danube (which always, every time, in some kind of residual attack of adolescent imagination brought to mind the gray-yellow Mississippi—"the lazy river"), it had been dark for a long time. I found a couple of mounds of dirt whose shadows would conceal me, exhaustedly put my pack down next to me (I figured I would spend the night here and in the morning take a few photographs nearby), and stretched out on the dry, hard, somewhat hostile ground. What a change from my soft, moist bed outside Brno! The river smelled of mud and fish: the immobile curtain of aroma hanging in the windless air was so dense and well defined you could have hit your head on it. The Danube lapped softly and smoothly against the stone raft landings; great rivers don't need to be loud for you to feel the power of their murmurings. I longed to swim and bathe in her, but I knew I couldn't, it was forbidden. Although the country on the other side of the river was only Hungary, I could see the flashing lights of patrol boats: they were guarding the surface of the water. Every couple of minutes the beacons licked the black, undulating surface, tracing fleeting bands of quicksilver. The river lapped and surged in her course, apparently unaware that she formed the border between a Soviet satellite called Czechoslovakia and a Soviet satellite called Hungary. For an instant I was possessed with an image of myself stripping and plunging into the Danube, washing myself, swimming with long strokes, escaping the eyes in the patrol boats and the watchtowers on the shore by submerging before the searchlights hit me—and finally, triumphant (and naked), reaching the other side.

The other socialist side.

If they didn't shoot me first.

I dreamed for a brief moment. Then the idea departed. And the mosquitoes arrived. They probably weren't used to unprotected visitors from distant regions, who didn't know enough to stuff their trousers into their socks and cover every quarter inch of their skin with a gallon of repellent. Only at that moment did it occur to me that it was August and I was in mosquito paradise.

They gathered slowly, like a pack of crocodiles converging on an overturned boat. There were a lot of them. Without thinking I reached for my pack, where I had a supply of cigarettes from Kurt. But I gave up the idea—I thought better of it, considering my inconspicuousness. I was a silent, dark speck in a desolate landscape and I didn't dare risk giving myself away with a red flame. Only my inconspicuousness protected me (and only God knew if it would continue to protect me) from the border patrol. This time it wasn't just a question of my insolent mouth. I was in a patrolled (though unadvertised and unposted) border zone, where I had no business being. Me, a girl whose passport had been officially revoked.

As the small, humming beasts settled their velvety feet on my hands, ankles, neck, and face, as swarms of blood-thirsty mosquitoes attacked my eyes and became tangled in my hair, as God knows how many dozens of them simultaneously bit and sucked at me, I didn't even try to brush them away. I didn't wave my arms around frantically, I didn't cry out at the piercing of those dozens of proboscises, I didn't sob in desperate and hopeless frustration.

I fed the multitude of parasites—resignedly—with my blood and sweat and tried not to notice them. I was learning self-control. I was ignoring the little beasts.

Then it occurred to me that I was somehow cleansing myself by having the blood sucked out of me, that I was getting a better bath that way than I could have in the Danube; at some level of semiconsciousness, it seemed that the mosquitoes were peeling me out of my (unclean) skin, that the soiled blood they sucked out of me was being replenished with virgin blood from my own stores. I let the mosquitoes attack me, although I knew that tomorrow I probably wouldn't be able to move because of all the poison they were pumping into me now.

After a time—like a scourged, fanatical flagellant—I began perversely to enjoy it, and in cathartic semi-ecstasy I even began to cry.

1

This beginning of mine didn't end well. I paid for my mystical initiation with unbelievable swelling, a fever, and near-unconsciousness. I have no idea how I managed to get home in that state. I know I hitched a ride with some old Hungarian guy who conveyed me wordlessly to Dunajská Streda—and then I made my way to Prague in two or three semis. I immediately fell into a half-sleep, half-faint upon getting into each one, and I guess my appearance was so unappetizing and repulsive that no one even spoke to me. The last of these unlucky drivers dumped me on the shoulder of the highway outside of Pankrác, five minutes from my apartment, and it took me at least half an hour to drag myself home along the walls and fences. The neighbors, especially the women, peeked out from behind their curtains—and I knew I could count on everyone for blocks around dragging my name through the mud once again. This was something of a local specialty in Nusle, a geriatric quarter where an excessively high percentage of the population had nothing better to do: people in our neighborhood, whom we knew by sight, never even said hello to one another; nevertheless, any poor fool who swerved so much as slightly from the expected path was meticulously scrutinized from a distance and slandered at every opportunity. And I was certainly a catalyst for such activity—undoubtedly one of the most rewarding ones. From time to time, with tears in her eyes, Grandmother would bring me the latest gossip she had been forced to listen to about me. I, of course, had gotten used to this years ago.

If a boiled lobster could feel, I imagine it would feel the way I did. I was red, puffy, and not very much alive. When I got home I collapsed on the couch and covered myself with some kind of powdery cream that was supposed to relieve the pain of the bites immediately. The problem was that I didn't have bites, I had a two-inch-thick burning crust, which instead of itching responded to the slightest touch with a stabbing pain, as if 450 rusty railroad spikes were being hammered into my suffering skin. I vomited. I put a bucket close to the sofa to help keep things pretty much in one place and concentrated on feeling sorry for myself. I told Grandmother, who now and again came running from the television to wring her hands over me, to get lost. Such insults always wounded her (I used them—in order to preserve their effectiveness—only rarely), and she didn't speak to me for at least a few hours. Which was a refreshing change.

This swelling was the continuation of that "afterward"—I knew that quite well. And as the enthusiastically constructive sounds from Grandmother's television reached me through two thick doors, I listened inside for the voice of my prompter and tried to rejoice in my ill-gotten Western gains. Everything was empty and hollow within me. I'd immediately hidden my hundred marks carefully in the safest place I could think of, and I figured I'd unpack the rest of the loot a little later, inconspicuously, so it wouldn't be so easy for Grandmother to make the connection between it and my trip. Thank God, my unhappy, insulted, silenced grandmother didn't even dare ask me where I had been or where I was going . . . Yet she was perfectly capable of asking where those pretty, completely unheard-of little items had come from—but still, what difference would it make?

It was worse that none of the booty consoled me, not even those hundred marks. I recuperated angrily and miserably on the couch in the living room (the room no longer smelled at all of Mother; not even the slightest scent reproached me from the corners). I called Patrik on the phone. In her honeyed teacher's voice Mrs. Fišer called him in from the corridor of the prefab, where he was practicing on his crutches. We exchanged a few meaningless sentences. I told him (through my hurting lips) about my situation and said I'd love to see him, but that I was in no shape to. I can't move, I sighed. Besides, they'd probably throw me off the bus and quarantine me in some isolation ward, claiming I had anthrax. And so Patrik—in spite of the protests of his mother, whose remote and unfriendly sounds I could hear through the receiver—headed over on the bus to see me, his Fialka. We talked and talked, and it felt so good to feel Patrik's warm and unpitying gaze on me! How good it was not to feel ashamed of my frightening puffed-up face; how beautiful that he didn't pity me or wring his hands over me! Suddenly I recognized a part of our friendship, an unchanging part that had endured throughout the years, although we were barely conscious of it: we never pitied one another. Suddenly I realized how nice it must be for Patrik that he and I could talk about something other than his illness, that I wasn't always examining him and asking him how he was feeling.

Patrik and I understood each other. I sniffed his characteristic scent when he sat down in the worn chair next to my sofabed and rested his crutches up against the headboard. His hair had just been washed, and I realized: his hair was always clean lately, clearly a result of Mrs. Fišer's therapeutic activities. I looked at Patrik and felt the powerful current, like a river of friendship that never ceased to connect us. Our friendship went beyond compassion, beyond the desire to help him somehow, even beyond the consciousness that Patrik was disintegrating, fading before my very eyes. I felt boundless sadness and loneliness, it was like watching elm trees die . . . but it was not sentimentality. I could sense something so absolutely sad in the way Patrik leaned his crutches up against the couch, a kind of acquiescence, a composed tranquillity. Patrik! We had a good, meaningful talk, as always. We could get to the bottom of most things the way most people could only get to the bottom of a bottle . . . and yet I felt that now I couldn't tell him absolutely everything about myself, that a tiny, still vague shadow was creeping into the cloudless understanding Patrik and I had . . . even though those hundred marks I still didn't know what to do with, even though those hundred marks were waiting especially for him, hidden in the safest place I could think of.

2

A long time after Patrik left, I lay lifelessly on the sofa, feeling that I had my tongue thrust out and buried between the enormous, eternally unwashed thighs of the universe; feeling that my swollen balloon of a body was rising into the air like a zeppelin filled with hydrogen, about to explode any second. I felt I was filled with poisonous gases ready to be showered on the deserving populace below. I still felt terrible—of course, I could have guessed on the evening in question that a hundred thousand mosquito bites would result in a little more than a few annoying scratches. I could have guessed that my immune system's response would entail headaches, weakness, vomiting, and perhaps even hallucinations.

Quantity had grown into quality, just as Marx had predicted. I was ripe for the hospital.

3

By a hellish act of concentration I managed to make it to the bathroom, where I collapsed into the tub and showered myself with cold water (there was no hot water anyway). My wounds (yes, I had already begun to think of them as sublime wounds)—my wounds were quieted for about ten seconds, but apparently only in order to gather their energy to explode an instant later like nascent supernovas. I was flooded with stinging, stifling internal heat. Even after the water I had crumbs of that powdery cream all over my body, and they fell onto the floor as I staggered out of the tub, naked and wet (drying myself off with a towel seemed like a bad idea). I lay back down on the couch, positioned my Political Economy textbook on my stomach (no less bitten than the rest of me; the beasts of the Danube could pierce T-shirts and jeans with their proboscises), and decided that I should study at least a little, or that moron of a teacher would boot me out again.

Pretty soon I fell into a sort of delirium, and in this half-sleeping, half-waking state a terrible nightmare visited my chest, right where that unappealing textbook stood open. A hundred and twenty thousand dragons, each armed with a proboscis the size of one of those flashlights that takes three batteries, were flying toward me like a squadron of sinister airplanes, deliberately puncturing my skin. They were tasting me. Sucking me. Checking me out. Deflowering me. But what transformed this feverish dream into a truly horrifying vision was the simple fact that each of those greedy proboscises had the precise shape and size, and even texture and smell, of the penis of a certain man I had the misfortune to know: the penis of a certain Kurt from Deutschland.

1

The pricks of conscience left me more quickly than the physical swelling. I put the bars of soap away in a cabinet, used the apple-scented shampoo to wash my hair (God, how mild and pleasant it smelled afterward!), and headed out for the Southern Road again. There was almost no need for the prompter. I am a modern woman, I decided. I can live a double life.

And my gestures (not just that important hitchhiking gesture), all my gestures acquired unprecedented self-confidence, arrogance—and (what surprised me most) effectiveness. My travels lost their focus on long-distance destinations. And acquired financial aims.

2

I was surprised at how quickly I learned. The prompter in my head ceased to function; her words and advice receded from me like the music from a portable radio someone has just carried by. In place of her, my second personality grew and took root, so that there were no more outbursts of idiotic self-flagellation. I learned a lot of things on the Southern Road I had never even dreamed of.

And never would have dreamed of if I hadn't traveled the Southern Road that way.

If I hadn't plunged into it up to my neck, like a pig into a heap of shit.

3

For example, I learned to recognize Scanias, Volvos, Mercedeses, Fiats, Renaults, and every other brand of Western vehicle at first sight.

I never had to look at the license plates or country stickers. I could tell immediately, almost without fail, where each truck that stopped for me was from—and I switched languages accordingly, from English to German to very, very broken Italian and, when that broke down completely, to hand gestures.

4

I stopped feeling embarrassed. And I worked out my second philosophy of long-distance travel. Fialka's View of the Southern Road. This was not a complicated philosophy. It's fundamental proposition was: They're all assholes, and as long as they've got the cash, you might as well take it.

5

I smoked the Marlboros offered me in cabs without the slightest embarrassment. And with the supplies I received from drivers I started lighting up more and more on my own. In pubs. At the tram station. At home. I was on my way to becoming a smoker.

6

It was an oral fixation, and I was becoming a professional.

An expert, if I was to believe all those passionate words

in every conceivable language and those sighs in every conceivable key. Not that I'd had anything against a blow-job
before, but before, I had thought of it as an expression of
genuine intimacy and trust. Purity. Desire.

Now it had become more of an expression of mistrust. I
started carrying a whole load of condoms around with me, but
the majority of men who bought me didn't want to wear them.
I had no other means of birth control and safe days were few
and far between.

I threw myself into oral gratification (both kinds) as my
salvation and got used to the idea that on long and distant
travels no one can be a perfect angel of purity.

Not even me.

7

I convinced myself that it didn't bother me to have encounters
with several suitable and eager men in one day. That it didn't
bother *me*; the most important thing was that it didn't bother
them. I became accustomed to certain (often not very fragrant) signs that a man had just been with another woman—
and hadn't had a chance, simply couldn't wash himself in the
interim.

I cleaned myself off with the paper towels and soft tissues every driver had an endless supply of. As recently as a
few weeks ago I had supposed that the pampered drivers of
the West used their paper towels to wipe the grease off their
hands. Oh, innocence!

8

I got used to not being able to comprehend every driver's
language—and none of their thoughts.

When they passed me on to their colleagues at rest
areas, evaluating me in a language I didn't understand a word

of—and unquestionably recommending to one another certain of my unquestionable charms—it didn't bother me. I got used to feeling like a pear that everyone could have a bite of.

9

I felt like a pear, but not like a powerless plaything in the hands of those highwaymen, who wanted to eat my flesh and throw away the core, so to speak. Quite the opposite: the more I understood this about them, the more these men became playthings in *my* expert hands; the truckers handing me over to their colleagues at rest areas could say anything they wanted to about me or share a conspiratorial laugh boyishly (assuming I didn't notice), but I, *I* was the one who pushed *their* buttons.

I was the one.

I was the one sizing *them* up.

Me. Me. *Me!*

10

I got used to the drivers' (expecially the more simple ones and the ones with whom I had no languages in common) limitless passion for keeping statistics on all the girls they'd gone through in their travels. I had to answer dozens, hundreds, maybe thousands of stupid questions. Each one wanted to know what my name was. Each one wanted to know how old I was (and no one wanted to believe I was twenty-five; they flattered me: apparently I looked seventeen). Each one wanted to know how many sisters, brothers, and children I had. If I was married. How old I was when I lost my virginity. They asked me about my life, where I lived, my whole family tree. Did I have a job? What did I do? Did I like it? *Gut? Gut?* What did my father do? What did my mother do? What did my brothers do? How was everybody's health?

My eyes became glazed—and I felt as if I was at a police interrogation. What do you care . . . what could *you*, of all people, possibly care about my mother and father; sometimes I couldn't believe my ears: I just couldn't understand how some *idiot*, some *moron* dared speak to me about my family in that kind of situation! And even though it was all part of a game whose rules I was gradually learning, each one of those questions (asked by someone it had nothing to do with) always pissed me off anew.

When it didn't piss me off, it made me sad. Put me in a bad mood. It dragged the original, vulnerable Fialinka into the second Fialka's business.

11

And mistrust began to fester.

Before, when anyone asked me about something unpleasant, I just said I didn't want to talk about it. Most of the time that was that. But now? I ground my teeth over the hundred and twentieth question about my mother—and I had to shield myself against that anger with barricades of lies. After all, I couldn't just say to them, Shut your mouth, you little prick, you filthy rich moron, what do you care about my father and mother, isn't it enough to stick your dick in me? I simply couldn't do that. These were customers, not the semi-friends of my countless adventures. In the West one always behaves courteously toward one's customers . . . Courteously. Obsequiously. Shamelessly.

Mistrust saturated both sides of these highway transactions. It was impossible to answer those stupid questions truthfully, impossible . . . And why bother! All that mattered to the idiots who started off in that vein was that the conversation kept moving, even if it was propelled by hand gestures. You just had to keep the conversation rolling, and the road kept slipping by—and a little farther on, at some suitable rest area, we would eat, drink, and screw.

The vulgarity of it, the *vulgarity* still made my head spin. It dumbfounded me. It was killing me. The seeds of mistrust and contempt, the seeds of spite and scorn, were sowed between my thighs together with the men's semen—denser, stickier, but essentially just as devastating. Neither party involved in these highway exchanges and petty contractual agreements had any self-respect, much less any respect left over for the other party. It was hard—and I understood that scornful, disgusted look on the faces of prostitutes. Lying was right, lying was honorable, lying was survival. I was learning.

I was getting used to it.

12

Naturally, there was little reason for trust.

I learned not to trust that I would be promptly paid for services rendered. Taking my example from professionals of the worst sort, I demanded to be paid in advance. I learned not to trust anyone who said he would be careful and to have somewhat arrogant but well-founded doubts about the venereal health of my customers. I became damned cautious and skeptical. I'd hardly ever given it any thought before: I had trusted my one-night companions naïvely and blindly—and I had never been stung . . . That was on the Northern Road. Perhaps Czech men were simply more considerate: a girl could be sure that unless it was mentioned beforehand a guy would never allow himself to come inside her. Czech guys were damned careful. They weren't in the habit of assuming that every unmarried girl was always protected by some kind of birth control. Czech lovers had concern for women. They were more tender. And when you got right down to it, they were protecting themselves, too, especially considering that the affected women could track them down easily enough by their license plates. There seemed to be more than enough freshly impregnated women already, roaming the earth, desperately seeking the fathers of their children. Someone to marry them—or at least to pay. (Blood tests? Ha, a woman specialist I knew used to say to me, They're useless, those blood types; the better the lab, Fialinka, and the more specific the tests, the more fathers are eliminated, believe me.) Nevertheless, whatever the motives were, the fact remains that I could feel free of worries in my Northern Road embraces. I had been safe on the Northern Road—and now, as I was being reborn as a hero on the frontier where East meets West, I began to envy myself: I envied the Fialka of the past. A Fialka just a few weeks younger, inexperienced, happy, and foolishly trusting.

Fialka Number One.

13

In the meantime, Fialka Number Two was discovering that Western drivers were completely inconsiderate—or simply used to an entirely different degree of emancipation. Perhaps the latter was the truth: from what I'd heard, almost all the more adventurous girls in the West used the pill. I'd heard that the pill in the West was incomparably better than its socialist counterpart, since after taking it your hips didn't immediately start swelling up and thickening, and your hair didn't fall out, which had happened to a few unlucky former classmates of mine. In the West you could buy birth-control pills you didn't have to remember to stop taking for a time every year, so as not to do permanent damage to your liver. (Of course, by the end of this rest period, most of the aforementioned former classmates already found themselves pregnant.) No doubt the imperialist pill had side effects—but in any case, Western men were unappealingly accustomed to that convenience. They considered it a sign of bad breeding or something for a woman to be unprotected. And a girl had to pound it into every guy's skull over and over again that he had to be careful. Western men didn't want to understand.

14

So traveling the Southern Road was not the magnificent and unending journey through space and time I had sought and found on the Northern Road.

Instead, hitchhiking was acquiring an unpleasant resemblance to a well-paid but damn stressful job with hardship pay.

15

What else did I learn?

That one definitely shouldn't throw paper or empty cans out the passenger window of a truck, because it might tip off the cops on the lookout at every crossing.

That it was advisable to stay hidden behind the curtain in the cabin, or at least to huddle down on the floor, when passing through especially closely watched stretches.

That it was a good idea to hide any money or gifts in the most intimate hiding places as soon as you received them, because it was not at all rare for girls exiting trucks to be searched.

That it didn't pay to stand around in polyglot conversations at rest stops, because that made it much easier to be noticed and then picked up.

That an ordinary citizen who dully watched as you went to have a pee at a rest area was not necessarily an ordinary citizen.

I learned vigilance.

16

Suddenly I realized what a diverse and unfathomed phenomenon hitchhiking really was: no one person knew it inside and out.

Hitchhikers' attitudes varied: for some it was a quick, cheap means of getting around. For others it was a quick and even cheaper means of meeting people. Or of making money.

I became conscious of the thousands of contradictory experiences, perceptions, and opinions that circulated among hitchhikers, each of whom thought he or she knew best. Events were as mutable as the hues on an iridescent butterfly's wings: they changed according to your point of view. Even if a lot of hitchhikers didn't realize it, hitchhiking gave them just what they expected and desired of it, nothing more, nothing less: most of their experiences were predetermined by their own attitudes, behavior, and goals. Some people hitchhiked daily—ten kilometers from their village to school—and those few minutes, during which they didn't even look around inside the car, became their hitchhiking experience. Others hitchhiked solely during school vacations and concerned themselves only with outdoing one another in kilometers traveled and how rapidly: how often I had listened with simulated interest to the naïve stories of my classmates' travels, events that sounded more than common for me, but for them were adventurous and sensational. Oh, these hitchhiking toddlers! I would say to myself—and I knew you couldn't explain the magic of hitchhiking to anyone who hadn't experienced it with his own skin. Before I turned professional, when I'd still had time for it, I had met a few true adventurers among the East Germans, people with brains and eyes in their heads, people who measured the landscape as easily with the tires of a semi as with the soles of their shoes. Among these winged hitchhikers, these genuine hitchhikers, these hitchhikers who were deserving and worthy of the name (of course, I considered myself one of them, too), among these knowing and comprehending travelers, every single one was a little different, unique, each one had his stories to tell, but only one of their own could comprehend these funny and beautiful tales. These real hitchhikers loved one another, and when two of them ran into each other it was a great day.

And the professionals on the Southern Road? They were such a hitchhiking extreme that I barely considered them hitchhikers. These girls knew nothing of distances and horizons. They moved suspiciously and cautiously (although self-confidently) over only those stretches of road they had already traveled a thousand times. They went where they were taken, knew intimately each stretch of highway, each junction and underpass; they recognized all the different lights on the trucks and the police sirens. For all that, they knew nothing. In the chaos of languages, customers, and half-loves, in the chaos of highways and junctions and whiskey and restaurants, they had forgotten how to think, if they had ever known how at all. They were unbearably lazy and comfortable; they had to have a permanent residence listed in their Citizen's Identification Booklets, but found it easy to get used to living in an endless progression of semis; they had to have a place of employment stamped in their IDs, and they managed to get that somehow—but it was so much easier to work in the horizontal position. Not to mention that the unexchangeable nature of the Czechoslovakian crown made even their tips, which they earned in hard currency, an unbelievable fortune. They had gotten used to it. They were much too used to the road to let it enchant them; they were used to sipping Scotch whiskey with and without soda and, for that matter, to being half-drunk all the time; they were used to the uncertainty. So the road was not an adventure but the comfort of alternating homes on wheels. And they had gotten used to looking for safety and the warmth of a love they longed to fall asleep next to in the questionable embraces of thousands of different, questionable characters.

They were used to fear. Fear of the police, of pregnancy, of disease; eventually even fear of their customers, who weren't always angels. They were not enchanted by the road, the headlights, and the azure sky. They only wanted a lot of money, a lot of comforts, and a place where they didn't have to be afraid.

The restlessness in them was altogether different from the restlessness I had once known.

Of course, they hated each other.

17

From the unwritten law of the Southern Road (which I hadn't known, but discovered quickly and easily enough, because it was as cruel and simple as the law of the forest primeval), it followed that it was impossible to trust anyone.

I didn't.

I didn't trust the paper bank notes (most of which I'd never seen before).

I didn't trust anyone's claim, no matter how solemnly he swore, that he was completely healthy in every respect.

I didn't trust anyone's promises that he would pull out.

I didn't trust the addresses or the telephone numbers.

Of course, most of that made no difference at all.

I didn't even trust the sighs and moans of pleasure, the arched bodies or chattering teeth; I didn't trust the beads of sweat that—supposedly wholly as a result of my services— appeared on foreheads and palms; I didn't trust the streams of sperm that didn't form rainbows behind the drawn blinds of the Intertrucks.

I didn't trust the avowals that I, and I alone, was the one and only most amazing woman in the world. Why should I?

Mistrust, or half trust—you could sense it in every movement and gesture of every girl on the highway. In every truck driver's every movement and gesture. No one ever bothered to tell anyone else the truth, and no one considered himself worthy of being told the truth. I didn't understand how the girls could be always on the lookout, and at the same time so lazy and complacent, but apparently they could. All they had to do was become a little numb. Have a little drink. Stay drunk all the time.

18

It really might have been pleasant to disengage your mind during long-distance journeys and long-distance sex. To listen to and believe the flattery. The drivers certainly never spared it. Flattery in every language.

But I (who had always let myself be rocked to sleep by one-night flattery on my northern journeys) never believed a word of it on the Southern Road.

And while once upon a time, long ago, I loved to curl up in someone's passionate one-night arms, as if into a cradle, and to fall asleep at the first blissful sigh, now I almost never slept at all. If I actually did let myself be talked into staying the night with someone, I never let him have the upper hand. It was never I who fell asleep first. I listened to their tranquil breathing, nasal whistles, dream whisperings, and snoring in every conceivable key (which I had already begun to associate with nationality, just as I had the quality and endurance of their cocks)—I listened to the breathing of the night and engaged all those senses I needed to protect myself.

I listened to the breathing of the night and picked out

the sounds that might have been dangerous. I didn't sleep. But the long-distance night no longer spoke to me, ever; it no longer inspired me with visions of rainbows; it was like being on the night shift: perpetually sleepy, bored, and constantly on the job.

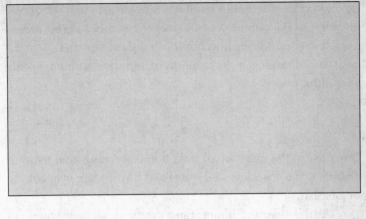

1

Time passed somehow incidentally, unobserved, measured only by the number of days remaining until the end of vacation and the beginning of the new semester and that dreaded exam in that damn Political Economy that awaited me in September. But I cared less and less about how I would do on it. Thinking about school got on my nerves more and more, and I no longer had even the slightest interest in being a model student. I let things go to hell.

Time was clearly dilating for me. Even when I thought about it later, in retrospect, that time, flat and expressionless, unfortified by any special events, swelled with dozens of small and identical diurnal segments marked not so much by the rising and setting of the late August sun as by its periodic exclusion with the help of curtains.

Time began to be measured in the mammon I stored away in little bundles of bank notes of all kinds and colors in a safe place at home. Time was measured in the piles of soap, shampoo, cigarettes, perfumes, and Western food which I was now absolutely unashamed of taking, even when I had no idea what to do with it all.

But time was not measured in the number of kilometers covered between Prague and Brno, Brno and Bratislava; it

was not measured in the number of departures and returns—
not even in the number of trucks or the number of rest areas.

It was no longer measured in magical instants.

Time became a gray, empty continuum without events
and without love.

2

One day, in the midst of all this, the phone rang (and by pure
chance it was I who picked it up) and a voice began speaking
in English.

At the time the phone rang pretty often, and voices in
every possible language issued from it (this made Grandmother so crazy that she finally refused to have anything to do
with the mysterious contraption), so it didn't really surprise
me. But this voice was entirely different from what I'd expected: it wasn't one of those haughtily insensitive or stupidly
beseeching voices I'd been hanging up on lately. This time
the voice on the phone was velvety, pleasant, refreshingly
young.

"This is Erik," it said. "Do you remember me?"

3

It was that nice Swede who had once upon a time (once upon
a time meant a couple of weeks ago) given me a ride to Brno.
That last driver in the era of my hitchhiking innocence.

He was in Prague.

And by some miracle I wasn't out wandering somewhere.

So we got together.

4

We wandered around the Old Town that moonless evening.
At first I acted as if Erik was a foreign tourist; only later did

I realize that he knew Prague very well. Erik had left his semi somewhere on the outskirts and met me in the center of town. Where else: "Wenceslaus Square," I said. "You'll find it. Under the tail of King Wenceslaus's horse."

It took a while for the conversation to get going. Erik obviously knew English much better than I did, and I didn't speak it too badly either. But from the very beginning I sensed that language wasn't the most important bridge connecting the two of us.

So what was it? Some kind of understanding?

Possibly. But not a transient understanding, it seemed to me. It was a kind of harmony. Implicit harmony: the kind of harmony of movements, glances, thoughts, and gestures that I had barely ever known before. I wasn't leading him in any particular direction, and he wasn't leading me either. The streets opened up before us—and they guided both of us in the same direction simultaneously. The corners themselves suggested the changes in our path—and the passageways and little recesses also beckoned us. Always calling us both the same way.

I wasn't thinking about anything. Somehow it was impossible—and luckily my English (which must have sounded bookish and dry to someone who had any practice) was implanted in my head firmly enough that the words and sentences flew out of my mouth without my having to translate them from Czech first. I just flowed with the intoxicating sounds of the language—and even here, at home, in the streets of Prague, I could feel its strength and power.

I loved English. I had nothing at all against German, or even Russian, or any other language. But I loved English. Its magical sound always made my heart pound whenever I happened to overhear it—and I half dreamed of, half thirsted with desire for the distances, for the purple mountains and the oceans, for that great, unknown, powerful land in the West: for that land I would probably never see, even if I suddenly sprouted wings. In English I heard the rumbling of the Canadian grizzly and the whispering of endless green forests. In English I heard the purring of trucks motoring their way from coast to coast, the trip Kerouac had made so many times—the trip I'd never make. English, in all those variations, accents, and dialects I would never know, was for me like a mountain climber's rope linking educated peoples; English (at least on the pages of the books I could get my hands on) opened a gateway into the world and stretched out the living hand of understanding to me. A hand I would never be able to grasp. I was nowhere. Surrounded by barbed wire, encircled by the distant, senseless, but nevertheless impenetrable walls of a prison; and I had no idea why I'd been put there. I had no passport. But the strong nylon fibers of that language reached even here, into this world of darkness. I clung to them tooth and nail. And English in any form, in written texts, sung in songs, on the lips of tourists walking in Wenceslaus Square—English made my legs tremble with travel fever and gave my soul wings. English alone of all languages.

That venerable language flowed from Erik's mouth so casually and easily that it made me envious. Sure, he'd had a lot of practice. Swedes travel to America all the time; Erik had even spent a couple of years there. Everyone in Sweden speaks English.

I envied them.

5

The more we walked, the more intensely I felt how here, on the centuries-old cobblestones of Prague, we were becoming intoxicated with this language and this bridge of understanding between the two of us. It was not an ordinary instant. Sure, this particular night showed all the signs of such instants, but this was much deeper. More beautiful. I wasn't just picking out pleasant things to say; I wasn't editing the conversation beforehand; I wasn't limiting myself to certain topics for fear of the other person's limitations. I walked through the Prague streets alongside the young Swede and I felt myself being drawn to him more and more by the sparkling silvery threads of the web he was slowly and deliberately weaving to entangle me. I could see that he was trying somehow to imprison me in that net of understanding, but I still didn't know why. We walked along through the dark and silent evening, and every brick, every building, every cobblestone still breathed the accumulated heat of the sunny summer day. Prague was familiar, but somehow new, and I understood that he had lent me his eyes, too. Nevertheless, there was still a need to carry on a dialogue somehow.

6

Out of the shadows at the foot of the Charles Bridge emerged a staggering bearded man in a khaki coat. He followed our steps for a few seconds. He was listening. I picked up the pace a little bit. The bearded man also walked faster, caught up to us, and grabbed Erik by the shoulder. "You're an Americano, aren't you?" he said in Czech. "You are an Americano, aren't you, buddy? A-me-ri-ca! Got any dollars, buddy? Dollars, dollars . . ."

In a cloud of beery breath he rubbed his fingers together in front of Erik's face to explain his desire.

Erik was taken aback. "What does he want?"

(I felt myself filling with shame. A shame that froze me for a second: shame for my people, for Czechs.)

"He wants money," I explained. "Nothing unusual. Let's go."

(Shame, shame for someone else? Now you're ashamed for someone else, Fialinka, you?)

The man stretched out his hand to block Erik. "Come

on, brother! What's a couple of dollars to you, huh? For a buddy, come on! Dol-lars. Understand me, brother? Dol-lars."

(Shame. You weren't ashamed of yourself, Fialinka, not on the Southern Road . . . But on the Southern Road there'd been no one to be ashamed in front of. But Erik . . . ?)

"Please, sir, leave him alone now. He's not an American, let him go," I said quietly. In Czech.

The man froze. He stumbled to one side. In the glow of the antique streetlamp his beard looked orange as he tottered for a moment, turning all this over in his head. I thought about who he might be. I wouldn't have been at all surprised to find out he was one of those painters who whip off kitschy little pictures while you watch and then foist them off on tourists.

"Ah, so she's one of us, who would've guessed it," the bearded man finally responded. "So she's a regular piece o' shit just like me. You gonna jump down my throat now, you common cocksucking slut? You of all people? Listen to her runnin' off at the mouth, oh yeah. So that's who's getting all those dollars of his; you are, aren't you? Got 'im right between your legs, huh? How much ya gonna cut me in for, huh? How much?"

The Charles Bridge suddenly seemed much narrower. And every possible way forward was blocked by the bearded man in the khaki coat, who had lost all interest in Erik. And had acquired an interest in me.

"Pull yourself together and get lost," I said dryly, focusing all my willpower on using the more polite *vy* form of "you"—and on trying not to cry.

(Shame, in the form of salty bitter drops, mingled with the saliva in my mouth and slowly welled up under my eyelids. Shame. Not just for the bearded man.)

The bearded man blocked my path—and I quickly started back when he tried to grab me by the shoulder.

"What—what's the matter? Is little Miss Spread-yer-legs afraid o' me or something? Or maybe we're disgusted by me, is that it, queenie? Are we disgusted by a good ol' decent Czech galley slave?"

He spat at me but missed, and the saliva dribbled down his beard, staining his whiskers like a lustrous, shimmering snake. He's not a bad-looking guy, I thought suddenly and illogically. An okay-looking guy.

(Just drunk. Begging. Gone astray. Like me. Maybe he has a good twin, too, Fialinka.)

Everything began to go dark before my eyes; it was probably the fumes from the beery sewage fermenting inside him. But maybe not. Why do I have to listen to lectures from guys like him, why? This flashed through my mind as the guy drained all the eloquence of Prague's gutters on me: "Ya know, just talkin' to you makes me sick, you make me *sick*, you disgusting, greedy, hard-currency *whore! Kurvo!*"

The next second he was picking himself up off the cobblestones and feeling his face.

"Let's go," said Erik. "That much Czech I understand."

7

A little farther on I rested my hand on the still-warm stone railing of the bridge, and a much larger hand settled on top of it. There was no longer any need to say anything. We went looking for a hotel.

8

I expect that if this whole little scene had been played out in, say, Sweden, I could have simply written that last sentence and safely left the rest to the reader's imagination. But we were in Prague.

At three hotels they told Erik flat out that there were no

rooms free. They probably wanted a little something for themselves, but I said nothing to Erik. I kept my Czech mouth shut, and it was interesting to observe the receptionists' efforts to speak a kind of universal language, which ranged from a dry "Everisink ful" to a dismissive gesture accompanied by the word "occupato."

Erik led me onward, arm in arm, and we almost couldn't walk anymore when we trudged into the Union Hotel, where a sleepy receptionist, who'd clearly seen her share of the world, asked for a fifty-crown tip and Erik's and his wife's passports. When she looked at my ID Booklet she just shook her head sadly and knowingly, saying, It's unfortunate, miss, but with a permanent residence in sector four of Prague we can't accommodate you. You must know that, so why do you even bother to come in?

I held the worthless piece of burning-red, plastic-covered cardboard queasily between my thumb and forefinger—and with my remaining hand, the one uncontaminated by socialism, I dragged Erik off toward the nearest alley.

9

Where, surrounded by the permanent odor of urine and garbage cans and long-lingering trash that had ripened in the summer heat, we finally started to kiss—and then we got to know each other better briefly and almost ineptly on the ancient rusted cover of one of the garbage pails, whose handle stamped a violet-yellow, almost perfectly rectangular bruise into the back of my thigh.

10

So even when Erik had taken me home and headed off again for the Middle East, the appearance of my poor stained butt in the mirror served as a reminder of the unappealing conclusion to our evening.

Except that this time the goodbye kiss didn't mean the end, as I had been accustomed to for years.

This time it was only the beginning.

1

World literature has treated the transformation of a virgin into a brothel whore innumerable times, to the point of perfection. But the tale of a girl of modern attitudes who gradually and almost imperceptibly becomes a commercial prostitute is one I believe I have yet to read. I have observed this neglected metamorphosis in myself; I have watched myself as a caterpillar in a jar: how she stops nibbling at the leaves, how she anxiously searches for a twig and begins to spin her miraculous cocoon. I have watched the cocoon splitting open within myself—and what crawls out of it? A hideous, scowling death's-head moth, haught and ostentatious, who laboriously inflates herself and spreads her wings.

I observed myself as one observes the subject of a psychological experiment: Fialka Number One (dwindling) scrutinized the development of Fialka Number Two—and was completely disgusted by what she saw.

The two Fialkas hated each other, couldn't stand one another, like two competing highway hookers, and the reverberations of their impassioned arguments had become desperately unamusing to me. But whenever it seemed to me that the two quarrelsome idiots in my head were about to come to any kind of agreement, I was almost paralyzed by the fear that they would soon become indistinguishable, that they would converge in a terrifying way and I would never be able to tear them apart. I was as frightened of the thoughts in my own head as I was terrified by the pervasive influence of television: I was afraid I would allow myself to be influenced, that I would begin to believe it, and that I would no longer be able to distinguish truth from inanity, sense from nonsense.

That I would lose the ability to distinguish my former self from my present self.

Until that spring, when Patrik got sick, I had always known very precisely what I really wanted out of life. I'd had goals—yes, I had, though they hadn't been squeezed into the same molds as the careers of my distinguished predatorial classmates.

I had lived for my goals, even though I was at a loss whenever I had to describe them to anyone. I'd had long-distance destinations, documentational goals, goals for my search for the rainbow and instants; I had the goal of photographing every deformed flower and of reaching out and touching everything that could be touched.

I'd had the goal of not dreaming, but living, remaining unblunted, childlike, young; I'd had the goal of contaminating myself with wounded nature and letting the droplets from a thousand streams dry on my face. I had wanted to exist simply and iridescently, to be as disobedient a little screw as possible, without being too conspicuous; within the boundaries of the space allotted to me, it had been my goal to love, feel, survive, and, in the end, just to *be*.

I'd been determined to be what I really was: not to let anyone or anything dictate to me how I should live or how I could think.

. . . But all that, Fialinka, is gone, remember?
No, I no longer pursued a pure goal down the Southern

Road. It was no longer that same searching, the same relationships. The catching of rainbows. Nothing remains, Fialinka, even of your instants. And the peeling off of layers?
When was the last time you pulled your skin over your
head, the last time you exposed yourself? When was the
last time?

(Not even there on that garbage can, not even there,
Fialinka. Erik arrived, and instead of the usual twenty-four-
hour transit visa he had brought much longer ones. Erik came
only for you and brought you books in English and would
have brought you much more if only you had asked him,
Fialinka. You couldn't even expose yourself to Erik; even his
marvelous, warm, tender, and ever more affectionate hands
could not burn a hole through your armor.)

You have changed, Fialinka.

And your journeys, originally without destination, yet
full of iridescent and pure goals—your journeys have become
tedious, gray, work-related obligations. They have become a
means to an end.

But to what end?!

Time was measured for me in the piles of bank notes
that I probably accumulated more easily than my average
highway competitor. But what to do with them? The problem was no longer just how to get my hands on that wheelchair for Patrik, although I still wasn't quite sure how I
would manage that. The new problem was how to get Patrik
to accept it.

Patrik had begun to have pains. Hard to define, elu-
sive, strange pains; "my spirits," he called them: pains that
seemed to originate in his state of mind but then shot
through his entire body until they overwhelmed him in an
entirely physical way and twitched and seethed like hys-
terical screams.

Curiously enough, in this respect Czechoslovakian

health care proved to be considerably forthcoming, and Patrik was given prescriptions for almost unlimited quantities of barbiturates, supposedly so he would sleep better. I had to admit it, dying was one thing Czech doctors always tried to make a little easier.

Nevertheless, Patrik refused to subsist on pills. It was our common policy not to let ourselves be stupefied, either by propaganda or by chemicals. We practically never drank a drop of alcohol—with the potential exception of Moravian wine. We always wanted to judge the world from a sober point of view and to allow ourselves to be intoxicated by mood alone. It had worked for many years. When we were healthy.

Nevertheless, I showed up once with my little bottles of capsules and pills of Western manufacture, which were supposed to relieve the pain without making you stupid. I brought a small armload from my private reserve and started to explain their effects to Patrik.

Patrik stared at me. He sized me up from head to toe, as if he'd never seen me before in his life, and said, "Where did those come from?"

"I got them on the road, Patrik."

"I don't need any pills, Fial. The last thing I need is to perform experiments on myself. Stick them up your ass."

Then he hung his head, puffed up his cheeks, and released the air slowly, the way only Patrik could. "You feel sorry for me, Fial, don't you? But I don't need it, understand, I don't want it, and if you ever . . . Anyway, let's talk about something else. What about that Political Economy exam?"

So that's what I get for my good intentions, I thought as I took my little bottles back home on the bus to my private stash. I knew that from now on there would always be a scar on Patrik's and my friendship; I knew that now I had absolutely no one to whom I could confide everything.

2

Suddenly I fit right in.

I exchanged my hard-to-define, at least partly unselfish, aims for a sharply focused goal, just as my classmates and peers had done long before me. I lost the ability to search, and all the youth evaporated from my soul. And even though my goal sounded completely unselfish—doing whatever was in my power to help Patrik—I could feel myself becoming covered with the scales of egotism, like some foul amphibious reptile hiding in a hole. It was harder and harder to communicate with anyone; embarrassment and the desire to know were converted into a practiced social smile that scared off anyone who had a genuine interest in conversation. I became alienated.

Serendipity ceased to function for me. There were no accidents, just lesser and greater degrees of success. Serendipity no longer served me, because I stopped relying on her. I had to be prepared. Always prepared. For anything.

And rainbows?

You could still see the rainbows on my eyelids, but not the slightest pastel trace of them remained inside me.

Yes, I now wore rainbows on my eyes. I had learned to artfully blend every conceivable color of Western makeup and to highlight this luminous creation on my brow with black pencil. To emphasize myself. To advertise myself. With carefully applied powders that protected me from the sun. And water-resistant mascara that allowed me to cry.

But I didn't cry anymore. My soul had become too desolate for tears to do any good. There was now nothing for those salty rivulets (which I had always saved only for the most profound, genuine sadness anyway) to wash away. And the desert of my soul was so parched and cracked that it couldn't have absorbed even a drop of moisture.

I had rainbows on my eyes. And I dressed in colors to match. At the age of twenty-five I unexpectedly discovered what most girls discovered at fifteen: that I actually had a feel for it. I unearthed in myself the ability to dress up and strut through the streets of Prague like the Queen of Sheba. And to my surprise, people took notice. Guys smiled at me and tried to pick me up; at night I almost couldn't walk around in Prague because of the inconvenient surplus of potential customers— and because of the interest I aroused in everyone in general, including the police. And once, when I got caught riding the bus without a ticket (those mushrooming piles of mammon commanded me to economize by forgoing a transit pass, too), I smiled at the inspector with such self-confident superiority that he only sighed and got off at the next stop. I discovered the advantage of being a woman. I never gave; I took. And it was the men (still only truck drivers, but God knew where it would all lead) who gave and gave—or paid, actually; they were buyers. And they were conscious of it, they knew the difference. I learned damned quickly how well they knew the difference.

I found myself more and more clearly situated on the bad side.

3

Curiously enough, I was also cultivating the shame inside me: Fialinka had started to feel ashamed in her old age. No, it wasn't shame as such, it wasn't embarrassment—more like an effort to act like a lady. What happened to the tattered jeans, to the faded holy-road T-shirts? How distant was the time when I had worn pants patched together seventeen times and when I had stepped out of my bra as if out of a skirt in front of my one-night companions? (I'd always had to knot them in the back, since, as a result of Czechoslovakian retail availability, all the ones with big enough cups were also loose across the back.) Where was the time of travel? The time of documentation? Now I left even my beloved backpack and camera at home.

I strutted down the access roads decked out like a lady, nothing but a handbag slung over my shoulder. My head was sleek with Western shampoos and lotions—and since a sprinkling of straw-colored gray had detracted from my overall look, I gave my hair a little assist in the direction of blondness. Just a tiny one.

And of course there was the self-confidently raised right hand to complete this portrait of a hitchhiker no private Czech driver would ever have dared stop for. I was radiant on the road, and my deliberately seductive silhouette raised whirlwinds of swirling dust in the wakes of dozens, hundreds of screeching foreign semis.

4

I had become a lady. A lady whose model appearance functioned as a compensation for her shameful acts.

It had been a damn long time since I'd last headed out on the Northern Road, or even tried to recall the former Fialka, standing by the side of the road with the hand of a supplicant emerging from a sleeve with a hole in it.

Maybe I wasn't even capable of being that kind of hitchhiker anymore. Maybe I had merged far too well with my new identity.

It was just this concrescence, this convergence of my beings, that I had feared most of all—I had been afraid I would be brainwashed, retrained. That I would coalesce. That Fialka would become Fialka Number Two, first in body and then this process would gradually spread to my soul.

I thought about the Communists. Even among my classmates there had been a few such cases: a person departs a little from his convictions, joins a Party-affiliated club he shouldn't have, thinking he's going to help change things for the better. Do someone some good; at the very worst, do himself some good. The little newfound Communist thinks his opposition is so solid that he's one hundred percent immune to the venom of all those forums and propaganda campaigns. But this is not the case. The effects of the venom are not like a hangover you can sleep off. The venom of forums and propaganda has cumulative results: a person makes speeches and memorizes them, thinks his own thoughts, but after months he becomes accustomed to logical patterns that once seemed absurd to him—and after years he can't even speak except in constructive socialist sentences. Then he teaches his children that "it really isn't so terrible, it's not as bad as it looks," and nostalgically recalls the anti-Communist indiscretions of his youth. And it's all over.

And me? True, I hadn't sunk so low as to surrender to the Party—and though I held many different rods in my hand during that infamous period, at least none had revolutionary banners attached to them. I hadn't done anything worse than joining a particular stratum of society. To put it bluntly, the alienated sisterhood of highway whores. I joined expecting that I would be able to do someone some good—and I certainly had no intention of harming anyone. I joined with the conviction that I really didn't belong there, that I would have to reshape myself and pretend in order to make it among them . . . that I knew, of course, in the depths of my soul, exactly what bullshit it really was. But the watchwords and slogans were already penetrating my soul; I stopped seeing the absurdity and idiocy in drawn curtains in the windows of parked trucks the same way the Party member stopped seeing it in the forest of banners.

I had learned to dress myself up in a social smile (I could even grin idiotically at Mrs. Fišer now!), and though my soul felt a thousand years old, I still appeared remarkably young.

Just increasingly more seductive.

1

I stopped at my department at the university to get a temporary registration stamp in my university record booklet. I still
didn't feel up to the Political Economy exam; I simply couldn't
force myself to sit down with that book and grind away at the
differences, according to the socialist pseudo-economists, between a cartel and a syndicate and a trust, and the reasons
why monopolies were disastrous for the imperialist economy.
I had a vague suspicion that the average Westerner had no
idea what the term "imperialism" really meant, and I didn't
feel at all like slogging through the "principle of worker ex-
ploitation" in those faraway enemy lands. A significant hatred
of economics had sprung up within me—and whenever I
actually did manage to martyr myself over that gibberish for
a minute or two, I always accompanied each page with at
least one or two exceedingly good, exceedingly sweet chocolates I had saved from my trips. I savored the chocolates
(molded—it goes without saying—by the exploited hands of
the workers), and this gustatory, physical pleasure balanced
out my spiritual suffering. Before too long I noticed a few
extra fatty deposits on my body.

I threw away my economics book and left the chocolates
out on a retaining wall near Jezerka Park, then—concealed in

a telephone booth—amused myself by watching a gang of local kids fight over them. Like a true lady, I was going on a diet. And I bragged about it to anyone who didn't immediately tell me to shut up.

2

I was trying to counteract all sorts of spiritual torments with bodily pleasures. I began to indulge my body—an entity I'd never really paid much attention to before—and I began to live for it alone. Before, pleasures of the purely spiritual type had been enough for me . . . my body had served merely as a kind of conduit between the surrounding world and my mind; it had been merely a system of sensors, a garden of antennae that I extended to receive the stimuli of holy iridescent happenings. My body had served as a link between inside and outside; it had functioned as a filter for my imagination.

But now? Now my body had become more a means of production than anything else. And—contrary to all the laws squeezed into my head by Political Economy—it had begun to exploit me. I had to admit it was a perfect means of production: it worked beautifully and without any help from the mind; my body always made the best of all those exceptionally strange and calculated couplings I wouldn't even have considered a few months earlier. It never let me down. I never had the slightest fear in surrendering it without a second thought into countless embraces while my spirit flew off God knows where. (Maybe to Sweden?) My body served me predictably and unflaggingly, with the staggering dependability of a perfectly programmed machine. My body received stimuli and responded to them. It even intensified the sensations of pleasure arising from commercial intercourse: superficial, simple, but nevertheless powerfully gratifying sensations that transformed my highway exploits into something almost pleasant.

My body served me like a well-trained employee. But I had to pay it a lot. A lot of attention.

3

For all intents and purposes I was no longer in school. I had lost all interest in that socialist psychology—and, for that matter, in everything else. I was even seeing Patrik less and less frequently—and when I did, I smiled more and more sociably at his mother, who now despised me quite openly. She even started telling Patrik that she didn't like his meeting with me, though Patrik snapped at her in response. But still, we saw each other less and less.

A certain religious girl whom I met now and then to have friendly arguments about religious questions and interpretation of the Bible told me I had changed. A lot. And she thought that my conversations with her weren't leading me any closer to the truth anyway, so she would prefer to devote her time to others. I resented that.

A few guys in the conservationist groups tried to pick me up—and the rest looked at me pretty strangely, as if to say, What's the glamour girl doing here?

I didn't show my face in the "better" bars and restaurants, because I started feeling sick before I even got there. And I'd gotten too pretentious for my favorite crowd in the sleazier dives.

Not a living soul in the whole wide world liked me.

Except Erik, who kept visiting, but so hopelessly, hopelessly rarely!

4

Once I walked into the kitchen—in a shitty mood, as usual—and without thinking took a rotten banana out of the refrigerator. While I was peeling it and slicing off the brown pulp at the kitchen table, Grandmother crept in from the television.

I ignored her as she took a cracked cup from the cabinet and filled it half full of low-fat milk, the kind that comes in a plastic bag. It was from the day before. And I could smell its sickly, half-spoiled, half-sour stench all the way across the room.

"That milk's gone bad, Gram," I pointed out. I mentioned it involuntarily, almost unconsciously; I just couldn't keep it in, although I knew from experience exactly what would follow.

"What are you talking about, girl? What? There you go again. What's wrong with you? You and that spoiled mouth of yours . . ." Grandmother dipped her soup spoon into the cup and took a sip of the milk. "It's perfectly fine. It's good," Grandmother stated authoritatively. "It's from yesterday."

"It stinks."

"I don't smell anything. So how bad could it be, right? I just bought it yesterday."

"Dear Grandmother," I said, "in the country it is our unfortunate fate to inhabit, one must, regrettably, buy milk every day. It goes bad by the next day. Please, pour it down the drain. I can't watch you drink it."

Grandmother, who was still busy tranquilly breaking chunks of a roll into the cup and mashing it up with the milk, was of course horrified. "Milk! Good Lord, child! You want me to pour *milk* down the drain?"

(Sometimes it was amusing to watch the reactions of my pious, television-crazed grandmother, who had no idea that she was the subject of psychological observation. Her responses were so simplemindedly conditioned it was a joy to see. Just as Pavlov's dogs salivated whenever a little bell was rung in their ears, my grandmother invariably came unglued—in her naïvely good-hearted way—at any suggestion of pouring milk down the drain or any lack of reverence for foodstuffs in general, let alone the idea of throwing out stale bread! Grandmother would drink any milk, as long as she could squeeze it down her throat; when it was too far gone for that, she put it up on the cabinet to turn sour—and if, instead of turning sour, it simply spoiled, she still consumed it. Grandmother habitually crumbled three-week-old moldy bread into her coffee—and one summer, when there was an electrical blackout, some meat went wormy on us in the refrigerator and Grandmother made goulash out of it anyway. She had a pious soul and a cast-iron stomach.)

When it came to the conservation of means necessary for the support of life in the socialist state, Grandmother was an exemplary creature. But as far as I was concerned, she was a nightmare. The sight of Grandmother sipping half-spoiled milk with bits of moldy bread in it turned my stomach, a reaction as conditioned and simple as her own responses. The worst thing was that hiding from her wasn't enough. For example, I could lock myself in the bathroom, but all I had to do was *imagine* my grandmother smacking her lips, digging her spoon into that mush, and gulping it down in big swallows and I immediately felt like throwing up. That was also psychology.

At least I got a little amusement out of Grandmother's reactions. In all those years of my suggesting she dispose of any kind of food, Grandmother never caught on that I was really just teasing her.

I listened to the endlessly repeating stream of rhetoric from my horrified grandmother's mouth (the point: bread is a gift from God and you can't just pour milk down the drain!), and I dryly remarked that the socialist beverage known as milk, for lack of a better term, was only homogenized water, colored with lime, into which cows had pissed beforehand, which the cooperative farmers then diluted with more water and detergent in order to increase the volume, and which was never pasteurized because—in case Grandmother didn't already know it—the majority of pasteurization plants in the Central Bohemian Region had long ago been taken off the shipping routes in order to economize on fuel.

I looked on disgustedly as Grandmother scooped up her dank bread mush with her poorly washed soup spoon and ladled it noisily into her mouth. Bloodthirstily, I added, "In case you haven't heard about it yet, there was an incident at the Progress Standard Farming Cooperative in the East Prague district where a bunch of gypsy women took a bath in the milk. To make their skin beautiful. Who knows how long they've been doing it. They just showed up, took off their clothes, jumped into the vat, and frolicked around; then they got out and wrung out their braids—and after that the workers simply started packaging the milk. Maybe some beautiful gypsy woman soaked her exotic body right in that milk you've got there. They even wrote about it in *The Evening Praguer*; pretty amazing that they actually wrote about it, huh? Can you imagine how many people are now going to vomit at the very thought of milk?"

I used to be able to supply Grandmother with such reports about twice a day. Milk anecdotes (which were not guaranteed to be true but were not at all unlikely, considering the catastrophic state of the entire country) were among the stories conservationists loved to relate to one another, always trying to outdo each other. Nevertheless, I don't think they were just ecological tall tales. Milk stories started with the cows, whose food was laced with leftover antibiotics; they continued with descriptions of what happened to the poor, ill-fated liquid itself—and they climaxed with narrations about the plastic bags the milk came in, which apparently made the milk carcinogenic. Every meeting of the conservationists brought some new milk story, or chicken story, or meat story, or vegetable story, or water story—and I got used to taking them down in a notebook that was already boiling over with treasonous truths. Of course, we ate and drank, too.

But these unceasing doses of data, these facts we had no way of defending ourselves from, aided in the fatalization, so to speak, of our philosophy of life. We knew that we were standing in line at socialist supermarkets for extract of hemlock sold in attractive if easily torn packets. But we had no alternative; we had to eat something. At least we accumulated information—and whenever possible, evidence.

Of course, there was no use in telling all this to Grandmother, and I'd realized that a long time ago. Even the television couldn't alter her simple outlook, her simple world of unambiguously defined things. She lived in a world where milk was milk—although it was a pity they didn't sell it out of a milk barrel anymore—and she never wavered from her reverent attitude toward bread, even the time she piously sliced into a loaf and found someone's crumpled dirty handkerchief. Grandmother lived in a world of simplicity, a world of principles without distinctions, a world where everything lost its luster before the merciful face of God. Sometimes I envied her certainty, her docile acceptance, her dogma, but more often it just got under my skin.

I hadn't succeeded in spoiling Grandmother's appetite with this story either. She probably hadn't even been listening to me. She sucked obliviously at her roll (most likely still immersed in one of the television plots that interested her more than reality), and when she finally raised her eyes, she noticed the banana peel on the table.

First she berated me for cutting off the slimy rotten parts. Then (as usual) she declared that our generation had no respect for anything—if only we had to work for a farmer out in the fields the way she had! After that she added that precisely the pieces I was about to waste were the sweetest part of the banana and that she had never even seen a banana until after she was married. She picked out the rotten scraps from among the peels and dumped them into her cup.

I turned away, as a precaution.

Then suddenly I heard Grandmother choking: "That was the last one! The last one! You took the last one out of the refrigerator, didn't you!?"

This time she was right. Usually—for the sake of domestic tranquillity—I made damn sure not to take the last of the cottage cheese or the last orange, or to eat the last leftover heel of bread. For Grandmother believed that she alone should determine if and when any leftovers should be finished off. She was convinced that she was the driving force that kept our household from collapsing, that without her I would have died of hunger long ago, that I was simply useless around the house. Many, many times she had told me the story she remembered, remarkably enough, from some television show: a father and son find the sugar bowl empty, pull a gnawed lump from the canary cage, split it in two, and put it in their coffee. "That's the way you would end up, too!" Grandmother asserted in a grand voice.

Although my worse half had always been bored by her claims, my better part had allowed that there might have been some truth to them. I certainly wouldn't have argued the point with anyone. But Grandmother didn't understand one important thing: I didn't give a shit. Grandmother didn't understand that I—probably surrounded by chaos and confusion—would have survived even without her. And almost certainly more happily. Grandmother simply took the housekeeping into her own matronly hands of her own accord—and I entrusted domestic matters to her without protest. Usually that meant being silent.

But this time I exploded.

"So we'll get more," I said.

"*Get* more, *get* more . . . ! Bananas don't just buy themselves, you know, girl! You've got to stand in line for them. Everything for you is *get*. Lord, child, what will happen to you when I'm gone . . ." Then she started quoting figures: "Three hours I stood in line at the grocer's for those bananas.

A good three hours. And you say *get* more! Just you try standing in that line sometime; your legs will fall off in half an hour, believe me, the younger generation can't take anything . . . Oh, if only you had to toil in the fields like I did . . . ! Eighteen crowns a kilo is what bananas cost these days, eighteen crowns a kilo! And they give you only three each; they say they're importing fewer again this year. So I stood in that line twice! And she says *get*!"

Usually it was easy enough for me to ignore Grandmother's speeches, the same way she ignored mine. As two quarrelsome women, we got on each other's nerves all the time, but we'd always worked around each other tolerantly and managed to survive the stroke of fate that had forced us into the same living space. I ignored her, just as I ignored official statistical oratory and those eye-catching constructive slogans on street corners. Fialka Number One was actually rather fond of Grandmother. But today, as chance would have it, I was Fialka Number Two.

"You didn't have to stand in line!" I yelled. "Nobody asked you to do that. So you didn't have to stand. You could've stayed at home gawking at the boob tube, for all I care. Bananas are expensive; so they're expensive. But, Grandmother, *whose* money is it? *Whose* money is it, *whose* money, *whose*!?"

In the whole time we had lived together, whenever Grandmother—sweating but triumphant—had arrived home from the supermarket or grocer's or bakery, in all those years, whenever—panting—she had unloaded her prizes from her bags and at the same time complained about how everything was so expensive these days—and how once again she'd spent a hundred crowns at the green grocer's alone—in all that time I hadn't once mentioned the source of that money. Of course, most of it was mine. But I felt I could afford it, paying for Grandmother's apartment and supporting her for the most part. I had faith in my abilities as a photographer and didn't expect that we would ever run into any serious financial troubles. I certainly didn't want to spend too much—and the difference between having and not having a hundred crowns was a very real one for me; nevertheless, I'd inherited a certain financial generosity from my father. No, it wasn't just a rationalization for squandering money: it was the conviction that, once you're already supporting someone and giving them money, you shouldn't be constantly hitting them over the head with the fact.

And so Grandmother, constantly thundering and dissatisfied with prices, would find behind the glass in the cabinet hundred- and five-hundred-crown notes that I had gotten at the bank and was sacrificing to the household. I didn't worry about how much we spent. And Grandmother took the payments for the telephone and utilities down to the post office; Grandmother also took the shopping into her own hands (though I was sometimes enlisted as toting muscle), and she marked down all the expenditures—which to her were fantastic numbers, becoming more fantastic all the time—on the calendar.

Sure, I didn't always behave like a boundlessly loving granddaughter. To be frank, I exploited Grandmother as a resource who carried in her head and in her shopping bags everything the household needed. I used her as a rudimentary computer which had a memory filled with all the simple data that I, as a result, didn't have to trouble myself with. I used Grandmother as a link with the harsh world of socialist reality and as a buffer that took the pressure off me. I had a convenient psychological argument: that Grandmother *needed* to do all this. That she needed to feel irreplaceable. Otherwise, she would have succumbed to melancholy. Gotten suddenly old. Died. So I would have been hurting her by taking over any of the household chores.

(Oh please, Fialinka, *you* take over—the household chores?!)

I took advantage of her. I'd become accustomed to having her around. At least, I never gave any thought to what might be the most effective way to get rid of her and free myself. We lived together, and that was that. It had never occurred to me to say anything to her about *my* money.

But now . . . now, with those piles of bank notes Grandmother never saw and would never comprehend growing in my room, now, because of them and in spite of them, there was growing in me a repugnant form of frugality, a thrift born of fear, you might say; obviously I couldn't take my multiplying deposits of mammon and chattels off to any bank, and the idea was gradually sneaking into my mind that any petty burglar could relieve me of it all at any time. You've become a miser, Fialinka.

"I wonder *whose* money it is, Gram, *whose* money?" I snapped. "Who do you think supports you, your measly little pension? Those lousy few hundred your lousy God-fearing husband left you? Screw it, so I took the banana, so what: what's the big deal?! Without my money you wouldn't have any damned bananas to stuff your face with in the first place. Without my money do you think you'd have a TV to watch? Without my money you'd be out picking through garbage cans, I might point out. Like that moldy old witch next door you watch out the window. And you bitch at me that I don't do anything around the apartment! You, of all people, complain! Without me you wouldn't have any place to live at all; you can't work, you don't know how to do anything, and you haven't worked a day in your whole life! You don't know how to do *shit*. And besides that, you can kiss my ass, kiss my *ass* with all your bullshit. No one says I have to take care of you here. Tomorrow you can get the hell out and go gawk at the TV at the old folks' home, if you want to know something. Tomorrow!"

I got more and more fired up during this speech—and I couldn't believe my own ears. I couldn't believe it was me saying all these things. Grandmother couldn't even defend herself; tears streamed out of the corners of her eyes and down her face, matching the driblets of milk and bread-crumbs that streamed out of the corners of her mouth. Grand-mother dropped her spoon and crossed herself slack-jawed. She trembled at each vulgar word as I released it from my mouth with the scathing tinge of satisfaction I used as em-phasis in an effort to wound this silly old pious soul as deeply as possible. Suddenly all my bottled-up rage, all my reserves of sorrow, which had nothing whatsoever to do with Grand-mother, everything I had been keeping inside because it would have been insanely cruel to vent it on an old person—everything burst out of me like stinking water from a punc-tured cesspool. It was a deep cesspool, and every word, tasting of shit, stung my tongue as it gushed out. Suddenly I sensed that I was even taking advantage of my psychology lessons: my perfect, ages-old knowledge of Grandmother made it possible for me to wound her as deliberately as pos-sible, to hit the most sensitive places. I knew my target and I had my Colt-45s slung damned low on my hips. "Do you think maybe I'd waste away here without you? Please, spare me. Here in my own apartment—oh yes, your highness lives in *my* apartment, in case you hadn't noticed—here in my own apartment I don't dare so much as fart without your permis-sion. Yes, you're the boss here, you cow! But I don't give a shit about you, you stupid old God-fearing cow. Jesus, a girl can't even fuck in this goddamned disgusting apartment—you can shove your damned rosary up your ass. Go ahead, hurry up and go to your damned heaven, I hope you have a nice time rotting among all the little maggots. Just give me some peace and quiet and leave me alone!"

Grandmother really was going to leave me alone. She got up heavily from the table and with broken steps headed for the kitchen door. She stopped—and if it hadn't been for the fact that she had just put her hand on the knob, her fall would have been far worse.

She was now lying on the kitchen linoleum (which she allowed to be washed only with the soapy water left over from doing the laundry), and her old-fashioned porcelain dentures had fallen out of her mouth. I looked into the toothless gaping hole of her mouth, where bits of bread and milk were mixed with saliva and tears. I felt like throwing up.

And I still didn't feel the slightest bit sorry for her. I suppressed the urge to kick her—and bent down to raise her off the floor. "Come on, my little cow, I'll put you in your chair in front of the TV. You can gawk all you want, you old cow, and everything will be fine."

But contrary to all expectation Grandmother took a swipe at me. "Do-on't tou-ouch me!" she wheezed, furious and out of breath. And as she lay on the floor Grandmother fixed her wounded, teary eyes on my painstakingly created face, now twisted in anger—and with surprisingly clear articulation she said, "Don't touch me! Don't lay a finger on me! God save me, what evil has become of my granddaughter? You look like a whore!"

That word, a word I didn't think Grandmother even knew, was strikingly precise. It stung more than I could have imagined. No, Grandmother hadn't discerned anything in particular about my appearance or character; it was worse than that: all my actions reminded her of the generic types on those televised serials and movies she watched all day and from which (most probably) she derived all her knowledge of the world. I didn't just look like a whore. To Grandmother I looked like a generic television whore, like the prototype of all the hookers that had ever flashed across the screen. Sure, Grandmother, who never ventured any farther than the dairy store on the corner, Grandmother had knowledge of the world . . . though it was only televised, socialist knowledge . . . She still knew the types, or pseudo-types, of characters the television assaulted her with day in and day out.

Later, when after two hours I finally left Grandmother's room, left Grandmother sleeping like a baby, not knowing which of the mingled tears on my face were my own and which were hers, I stopped at the mirror in the bathroom and examined my face with unconcealed disgust: wet, red, blotched, puffy from tears, painted. Things went dark before my eyes as I stared at that face, that repulsive, wrinkled, billion-year-old monster grimacing at me from the mirror.

5

I stared into the mirror and said the word aloud.

Whore.

I repeated it over and over, forcing it out between my throat and tongue and lips.

Whore!

Whore!

Whore!

Onomatopoetic. Few words in any language seemed to capture their meanings so perfectly in sound. To express their essences so directly.

Whore. Thighs. Fuck.

I repeated the words several times. I screamed them at myself, until they resounded through the airshaft and the bathroom tiles echoed with them. I screamed at myself until strands of spit spurted onto the mirror and covered my face.

Whore!

Whore!

Whore!

I couldn't cry any longer. Comforting Grandmother (God, how easy that had been! How simple and undemanding it had been to ask her forgiveness!), comforting her had exhausted all my tears of pity (and self-pity) and everything was all dried up inside me again.

All dried up.

All dried up.

All dried up, *whore!*

I picked up a graying, repulsive piece of cloth from the edge of the sink. It was one of the scraps Grandmother in her infinite thrift called washcloths and—despite the fact that they had acquired a noticeable stench over the years—used to rub the various parts of her body, a procedure she called bathing. I picked up that gray rag from the porcelain, wet it with cold water, and wiped half my face with it. I flinched as it touched the white of my eye, which I had forgotten to close in time, and its sour smell overpowered the oily taste of carefully applied lipstick on one side of my mouth.

I looked into the mirror at my divided face.

Where was that girl with the clear eyes who used to joke around with Patrik? Was there anything left of her? Where was she hiding? Now I could see the exhaustion in the old, unadorned complexion on the free, newly liberated side of my face; I could feel the exhaustion in the structure of the pores of the skin; a thousand years of exhaustion from round trip after round trip. I ran the back of my hand across my forehead. This gesture had belonged to me for a long time; it used to wipe the sweat and cobwebs from my brow in Indian summer. It used to gather the heavy thoughts from my head and fling them aside. It was simply Fialka's gesture.

But it must have been a long, long time since I last used it. I had forgotten about it, lost it—just as I had lost a whole series of mannerisms and gestures . . . I no longer drank out of streams or directly from taps, no longer touched my eyes or plunged my nose and face into the soil of ditches to inhale the rich fragrance.

I carried my painted face with great care and at a certain distance, the way a painter carries his work under his arm. I drank out of glasses with a reserved extension of my lips— and I used the smudge on the edge of the glass to gauge how badly I had smeared my lipstick. And I kept myself in one piece throughout the day by means of a series of pocket mirrors, little bottles, compacts, and brushes.

Where has that little girl with the clear eyes disappeared to, Fialinka?

And suddenly that word sliced through my mind.

Vulgarity.

Yes, this face, this face of yours, Fialinka, is infected with vulgarity. A severe case.

Vulgarity curled the lips in scorn and turned the corners downward.

Vulgarity had begun to form lines in the skin between the nose and corners of the mouth, not yet folds certainly, just inconspicuous but prophetic little creases in the muscle tissue that hadn't been there just a short while ago.

Vulgarity curled like microscopic worms from the thickened and blackened lashes and collected under the eyes like fine black soot.

Vulgarity shone like silver from the perfect rainbows on the eyelids; vulgarity sneered at me in those shades of makeup, carefully chosen and sensitively balanced, but somehow far too cheerful.

I was wearing a mask—and this realization struck me for the first time in all its horror.

I was wearing a mask, like a circus clown in the ring.

I was wearing a mask, like an Indian on the warpath.

I was wearing a mask, like a camouflaged soldier behind enemy lines.

I was camouflaged.

I filled both hands with water from the tap and splashed it on my face. The cold took my breath away—and I scrubbed my face with the coarse soap for a while, until I was looking that denuded clown in the face. That clown who, until recently—and God knows why—had been me.

The red eyes of a pig squinted out at me; they were still

blinking from the soap. I dried myself off with a towel, and when I raised my face, I just had to grin at that white, unaccustomed, bizarrely alien oval.

I smiled.

At first just a little, as if just learning to smile: it was a cheerful and innocent and experimental smile; it had none of the practiced smoothness that had characterized it recently.

The corners of my mouth turned upward—a pleasant surprise for me. My cheeks regained the rosy roundness of sun-kissed apples. And my eyes? In my eyes there flashed that little flame, not yet clear but already playful, that flame I had almost forgotten about.

As I admired myself in that shining surface, as I salvaged the remains of that ancient and naïvely sacred Fialinka, I suddenly caught sight of my hair.

I was used to its rich, golden, artificial tint. I had liked it. It had been the finishing touch.

My hair danced around my head, clean, light, styled; finished with all those imported shampoos, finished with the golden-blond rinse I'd used on it.

Finished?

Yes, finished: I looked like a sunflower with the center all pecked out by crows. I had looked like a sunflower, a plastic sunflower; I had been perfectly done up, pretty and inanimate and without a breath of scent.

It still wasn't me.

So I went to my room and got the scissors, which, by the way, I had stolen long ago from Grandmother's sewing table; we'd been fighting over them ever since. These scissors had been forged of good, prewar steel; Grandmother had used them long ago to tailor my mother's wedding gown—train and all; these were the scissors I had used to cut clippings from newspapers and conservationist pamphlets . . . these were the scissors I had used to cut apart my developed slides of deformed flowers. I took the documentational, still sharp, though long unsharpened, good scissors—and I cut into my hair.

It was painful.

Not just because I didn't know how to cut hair.

I cut close to my head, pulling out the locks one at a time and letting them go; the streaming sunflower-yellow snakes fell to the ground and curled up into coils.

I cut with the scissors held right next to my scalp and threw the snakes from myself with loathing.

I was freeing myself from the bonds.

I was cutting the noose.

In that bright, rich tangle on the floor lay everything from the past.

The hair I used to let fall over gearshifts . . . out there on the forgotten trails of the North. The little conduits of temptation and holy nights. My raised antennae, my velvety feelers.

The hair I used to toss from my face the way one throws the curtains open in the morning; the hair all kinds of men had longed to run their fingers through.

I trampled the heaps of shorn locks underfoot obliviously—I looked like a convict. Only little mossy clumps—spotty and uneven—were left sticking out of my revealed skull. They were still the color of sunflowers, but that didn't bother me nearly so much now. It would grow out, there would be new hair.

You will be new, Fialka.

Your hair will grow back, and so will your soul.

I smiled at myself with fire in my eyes; it was a completely sincere smile. It pretty much had to be, considering that moss all over my head.

Mangy but likable, I thought to myself with satisfaction. Mangy but likable.

1

"You don't know shit about Eastern philosophy, absolutely nothing, Fial," Patrik declaimed in his typical style. There was no reason for this to surprise me. "You don't have a clue about Buddhism, Zen Buddhism; you've got no idea who Ramakrishna was and you've never even heard of reincarnation. You're just completely unenlightened, my friend. But look, I'll explain it to you."

(Lately Patrik and I were getting along much better. I enjoyed going to see him much more now. I wore my ski hat over my crewcut during the November flurries, and exposed to all the elements, I was myself again. And being myself meant being with Patrik every chance I got.)

"Have you ever wondered, Fialka, have you ever thought seriously about why it is we're here in this world?"

"Oh, I don't know. I'd rather not think about it," I said. "I'm alive, and that's it."

"Fine, but that's not the point. So am I, pretty much, even though, I don't mind telling you, I've been more alive in my day." (Patrik could barely walk at all at this point; it was hard enough for him just to hobble as far as the kitchen on his crutches. The day he would need that wheelchair was approaching damn quickly. That doctor had been right.)

"But that's not the point at all here." Patrik waved away the thought as if it had been a nagging fly. "Have you ever thought about reincarnation?"

Patrik rambled on about his theories of life and death for a while. It certainly was no nice neat presentation; it wasn't an organized, well-planned lecture or even a rhetorical argument that might have convinced anyone he was right. It was a search, I understood that: Patrik wasn't communicating a theory to me, he was using me as a quiet listener, a freshly stretched canvas on which he could sketch a disorganized outline of his thoughts—and which had just the right amount of resistance.

"Fialka, we've never really thought good and hard about where we've come from and where we're going, we're always just rushing off in pursuit of something—have you ever noticed that? No one ever thinks nowadays. No one knows how to stop and think. Everyone's always running somewhere, or marching somewhere, whether it's toward Communism (in gigantic strides, of course) or toward the grave, or just straight to hell. What do you think you're doing when you go riding around in trucks, there and back, there and back? What do you think I was doing when I could still take pictures? We're rushing headlong, Fial, we're running away; we're always running away, understand, from any kind of great knowledge—we're scared to death of it!"

Patrik held his temples with both hands, as if he thought his head might fly off at any moment. "Has it ever occurred to you, Fial, why it really is that people go insane? Or have all those psychological theories of yours already made you crazy? Have they gotten to you yet? People go insane from *too much* thinking, not from too little. People go insane because they're able to *stop* and *think* . . . But as soon as they come upon even the smallest sliver of truth, you psychologists immediately sic the body-snatchers on them with the straitjackets, declare them certifiable, and stick them behind bars.

Then you fill them up with Valium. To pacify them. To re-orient them. So they become stupid and *normal* again . . . behind bars and on drugs!"

Patrik looked at me combatively, as if I myself, neophyte psychologist, were the body-snatcher who had come for him, Patrik, with hypodermic syringes full of unknown substances. But I didn't protest. I went into the kitchen to put some water on for tea. Now that Patrik almost couldn't walk, he could no longer spare me this extra exposure to his parents, who despised me more openly than ever . . . On my way through the living room I ran into Mrs. Fišer, of course, who greeted me with her prompt, wide smile. She checked out my recently-escaped-convict look: my own hair color was beginning to show through a bit at the roots, and I intended to get the rest cut off soon. Most people looked at my poor abused head with undisguised disgust—and I'd gotten used to these looks. Only Patrik hadn't even noticed the change. He didn't look at me as a woman, which flattered me; Patrik examined me on the inside.

2

He seated himself more comfortably on the couch, moving his legs with the help of his arm. I watched the whole procedure without blinking; I no longer had to suppress the nervous urge to run over and help him in some way, to speed up his efforts . . . Whenever someone with a cane, or even on crutches, had walked by me, I used to get this nervous pain in my back and my hands started twitching. Since childhood everyone had always pounded it into my head that one had to help sick people, slow people; that you should help blind people cross the street and give up your seat on the tram to the elderly.

Until Patrik: Patrik made me understand why you *shouldn't* help everyone in every situation; that these weaker (or seemingly weaker) people also needed the space to achieve things on their own, to provide for themselves . . . I understood that the weak had little patience for even the most eager helpfulness on the part of the strong; I understood why you shouldn't look away when someone limps torturously by on crutches; I understood why it's sometimes better not to leap up and politely hand an old man the cane he is stooping painfully to pick up.

Unlike Mrs. Fišer, I comprehended the destructive power of pity. And that was probably why Patrik and I got along so well. Because at home with his parents Patrik was feeling more and more like a babe in swaddling clothes, even though in September he had advanced, according to his mother's four-year cycle, from second to third grade.

3

I squatted like a duck beside the desk, sipping cheap but strong tea (I'd learned how to make this stimulating brew from Patrik), and holding my cup more and more piously between my palms, like a Tibetan monk, I listened to Patrik's exceptional monologue and my poor shaved skull began to ache dully. Insufficient mental training, Fialka . . .

Patrik talked on for a long time, interrupted only by two separate visits by Mrs. Fišer, who put me in my place with her smiling look and asked worriedly how Patrik was feeling. (Which Patrik answered with a disgusted grunt.) Patrik spoke about the ability to drop out of the inane rat's marathon of life, about freedom of thought unlimited even by incapacitation of the body. He held forth on dualism and monism, and got the two hopelessly mixed up; finally he concluded from all this that modern society had completely forgotten about the soul, and hence the soul had atrophied. Anything you didn't use, according to him, withered away—it was even possible to neglect the body, to leave it behind, and it would atrophy, it would die, as some might say—but the soul, the soul would still soar freely through space. Only through great knowledge was it possible to redeem oneself from afflictions of the soul and body.

When he talked about Oriental philosophy, it seemed to me at times that I had heard all this somewhere before: probably in clinical case studies at school—but I chose to keep my mouth shut. Because any time I even tried to force my way into the conversation, I was chased away like a bothersome insect by a wave of Patrik's hand. Patrik concluded with an interpretation, universal and undoubtedly exhaustive, but muddled beyond imagination, of more or less all the Eastern philosophies, freely importing elements of one into the other in the process. The result of all this speculation, the end toward which he had been working, turned out to be surprisingly simple: people who could somehow drop out of Western, so-called advanced society, who could stop and contemplate in the Oriental style, they, in a certain sense, would always derive great benefit. And the ones that *didn't understand*, normal people and the guardians of normality known as psychiatrists, were always gagging these people's mouths and sticking needles in their arms—and burning them at the stake.

I sighed.

But now Patrik had dropped out: now that he was handicapped, only now was he learning how to contemplate. He was going to make up for everything he had neglected. He was going to train his mind—now—now that his body was becoming useless. "I'm going to train, Fial. And whether anyone understands it or not, I will know what the absolute truth is!"

I nodded; quarrelsome Fialka just nodded at him—and it made me sad. I said, "That's all very beautiful, Patrik, but you'll never get the materials you need for your studies. You think you're going to discover something new, but it's just the opposite. Do you know how many books—in the West!—must have already been written about it, books we just haven't read and can't get our hands on? Patrik, you haven't got the literature, you'll scare up a couple of idiotic books that find fault with Buddhism and glorify the power of the working class. Because the majority of decent books are either locked up in restricted stacks or aren't to be found at all in Czechoslovakia. There's no one to lead you through it sensibly, to keep you from going completely and irreversibly nuts, like so many others before you."

"Hm, you've got a point there, Fialka, you've got a point. But I still think the real knowledge has to come from *inside* you. Would you believe I've already made progress? I can sit here, without reading, without drawing, just sit and concentrate. And as long as Mother doesn't come barging in with some bullshit, I can actually achieve happiness for a while. Happiness—can you imagine it, Fial? Have you ever been truly happy, except for those two minutes after sex? I used to think I could be happy in other ways, but now, it seems, I never really was . . . I didn't want to tell you about it before, I wanted to make some progress first . . . By the way, aren't you going to ask me what's up with my cock?"

"What's up with it?"

"Zilch," said Patrik proudly. "Absolutely nothing is up with my cock. I might as well use it to clean my glasses. That's about the size—and consistency—of it. But I've worked it out, Fialinka. I've trained myself. I haven't had sex since I don't remember when, but even without sex I'm happy. I'm actually *happy*, Fialinka, can you imagine?"

4

I can't honestly say I found Patrik's enthusiasm for the search for the real truth (as he called it) infectious. Nevertheless, I did believe that within every normal (normal?) human being there survives an atavistic desire for the unknown, for the distant, for the mysterious. For most of us, the unknown, the mysterious, and the distant converge in a single desire to *go*: to tear through the membrane of daily repetition, to rush after something secret, dangerous, and boundlessly pleasurable . . . In a certain sense my long-time need to hitchhike was an expression of these human desires: my nighttime dialogues in warm semi cabs on the road were always with someone unknown, I rushed headlong across distant landscapes—and the darkness all around breathed mystery . . . I opened myself (there is a longing in each of us to open up) and eagerly absorbed the vibrations of unknown, ever-changing secrets. This was searching, too. Breaking the leash destiny had used to train me. This, too, was dropping out of the deeply rutted, tried, and supposedly true path of fate.

I was sure that within every human being this atavistic desire for the Unknown was fueled by tedium and feelings of powerlessness.

Tedium and impotence were its sources . . . tedium, impotence—and the consciousness of death.

Patrik now had all three of these inside him. Sitting there in his cubbyhole, Patrik was beginning to suffer from impotent, frustrated tedium. And it was precisely this, I believed, that had brought him to his theory.

It wasn't any kind of finished theory, actually. We really were good friends, and so I got to see many of Patrik's ideas in advance, almost before they were hatched. Patrik never placed before me the finished, framed picture a painter unveils to the public. No. And just as I had known Patrik's paintings when they were still just insane flurries of seemingly meaningless lines and strokes, I was also presented with the barely conceived torsos of his intellectual works-in-progress. Patrik was the kind of person who always started with chaos. As a photographer he had always cut up huge piles of negatives, of which he later used only very few. As a lover he had always auditioned—so to speak—many women, eventually deciding that he liked only a few of them. (He almost always did his choosing after the fact.) And as a painter he suffered the vice of a rather recherché style. In living, fucking, and documenting, he used the trial-and-error approach.

And so I could imagine that as a discoverer of truth Patrik would begin with a complete goulash. I could imagine Patrik half sitting, half lying in his cubbyhole—buried under great heaps of wise books, both truly wise and so-called, that he had picked up wherever he could.

(That *I* had picked up wherever *I* could, because Patrik was becoming more and more handicapped all the time.)

5

Of course, I was afraid that with his dropping-out theory Patrik might drop so damned far out that I wouldn't be willing to follow him; that he would finally reach some undoubtedly absurd philosophy that would probably destroy him.

No, philosophizing was not exactly my strong suit. I didn't enjoy meditating at tedious length on truly bizarre themes. But I was tolerant. I had no problem letting everyone believe whatever he wanted when it came to questions with no unambiguous answers. I accepted the fact that different climates could engender different philosophies, so it wouldn't be right to condemn any one of them outright.

I tolerated all kinds of different philosophies. Climatic, situational, personal.

So why, why, I reproached myself as I thrashed over the previous evening's truths in my mind, why can't I tolerate Patrik's? Patrik's medicinal philosophy?

6

Needless to say, Patrik was forced to go through a period of real suffering, a psychological reaction to the disintegration of his body. He had always been convinced that he was incapable of going crazy, that he was perfectly armed against insanity—then, suddenly, he panicked: multiple sclerosis is, after all, a disease of the nerves: the myelin sheaths around the fibers deteriorate and can no longer transmit impulses (thoughts?).

Patrik was terrified of his internal enemies, he was afraid his thinking would change, become diseased; that the diseased sheaths of his diseased nerves would eventually lead to diseased thoughts . . .

Why, oh why, couldn't he deepen that gap between mind and body, sever them one from the other? That split that even socialist, materialist psychology acknowledged—at least in its nomenclature. Patrik had always believed that his soul, or quasi-soul, was still absolutely healthy, unaffected, logical—but where was that retaining wall that would protect him from his crippled body? Patrik couldn't find it. Or perhaps . . . it had never existed!?

Patrik placed all his faith in his soul, and now he was afraid he was losing it along with his body.

Was losing, not *would lose*: the one-time, simple, generally comprehensible fact of death didn't upset Patrik so much. He was afraid of *dying*.

Withering away. Decay.

The decay of his own body and soul, a process he might no longer even be conscious of.

1

The crammed bus carrying me from Patrik's made its way through the gray winter mud, and there, in that gray world, the colors of the rainbow appeared to me.

I thought about the emotional reserves that each of us carries within himself—and which we don't have time for in the daily shuffle. I thought about the human senses, which lie hidden and neglected but which nevertheless have the power to beautify the life of anyone who learns to use them. Who learns to use them through an awareness of his own handicaps . . . I thought about the acute senses of touch, smell, and hearing in blind people. About deaf-mutes who can read the words on your lips.

Our success and happiness are determined by our limitations, Patrik . . .

We search for rainbows. We crawl after them, lift our eyes to them, try to smell them any time a tearful cloud covers the sun. But what if the most brilliant rainbow of all is right inside us, what if we could learn how to make contact with the things around us—not only with the surfaces of our bodies, but with our insides, like a glove? To touch our insides, and to touch the insides of things. To search inside ourselves. Deep inside.

We needed to learn to seek the rainbow within—as Patrik was learning to do. He was searching inside himself for the primal security of the internal rainbow that no person or thing could ever take away from him.

2

At that particular time, of course, rainbows were not exactly promenading down the streets of Prague. I wiped an opening on the fogged window with my hand—and I looked at the thick black grime it left on my palm. The bus was packed, as usual—even I didn't have a seat this time, but I had a swaying grip on a pole above the head of some gloomy lady who— whenever she thought I wasn't looking—eyed me with suspicion and loathing on her face. Everything was gray, including the mood. And when the bus turned suddenly and threw me to the side, I landed lightly against the woman. She snarled threateningly but didn't even glance around at me. I mumbled an "Excuse me." No response. That's nice, I thought, before too long our only common means of communication will be grunting. The entire Czech people is losing the faculty of speech; the harassed populace can't speak anymore. Perhaps someday we'll forget even how to swear at each other.

I hung from a pole on the bus, on a filthy bus on the outskirts of Prague, on a foul bus packed like a sardine can with crowds of the nervous, glowering, grayly silent people of winter. Sardines: all they needed was to have their heads removed. They were probably all pissed off. I alone was in high spirits, because the grayness didn't apply to me. I looked around: the floor of the bus shook slightly as we rode—as the wheels bounced and fell through potholes dug into the asphalt by winter. By a series of winters, actually. The streets formed one huge puddle, a web of canals clogged with slush—and every depression you stepped in turned out to be an unfathomably deep reservoir of filthy, dubious water that sucked you in. It wasn't a good day for walking, and everyone dripped with mud that was as gray as the general mood. The passengers in the overcrowded bus only watched helplessly as everyone stepped all over their feet and legs, covering their pants to the knees with Prague's traditional winter concoction of salt, sand, and ash, which the building supers sprinkled on the sidewalks. In the winter months the dried salt congealed into dazzling white lace on every shoe. Even this, then, is beautiful, it occurred to me, even though oversalting had killed entire avenues of maples a couple of blocks from my house . . . Even though every footprint in the foyer was just the crystallization of salty filth from the street.

The floor of the bus shuddered lightly, and by concentrating I could feel those pleasurable sensations begin to climb up my legs . . . up my thighs toward my crotch. They caressed me. I was bundled in a ski jacket, which was now unbuttoned, and beneath my cotton pants I had on Father's old long johns. Not exactly the sexiest outfit; I didn't want to catch cold. In any case, I wasn't at all in the mood for sex. All the same, that shuddering, that Freudian, semiconscious pleasure from the jolting of the bus still found its way to me, through the clothes, to the skin, to the little hairs in my crotch . . . I recalled Freud gratefully. The sensation of my opening thighs intoxicated me slightly; I paid purely private attention (with a perfect poker face) to the little shuddering ripples tugging my knees apart, to the coarse, large, welcome something making its way into the warmth of my crotch.

(It had really been a terribly long time since I'd last felt that true, internal pleasure of opening: since I'd been aroused by thoughts—especially in as public a place as the bus. I hadn't felt so open for a long time—and so receptive . . . to thoughts, to caressing, to everything. Suddenly I was myself again: I had recuperated—I no longer had anything in common with the highway whore I had been as recently as six weeks ago. Yes, I existed again—me, Fialinka, me, me, me!)

At first I hadn't even noticed the light touch on my buttocks; who knows how long that broad, furtive hand had been there? I felt a tingling in my soul.

It wasn't for nothing that I had nicknamed the buses on the edge of the city "sexual transports." Over the years—since puberty—wandering hands had now and then turned up on my buttocks, on my thighs, on my breasts, or on the curve of my hip. Of course, Prague buses were "open for gropin'," as the girls used to say in high school. Always packed to bursting (because unless it was rush hour they were separated by such long intervals that giant crowds of passengers accumulated at the stops), the zoo-like Prague buses breathed a mixture of warmth and underarm deodorant, which still couldn't overcome the odor of bodies; the buses somehow broke down the touching taboo in people: even passengers accustomed to keeping a safe and private distance, day after day, year after year, had to grapple for their quarter of a square yard with alien people with alien smells whom they wouldn't have allowed anywhere near their bodies in any other situation. A perfumed boy in a suit, apparently on his way to his dancing lesson, jockeyed for position with a sweaty plumber who—with his soiled equipment bag over his shoulder—was returning from a shitty afternoon, literally. Distinguished ladies with umbrellas swung from poles above preoccupied-looking teenagers, and the pensioners—schooled over the years in the practical basics of the transport system jungle—used their canes as machetes to cut a path to the seats reserved for invalids, insisting gloomily and willfully on their right to be seated. In the crush, timid young girls suddenly found themselves surrounded by male bodies, so it's easy to imagine how hands occasionally wandered. They weren't rare, these hands, and adolescent girls, quick to adapt, exchanged among themselves "horror" stories and adventures that took place on the transportation routes of Prague. In my day I had even produced a naïve but I thought charming treatise on the influence of public transportation on premature sexual development. I had entered it in the student competition my first year in the psychology department. The treatise was written (thanks to great expenditures of self-control) in completely acceptable language and concerned the compacted crowds on Prague's trams, buses, and metro—it talked about the consequences of the violation of the distance that, according to traditionally accepted analyses, could be observed in various spheres of interpersonal relations. It examined the way strangers standing in Prague's trams and buses were crammed together body against body like sardines. Now imagine a young girl, innocent and (so far) chaste, her budding nipples, whether she likes it or not, making contact with the buttocks (and God knows what else) of the man pushed up against her. Her privacy is violated. That psychologically maintained layer of space around her, that imaginary buffer zone that no one may enter, has collapsed all the way back to her skin. With great effort the girl overcomes the shame she feels. And she becomes accustomed to the nearness of completely unfamiliar people who are making it difficult even to breathe. In my "competition" essay I analyzed this situation from every possible and impossible angle, citing a few learned books for good measure. Obviously, I hadn't discovered anything particularly new—the essay was more a reflection of the less than incisive personal viewpoint of an adolescent girl, which I was at the time. I analyzed the feelings of innocent girls and somewhat less innocent girls—what they might think, how they might feel when someone put his hand on their behind in a bus. I contemplated the collective odor of human bodies—which is known to be an aphrodisiac—and the involuntary contact of the defenseless young creature. I discussed the particular sort of internal hypocrisy that could force a girl to expose herself to these influences without admitting to herself that they made her feel good . . .

No, I don't think my little masterpiece had the slightest scholarly value. I entered it into the competition—and needless to say, it didn't win any prizes. Nevertheless, I don't understand why, out of all the contributions on themes like "The Education of the Socialist Citizen," "The Socialist Union of Youth and Its Task in Overcoming Remnants of Bourgeois Mentality," and so on—why precisely my little oeuvre, modestly titled "A Reflection on the Potential Influence of Urban Mass Transit on Premature Sexual Development," had to be the only one that was lost without a trace in the course of the judging.

I was riding the bus, and an unfamiliar, groping hand explored the curve of my ass and the crease where it merged with my legs. It savored the crevice between the buttocks and made its way between my thighs from behind. It felt so good combined with the slight concussions of the bus, shaking and panting and so warm inside!

Of course, when I'd been younger, this sort of thing had embarrassed me terribly.

I had no idea what to do: such was the psychology of Prague's sexual transports. Should I let the hand stay where it was? And let him get his rocks off at my expense? Or turn around and ask him to . . . ? That was unthinkable.

Among all those bodies packed one on top of the other, as they always were during the all-day rush hour, a hand could easily turn up in all kinds of places entirely by accident. Although in this case that seemed rather unlikely, to turn around and ask the groper to stick it somewhere else might still have been an invitation to the groper to frown ironically and say, "You don't by any chance believe, your ladyship, that my hand is there *on purpose*, do you?" And,

God knows why, but this accusation represented one of the most terrible insults a young woman could receive.

And so, for abnormal (and normal) young (and not so young) men, the packed buses were a groper's paradise. And many of these gropers, incredibly many, sooner or later mastered the art of inconspicuously creeping closer to the chosen victim, the art of the perfectly neutral face (so that sometimes their actions were revealed only by the confused and blushing face of the girl being groped), the art of inching closer and closer with every jolt of the bus, the art of synchronizing the rhythm of the bus and a rhythm of a different nature. It was an art, pressing up against the victim as closely as circumstances allowed—and apparently only because another passenger was digging his elbow into him in the laborious effort to push through to the exit. It was an art, fingering whatever could be fingered—and hiding oneself inside a bubble of inconspicuous indifference.

All kinds of men allowed themselves to slide down this slippery slope into depravity. And the opportunities were limitless.

At first, when I was young and naïve—and untouchable—I considered these groping scavengers insipid. Obscene. Disgusting. Later, I got pretty much used to them and began to distinguish different types. There were the Neophytes, almost timid youngsters, boys with barely sprouting whiskers, who were most likely preparing their hands for sincere caresses with their proper and chosen beloveds. There were the Apprentices, slightly more mature, but still young, who groped with a kind of exaggerated, overly contemptuous professionalism, the professionalism of the pickpocket. These were among those I liked least of all—it was the representatives of this most insolent strain who, when actually confronted with an objection, were capable of pointing out to the girl that, really, she had no business sticking her ass there in the first place. The next type were the Wankers, perpetually horny adolescents who, with fly unzipped, introduced between the unlucky female's nether hemispheres something rather unpleasantly moist. They were fairly disgusting, but from a psychological standpoint you couldn't get too mad at them. And the last were the Walruses, melancholy older men with St. Bernard eyes, perhaps fathers of families, perhaps all alone in the world, who simply couldn't resist the innocently pursed little asses of those enticingly young girls. At one time, when I, too, had belonged to the ranks of the enticingly young, this had seemed entirely repulsive to me. But as I grew older, all these furtive old gropers—these clandestine libertines with stealthy hands and evasive eyes—became more and more understandable.

In time, I became so used to them that I almost had sympathy for them, and I was sorry if a long time passed without one turning up. Because their regular appearances were good for my self-confidence.

More often than not, they were the only ones who at least noticed you a little in the gray mob of nameless strangers.

I felt the hand on my buttocks: it was sweaty and warm and seemed somewhat bewildered. Probably not the youngest type, but I didn't have the least desire to be acquainted with its owner.

It felt good: suddenly someone had noticed me; in the crush of waxwork figures, someone had at least taken enough interest in me to feel me up. It was probably a Walrus. He furtively spread the cheeks of my ass and yearningly inserted his hand into my crotch. I didn't resist. I didn't move away. I didn't turn around to snap at him. In some kind of semi-conscious response I made room for him with a relaxation of the muscles—and around a turn that threw us all to one side I let his hand penetrate further. Actually, I drew it in. I was

flirting. I adjusted my bag over my shoulder so that the glowering woman on the seat beneath me couldn't see anything; I
wiped the frosted window again with my hand and gazed out
neutrally at the gray darkness. And the lights. The bus trembled slightly with the rhythm of the road and snorted—and
between my thighs, I took advantage of the hand of an unknown man, whom I could hear panting behind me in surprise and excitement.

With a completely expressionless face, without any conspicuous movement, and without a sigh, enveloped in the
smells of sweat, cheap makeup, damp clothing, and intrusive
deodorant, I succeeded in experiencing one of those sudden,
rapid, unexpected—and therefore that much sweeter—feelings of gratification.

3

Of course, Patrik's decision to study and train his mind kept
kicking around in my head. I myself wasn't going to school at
all: I just couldn't stand the boredom of those lectures anymore, I couldn't stand grinding away at that damned economics (the only reason I still had a temporary registration stamp);
I knew that no good little socialist psychologist could ever be
made of me, even in a million years. I simply gave up on
school—that's what Father would have called it, giving up,
and he would have bawled me out terribly if he had known
about it . . . I stopped going to the university, and my life lost
neither flow nor direction as a result. There had been none to
begin with.

But I felt happy, as happy as I could feel—it didn't feel
like giving up to me at all. It was as if I'd done myself an
enormous favor by deciding to stop filling my head with
pseudo-information I had no interest in. I knew that I had
before me almost a whole year of joyous free time: I wouldn't
have to go to school at all, but my registered-student status

would remain valid. I'd salvaged at the very least a few months during which I wouldn't have to work—and they wouldn't have any obvious reason to lock me up for "parasitism." I intended to take advantage of this time. To use it for reflection. For acquainting myself with new social circles. For my meetings with Patrik. And—of course—for analyzing my love relationship. The first and only relationship I had ever been willing to call love. Erik.

I didn't travel anywhere outside winter-stricken Prague. I was taking a break. In our "communal villa," as Grandmother's and my dwelling was so grandly classified by the bureaucrats, there were the usual problems with the heating: the District Housing Office had been unable to find a steady stoker. And so it was freezing or bearable by turns—depending on the weather more than anything else. Now and then, some pathetic character staggered into the boiler room, scrabbled around in the furnace with a poker, threw a couple of shovelfuls of coal in, then ran back to the pub. A certain lively old pensioner offered to stoke for us, on the condition that the building come up with two or three thousand a month on top of the four hundred he would get from the state. The building committee took this offer under very serious consideration, since the old man seemed reliable enough, but finally it was decided that he was too forward. And so we had to manage with the shifting series of stokers sent from the Housing Office (I warmly called them the icemen), who would finally come and stoke the furnace, managing to waste an enormous amount of fuel in the process; then they departed, leaving the whole building to get good and frozen, perhaps so we would learn to appreciate the little warmth we did get. And so it had gone, round and round, for years, during which time the tenants had more than once announced that they would do their own stoking. However, we were not allowed to do this—for safety reasons, supposedly. No one in the building was a stoker by profession. And so we had a string of perhaps dozens of professional stokers, mostly of gypsy origin, who often spoke no Czech at all; who, instead of stoking, preferred to curl up around the lukewarm furnace; who went now and then to warm themselves at a nearby pub, where—leaning against the radiator—they fortified each beer with two or three shots of rum and, with their eyes fixed on the distances to the east, quietly cursed the difficult life of the stoker.

I didn't like winter.

Not to mention that I, in place of Grandmother, had to trudge through the streets—covered with clinging sheets of ice, in addition to the oily, salted slush—to do the shopping. I always took her place in the winter, and it always pissed me off. Though Grandmother claimed that in the winter she couldn't go out to bring home "our subsistence" because she might slip, break a leg, and freeze to death, this didn't prevent her—I noticed—from going out for walks and trading gossip in the streets, probably about me. Nevertheless, I was shopping in her place, and I had absolutely no idea what I was doing in the nervous pre-Christmas bustle of housewives. I saw for myself the serpentine lines that stretched all the way out of the stores where you bought things over the counter and the dual lines in the supermarkets; one for the baskets and one for the checkout stand. It was enough to make you furious, having to go shopping twice a day, for example: once to get milk, which was delivered in the morning, and again for bread, which came around three o'clock. It was a pain to jockey for position in a crowd of twenty people waiting for one of the five baskets in circulation in the whole supermarket. This was one of the special characteristics of life in Nusle: supposedly the salesgirls' greatest concern was keeping the gypsy children and teenagers from shoplifting. And so, of the three registers in our Nusle market, two were always closed, and of the three checkout girls on a shift, two always stood by the shelves, suspiciously observing the customers. The number of baskets was reduced to make the watching easier, since you weren't allowed into the main part of the store without one. As usual, people's frustration was channeled in such a way that they only screamed and cursed at each other. And did they ever scream. It was interesting to observe how each person gloomily and selfishly guarded his hard-won place in line; it was instructive to watch how old women and old men spitefully stepped on one another's toes, how dignified-looking people bitched and hissed at each other . . . It was interesting to see people's faces become combative when they so much as walked past a store, to see their elbows sharpen, hear their voices become harsher—to see how the law of the jungle ran wild and flourished in Prague, the law that the winner would be the one who fought the hardest and offered the best bribes . . . It was interesting to observe these instincts in humans enclosed in a barbed-wire cage, it really was. Too bad I had to live there!

Since I wasn't going to school and consequently had some time on my hands, I started to notice the normal, everyday street life of Prague more and more. I became attentive. I began to see things in a slightly bourgeois light. I became that frantic, rank-and-file female who has to worry about subsistence.

I saw how that ingrained way of life wore away at people. Myself included. The neighbors barely even acknowledged one another, and only the loneliest, most garrulous windbags ever stopped to exchange a few words in order to complain about something or slander someone. No one smiled at anyone else. And the only language they had in common was swearing. Cursing.

Now, all of a sudden, I had become a more integral part of that society it had been my destiny to be born into. I lived with others, right in the thick of it; I was coming to know my surroundings like an ingenue who has just turned thirteen. I could feel how vulnerable I was, I worried about my own self. I lived in the middle of life on the streets among the Nusle tenements and I wasn't looking for those other social circles. I wasn't trying to feel different.

Nevertheless, I *was* different: once again I fit into no category: I wasn't even a student anymore.

I was one of those extremely few young fortunates who had months and months and nothing steady to do.

And I was coming around to the thought that the gray, homogenized, carcinogenic hell on earth in which I was forced to live pretty much compelled any rational person to escape it.

Some to the West, like a number of people I knew.

Some into thought.

So it finally turned out that I crossed my fingers for Patrik and his speculations, looking forward to the time when I, too, could derive sustenance from his discoveries.

I

Erik . . .

Erik became an inseparable part of the winter of that year.

He would return with enchanting and reliable unpredictability to telephone and tell me he was in town.

Suddenly it was much easier to reach me at home in the apartment with Grandmother. I waited entire days, entire weeks for his calls. And Erik, swinging back and forth between Stockholm and Baghdad or God knows where, always called when he passed through Prague. I became his stopover en route.

As winter advanced, we gave up the embarrassment of looking for hotels and the frosted breath of alleyways filled with garbage cans. I simply took him home at night after our walks. This meant first sneaking through the gate of the building unobserved by the sharp eyes of our local scandalmongers; then it was just a matter of some nimble steps up the stairs before we were at my place. Erik became one of the extremely few men I had ever allowed to touch my body between my own down covers. With others I had always preferred neutral territory. And since the door to my room couldn't be locked, my safely snoozing grandmother added an air of mystery and excitement. Erik was bewitched by this and kept coming back.

In the morning, if Grandmother happened to get up first, I would hide Erik in the storage closet. It was in this closet Grandmother stockpiled the mountains of baked goods she had been saving up for Christmas since October.

Thanks to Erik there occurred a noticeable reduction in the supplies. Unlike other kinds of Czechoslovakian food, these cookies suited him fine. Grandmother began scrupulously searching all the utility spaces in the apartment for mice.

As I've said, at the beginning I modestly considered myself just one of the girls on the road. I believed that it must have been pleasant to sleep in a real bed once in a while, beneath a real down comforter made of real feathers, next to a real woman of the East, who caressed him and warmed him and slept with him. I believed that this was pleasant for Erik, because it was pleasant for me. I can't deny it.

And so I placed no conditions on our love. I resolved not to feel lonely, I resolved that I would remain independent, and—although it's true I wasn't traveling anymore at the time—I reminded myself over and over again that I had no right to expect it to be anything more than pleasant and charming.

And I didn't expect anything more.

But with time I began to become unpleasantly accustomed to having that body next to me.

No, it wasn't at all that passive habituation to a body that lies next to you night after night, so that in the end you can't even imagine it any other way: because you never even consider it. It wasn't because Erik's body did things to me no one else could do; I was too flighty for that.

It was something worse: I was beginning to get used to Erik.

I looked forward to him.

I thought about him. I masturbated with his image in my mind. I lay wide awake on my bed, preparing the English monologues I would deliver to him when I saw him next. My heart started pounding whenever I recalled his touch, and my head spun whenever I thought of our conversations.

I resisted this for a long time.

Until I finally realized that I was simply, completely, classically, normally, unhappily, perhaps almost adolescently—in love; at the age of almost twenty-six.

With a foreigner.

2

Of course with a foreigner: who else could our Fialka have fallen in love with?

The fragile beauty of that relationship based on Erik's visa, my bed, and Grandmother's sound slumber had fascinated me, intoxicated me, attracted me from the very beginning. And now it was beginning to alarm me, too. Our love (yes, after a while I was no longer afraid to call this feeling love) was built on thin ice, and any one of a million trifles or accidents could have sent it crashing! And I—I was terrified. What if I happened not to be home when he called? Grandmother wouldn't understand a word he said, and I'd never even know he had called. Missing his call just one time would have meant waiting through at least one leg of his journey, and that would have been too long a time. Too uncertain a time.

With each of Erik's visits I became more and more sure I wanted to be with him.

Only with him.

I had fallen for him. All the principles I had maintained through all my relationships were turned inside out, those almost male principles. First of all, I had never wanted to be with most guys more than once, and if I did want to see them again, it had always been *they* who had waited for *me*. It had been my companions of more than one night who had waited meekly by the phone. I had guided these relationships in such a way that they depended on me alone, and I had never been a number in any man's little black book.

It wasn't until Erik that I became that stronghold, that harbor to which a man returns again and again. I approached him differently. I looked him over. But not just superficially, not just as a connoisseur of men, as I had with other bodies. I got to know him. And I fondled him with experienced movements, experienced caresses, and experienced kisses (not experienced in that other, general sense, but in the sense of *familiar*: familiar with him and for him alone!). I knew his penis (I called it "my little bell"), I knew every curve of it, and it was magnificent how that shape—the same fixed and tenderly changeable shape—returned to my waiting hand over and over again like an obedient migratory bird. It was the shape of a bell tower: the wide base tapered toward its slender crown, which fit into my palm like the cap of an oak mushroom, into that little cup formed by touching my thumb to the other fingers of my hand. Why is it that when two people are fond of one another it seems as if Nature herself has made them compatible, so compatible that one fits the other perfectly, so perfectly you feel the other was tailored to your precise measurements? I didn't know. But I made the most of it every time Erik visited. I always took that voluptuous little object in my hand for the night's half-pilgrimage from the evening's lovemaking to the morning's, from the *before* to the *after* . . . and I held it with an almost desperate tenderness, like a hose in the garden, flowing with life-giving water.

I was used to Erik and I wanted him more and more. And to him I was becoming less like a mere stopover en route and more like an oasis, a flowing spring in the desert across which he wandered in his caravan of semis. I had become the star in someone's sky, in the sky of someone whose heavens I adored . . . although this left me no less lonely during the interludes. I was an oasis, a source, a wellspring to drink deeply of; a clear stream to wash away the dust of the highways and scorched roads.

I kissed off the desert sand and stardust from his body; I asked him to wait until later to wash (which he did, by the way, at the kitchen sink, since the bathroom was too dangerous). I tasted the fragrances of distant lands and myriad horizons under his arms, I caressed my cheeks with his hands grown hard from the wheel (those imperfect driver's hands, the kind I liked best), and in doing so I stole from him the remoteness of the kilometers, the remoteness of the road. Erik said that I was amazing, like an animal, unique; that it was so magnificent, so unforgettable to entrust himself to my hands . . . that through me, through my caresses, he understood himself far better. And I stole from him. I stole the blue horizons where roads vanished into infinity. Roads I had never traveled and probably never would. Stories. Loves. Yes, I secretly stole even his loves, the other girls, in other times and other spaces, who had touched his body and soul just as I was touching him now. I stole Erik's past—but not because I wanted him to shed it as a lizard sheds his old skin so that I would possess him for myself alone. I was getting to know him, feeling in his skin (I didn't ask, I could feel) the caresses of those other, strange, foreign women and girls, the caresses that furrowed his body just as my contacts had long ago left their signs on me. No, I don't think it was jealousy. Perhaps it was just that I, as they say, truly loved Erik . . . deeply, wholly, completely, past and all. Or . . . or that this relationship was just extraordinary . . . inexpressibly so. Erik was gradually entangling me in his silvery web, like a spider putting a fly away in his pantry. He wanted to capture me. He wanted me, and this feeling emanating from him was so intoxicating and powerful that there was no need to talk about it.

With each visit (perhaps even more so between visits) Erik was weaving his net around me, a web of lace. The intricate lace of a wedding gown.

3

It was obvious that sooner or later the proposal would come— and I'd been expecting it for a while, though I still had no idea how I would react. The periodicity of our relationship had its own momentum and it was threatening to become critical: Erik swung through on his way from Sweden to the south and back again, and came closer and closer to me, like a pendulum gradually coming to rest in the middle of its orbit. I was the gravitational center. And Erik was like the pendulum of a clock, drawn toward the center of Europe, the center of his journeys, the center of me. The relationship had its own momentum.

Some would say it was a relationship centered around bed.

I knew a lot of people who would say that.

It was largely centered around bed, but in a beautiful and refreshing way. The better part of it was enacted on my cotton sheets and on my pillow, beneath my checkered down comforter. This bed played a large role in our relationship, but it had more to do with setting than with plot. It was already too cold for walking outside, and the pubs and wine bars were always packed; besides, there was no privacy there. Our relationship was centered around my bed, because this was the most sheltered place in an apartment haunted by Grandmother. My relationship with Erik was not one of those carefully balanced relationships of touching that I'd had on my long-distance journeys. Erik was not the goal of contrived conversations precisely conducted so as not to come to a crashing halt, so the conversation wouldn't become embarrassingly trivial or lose its spark. Erik was not an instant severed from the flow of time for the sake of one brief moment, iridescent though a bit threadbare around the edges. Erik and I—we both had our pasts—and the future (according to him) lay before us. Before the two of us together. The past was the past, and the future was beckoning, and there was no need—as there had been at other times—to shield our eyes from anything.

Except for one small detail that was beginning to worry us more and more: he was from Stockholm while I was from Prague.

4

"Why don't we get married?" Erik said to me suddenly, during one of the times that filled the space between our always enchanting and now familiar *before* and *after*. "You could come live with me in Sweden . . . Or, if you want, we could go to America." (Erik knew that I loved America—based only on what I'd heard of it—and that its unattainability tormented me.) "We could be together."

He spoke and his speech was automatically translated for me into Czech, or perhaps into a sweet Moravian dialect; that was how much I loved English, that was how well he had taught me.

"Do you really want to be together with me?" I asked. "After all, we see each other so rarely . . ."

"That's just it . . . we see each other so rarely," said Erik. "And I worry about you. Every time I call—I've known the number by heart for a long time—every time I worry terribly that you won't be home, that you've gone somewhere . . . by yourself, or to see someone else . . . And I even worry that something might happen to you, here in Czechoslovakia. Sometimes it seems to me that it must be terribly dangerous to live here. Do you understand? I grew up in a completely different place, in a completely different way; it's hard for me to understand all this. I just want to be more sure that you are mine. No, I don't mean it like that, it's not that I don't trust you . . . It's just that if you move with me, you could have Swedish citizenship, you could travel with me all over Europe, all over the world. We could go to Japan; I've wanted to go there for a long time . . . Or, you said you want to study Eastern philosophy . . . so maybe we could go to India."

(My throat went a little dry in the course of all these distant travels—and I held Erik a little tighter. As if he were the ship taking me on this tour of the world's horizons.)

"I could show you what you've never seen . . . because this land"—and he moved my hand a little lower on his body—"this land you have seen from end to end, my love."

Everything was going cloudy before my eyes, and it's hard to say whether it was because of erotic passion or the longing for distant lands and blue oceans: the two temptations were so closely merged in me.

I said, "If you want to marry me just to be with me more often, that's stupid. First, we have known each other for only a few months, and we see each other so rarely, you have no idea what I'm really like. And second, when you go to the Middle East you see me twice: on your way there and on your way back. If I'm somewhere in Sweden, I would have to wait twice as long. That's how it is, Erik. By chance I am in a very strategic place here. I am right in the middle—and all your other lovers in Sweden and Arabia—they all have to wait twice as long!"

Erik laughed. He kissed me. "You're funny. But really, what more could you want: you're great! And I love you! That's why I want to marry you. Don't be so afraid of me!"

"Oooo, v-v-very s-s-scary! I'm not af-f-fraid of you, not at all. But please don't s-s-scare me like that."

"I'm only saying that I want to marry you."

"And have you ever wanted to marry anyone else before? Ever?" I probed. "Confess. You have, haven't you?"

"That doesn't matter. It was a long time ago. Don't be so jealous."

"I'm not jealous at all," I lied. "And I don't need to know all the details." (I lied again.) "I just want to know how serious you are. I'm a respectable girl, don't worry, I'm saving all my nagging for marriage. But I have to be careful. Maybe at home in Sweden you have your own little harem and you only want to show me off there. How do I know? You imperialists . . ."

Erik laughed so loud I was afraid he would wake Grandmother. Made yourself right at home, haven't you, I thought to myself. You're not afraid of anything anymore. And Grandmother would have a heart attack just from the sight of you here.

"I'm not asking *you* if you've ever wanted to marry someone, my Violet. You're almost twenty-six . . . and, by the way, pretty depraved already, even though you may look like a teenager who's never been kissed, to tell you the truth. You're magnificently depraved in the Slavic way, natural and free, like a Russian girl who's managed to break her chains . . . Please, don't get jealous again. I've never had another Czech girl, I swear to you. Do you know what I am really offering you? I am voluntarily throwing myself into the clutches of some Commie from the Soviet Bloc! I take you to Sweden and then you collectivize me. You see the risk I'm willing to take? And she calls me an imperialist!"

"Listening to you, Erik, and your expert description of Slavic women, I don't think I would have to collectivize you at all. You've managed to collectivize yourself quite successfully on your own in all your travels. Or at least one part of your body . . ."

We joked around like this for another hour or so, though

the subtext of the conversation was serious, almost too serious. We had a big decision before us. And even if Erik hadn't hastened the arrival of that decision, it couldn't help wandering into our thoughts and actions. Even with the added spice of my pious sleeping grandmother, my bed, together with the caresses that fascinated us, was probably doomed to become monotonous sooner or later. And that would be too great a shame.

Besides, this Erik from the distant, snowy North, my knight in shining armor, was longing to rescue me. He wanted to buy me out of bondage by marrying me, like a serf girl. He wanted to liberate me.

5

It was just before daybreak when we awoke from our half-sleeping embrace and Erik came at me again, this time by stealth. With eyes closed I let his face caress mine, and with my happy morning smile I tasted his. I was dying of bliss. When he slowly put his hand around my waist and familiarly and expertly slipped into that opening, still moist for him from the night's passion, I felt delicious in his warm arms and thought about how a woman's body resembles a fortress; I thought about those concealed places where the organs of love had been placed—yes, as if Nature had wanted to remind man that not just anyone was allowed to get that close. The body was built to converge toward that opening, so that to conquer a woman one had to open her like a rose blossom. Somewhere in the recesses beyond consciousness I was experiencing the loves of generations, the long-ago love of my mother when she conceived me—that intense pleasure of lovemaking, of conception. Suddenly—perhaps for the first time in my life—I felt more than mere sexual desire: it was multiplied desire, the desire to multiply. With Erik, for the first time ever, I understood that to want a child and to make a child could be a pleasure stronger than any other. Oh yes, I had always been rational in word and deed, but still, in that perfect understanding, that perfect joining of the bodies that belonged to us, I longed to multiply the perfection, to project it along a vertical line, to continue the history of pain and blood.

Amid the ancient, thousandfold, all-embracing pleasure I felt only desire. My thoughts drifted off into clouds of recollection . . . perhaps sometime before . . . no, in love there is no comparison, no repetition; not in love—all of that is just love of self, egotism. In other embraces I had remembered, fantasized . . . not in order to excite myself, I had remembered even when there had been no need of it, for with other bodies and by means of other bodies I had been satisfying my own body. And the experience of pleasure I derived from satisfying other bodies, that had also been only the pleasure of my body, the blissful love of self: yes, egotism. Everything repeats, it is only in love that there is no repetition, I realized. Only the motions are repeated, eternally repeated, those amazing and painful motions, like labor pains, like menstrual cramps . . . these soft and hard, escalating, converging motions are repeated like leitmotifs in a symphony. Over the years I had experienced in myself a symphony of caresses and now I was experiencing all the music at once. It was good to know that everything was converging, and that I still didn't have to concentrate on convergence . . . not yet . . . I didn't need to rush to snatch something for myself before it all came to an unexpected end. It was good to know Erik, it was good to know that soon he would lead me up to the gates of paradise, which we would enter together. I let myself drift slowly away like a fishing boat on the ebb tide . . . the shore of consciousness receded, the wind flapped in the sheets—suddenly nothing remained for me but Erik, Erik, an ocean of Erik, no recollections, no past, no future. There was only Erik, and even the name sounded so sweet, so sweet that it must have unexpectedly slipped past my lips as the gates of paradise already summoned us with the once-bitten blushing red apple of sin.

"Will you marry me?" said Erik with closed eyes. "Will you marry me, will you marry me, will you marry me?" Then he opened his eyes, made deeper by morning, and repeated, "Will you marry me?"

"Yes," I said almost with the voice of Fate herself. And while I repeated my own "yes, yes, yes" together with him, I clung to him in an arc of convulsion as if he were its only reason and my only redemption from it, and I screamed until the panes in the windows rattled; I screamed at the top of my lungs, "Ye-e-es!"

Then of course Erik had to retreat immediately to the storage closet—and an hour later, when Grandmother had been calmed down and seated for her morning dose of television, I already knew without a doubt that my promise had been a lie.

6

I don't know how, in capitalist Europe and in countries even farther west, there could possibly be so many madmen who wanted to and often did marry Czech girls. Particularly among the refined super-girls, who were hopelessly ashamed of their East European origin, it was simply a sign of a good upbringing to have at least one (the more the better) admirer from the West and to boast of it at every opportunity. If one didn't get married right away, it was fashionable at least to have a couple of broken imperialist hearts to brag about and to wear a ring on the middle finger, which one could occasionally glance at languidly, saying in dreamy introspection, "That's from Wilhelm. To remember him by." Or from Francesco. Or Sebastian. Or any other exotic-sounding name that, when sighed with the correct foreign accent, immediately told the whole story and aroused the envy of one's girl friends, and in potential partners stimulated curiosity about this experienced woman of the world.

And so it went in Prague, day after day, in the ongoing armed hunt for foreign spouses. Surprisingly enough, the foreigners allowed themselves to be caught. They all seemed to suffer from some sort of mawkish sympathy for Czech girls: they wanted to save us. For them we were like pretty little monkeys in a barbed-wire cage, pretty little monkeys who needed to be liberated, cleaned up a bit, and taught to speak like humans. Someone had to look after them. Someone simply had to save them.

Salvation hysteria reigned supreme in the little pubs and wine bars of Malá Strana; girls longing for salvation stormed the groups of tourists, who must have found Prague very much to their liking. And a surprising number of these hopefuls actually succeeded sooner or later, although many (otherwise chaste) girls, just to be on the safe side, took a tumble with every fool they met who spoke a language other than Czech. The hunt for husbands resembled the hunt for hard currency.

It was not at all a matter of the man's education, position, or his sympathetic qualities as a whole (viewed, in any case, only through the latticework of the broken languages in which most of these eager girls communicated); even his appearance and age were of no interest. And the girls' feelings? These were at best kept on a short leash or masked with makeup. Ninety-nine percent of them assessed their Western lovers according to the money they were willing to fork out; they hawked their goods on the black market just like the teenage boys selling jeans in front of the hard-currency stores. Just like those boys, they tried to outtrump one another, tripping over their own feet to bag these profitable (and love-stricken, to hear them tell it) husbands-to-be from forbidden lands. Bagging the best one, that was the mark of resourcefulness, cleverness, and beauty in a girl. The sign that she was a lady among ladies.

When one looked at these stories a little more closely, it became clear that these foreign grooms and spouses were not exclusively a bunch of well-meaning idiots throwing their money around. Some of them had genuinely serious intentions, while others were victims of the universal salvation trend—but still others traveled to Eastern Europe simply to get laid. A few caught on almost too quickly and cashed in on their exceptional position quite happily. And every once in a while it happened that a successful husband hunter unexpectedly found herself in a Turkish harem, where she had to serve her husband devotedly and faithfully, until he—as punishment for disobedience—bartered her for an elephant. There were all kinds of stories floating around about Czech girls who had been duped—and no wonder: after all, we lived in the tranquil backwater behind the Iron Curtain, in the tiny world of Czech disinformation, and—though we thought ourselves more clever than we were—we really had no idea whatsoever how things worked out in the great wide world beyond. A lot of girls got married (some perhaps even out of love) and then wrote strained letters back about how well they were doing in the West; it was easy to guess they were pretty homesick. In our small world of Czech disinformation, we could hardly know what émigré life was like over there—many a reckless girl, led on by the fool's gold of empty promises, later bitterly regretted her emigration and longed to return, just as it happened in the heartrending stories with which the organs of mass media occasionally regaled us. Like emigration, marrying into the West, it turned out, was also a more or less irreversible step into the unknown. Only the biggest fools went without doubts. Nevertheless, when it came to so-called advantageous marriages to foreigners, most girls didn't think twice.

But I thought twice. I'd never participated in the universal hunt before—and *voilà*: this proposal, like a bolt from a clear blue sky, a proposal based on love. Or was it another attempt at salvation? I didn't know. I didn't know whether Erik really wanted me to sail with him into the future or if he was just throwing me a life preserver out of human decency.

I wanted to be with Erik, to live with him, but why, for God's sake, why did I have to emigrate to do it? Of course, if I went ahead with it, I could always return to Czechoslovakia later, but that might make things worse. I would never be able to feel settled.

I still didn't know Erik. And when I tried to think about it logically . . . Erik was great whenever he came to visit me, the smell of distance on him was amazing—he was perfect for that international relationship of intoxicating distances centered around our bed, the relationship that was taking deeper and deeper hold inside me. But did I really understand him? Did he understand me? Walking through the deep, pure Swedish night, wouldn't I feel homesick for the gray chaos of the Prague streets? Wouldn't I miss that small world of the Czech spirit that I happened to despise at the moment? Buried in Western photographic equipment, would taking pictures still be enjoyable?

I didn't know.

And what was worse, it was something that couldn't be thought about logically at all; it couldn't be imagined or deduced. No one could give you advice, although no one would have refrained from suffocating you under the weight of their lengthy opinions. It was like thinking about sleeping with a boy for the first time: all the concrete facts were common knowledge, but no one could tell you how *you* would feel when you did it. Even so, the girls who were still in your position were only guessing just like you, and the ones who had gotten past this hurdle had already changed their thinking somewhere along the way. No, I didn't talk to anyone about Erik—it would have been like discussing sex with twelve nuns fingering their rosaries.

I loved Erik far too much—and I knew my own inconstancy. Our relationship, as it was at the time, was delicate and breakable, but then that was the cost of its crystal clarity. If it had to happen, it would be more sensible to let it happen right now, with a minimum of shattering, than for one of us to take a hammer to it somewhere in Stockholm (perhaps after years), then try to glue all the pieces back together. That's the way it had always been with me; and with Erik, I couldn't even imagine the horrible ending. So I preferred not to take the risk of someday destroying our love ourselves. It was probably better to blame it on the Communists.

All of a sudden something occurred to me, something completely absurd, if not outright conceited and stupid: my homeland needed me. Yuck!—my homeland! I hated that term, with its socialist-militaristic overtones—my homeland as a strategic battle zone where we lived ever better and more happily, and which it was our civil duty to build and defend. Yuck! Such a beautiful word and so disgustingly degraded nowadays that you could use it only at Party meetings. But still, my homeland was the trucking routes. My homeland was traveling from horizon to horizon, horizons enclosed by barbed wire. My homeland was expeditions to hunt monstrous wild snowflakes, snowdrops, anemones, and saffron. My homeland was the narrow winding streets of Malá Strana, without which, perhaps, I couldn't have existed. My homeland was the Lost Meadow in the Bohemian Karst and the white beech trees above Třebová, the whitest beeches I had ever seen in my life.

I raised my feet off the floor—no roots! But I could still feel the delicate silver fibers of the web that bound me to everything around me.

Maybe everyone felt this way. Most people just never thought about it.

Or maybe I simply feared that step into the unknown more than the others, just as I had feared diving into the pool off the three-meter board more than others as a girl? Was I old? Had I gotten old, after all?

Patrik was studying different unknowns, different spheres in the books I brought him, the books which Mrs. Fišer immediately tried to take away with tears in her eyes, fearing that her son was drifting away to a place where she couldn't follow. Patrik told me I was stupid, that I was indecisive, that I was more likely to rot away in this hell than even he was; supposedly one of the symptoms of the decay was the reluctance to leave it behind. Patrik was aiming way beyond Sweden in his studies.

Still, my homeland was the hairpin turns on the Northern Road, the steep inclines where every driver always had to downshift to third; my homeland was the rest areas and dozens of fragrances of nights even Erik couldn't erase. My homeland was the sprouting . . . an inhospitable wintry landscape where the breath of spring already warmed the buds on the trees. No, everything was not lost here—and even now, in December, I could sense the flutterings of spring.

Patrik said to me, "Get married. You'll adapt to a new place without even thinking about it. You'll adapt; it's just like getting used to a new guy, that's how easily you'll adapt to a new country."

But I didn't want to adjust. Sure, I could forget, it was possible to rebuild my entire personality and start anew. With Erik. With someone I really loved.

It was just that I didn't want to reshape myself. I refused to make myself different.

My homeland was the curve near Hradec Králové where long ago—almost eight years had passed already—something terrible had happened. My homeland was filth and grayness and the prefabs, Garden City, where Patrik was fading away.

My homeland.

No . . . I didn't want to forget and adapt to a more comfortable life, to roll my good fortune around on my tongue like a piece of delicious cake you eat in an attempt to chase away your clinging sorrow.

I simply wanted to be myself. Let everyone think they know what's best for me, let them think whatever they want. Let them think I'm odd and stupid.

7

After a couple of days—before Erik appeared again—I already knew for sure that I wasn't going anywhere—and just as I had with most of my former loves and infatuations, I began to predict when and how our love would die.

It was withering.

We made love again and again in my bed beneath my comforter (whose cover, according to Grandmother, I washed altogether too often), and I still trembled from the pleasure of distances with which Erik glowed; but what we'd had now lost its direction and momentum.

And we two happily desperate and desperately happy people from different parts of the world could do nothing about it except to make love and caress and make love—and constantly reassure one another over and over of our mutual love, over and over and over again—until it passed away completely.

8

One time (Erik had trained me in English so well by then that I could communicate the nicest subtleties of my thought) I told Erik about my friend who had multiple sclerosis. I told him how he couldn't walk at all anymore, even on crutches, how badly he needed a wheelchair, and that he had one coming to him from the state—in five to ten years. Then (as lightheartedly as I could) I told the stories of my attempts to get my hands on a wheelchair for him—that is, only about the most innocent and hopeless attempts, climaxing with the German marks which I, like an idiot, in exchange for nothing but a word of honor, relinquished to a certain black marketeer who, needless to say, never showed his face again. Finally I asked Erik, as suggestively as possible, whether he happened to know how difficult it might be to get such a wheelchair in Sweden. Erik asked for Patrik's measurements, and on his next visit he lugged with him an excellent motorized chair, for which he'd paid customs tax at the border in the form of several cartons of Marlboros: a handsomely constructed wheelchair of steel, wrapped in plastic, with instructions in English.

I thanked him and asked him how I could pay him back for it. Erik waved his hand. There was no way I could pay him back.

Soon after that we broke up.

1

It was spring again. Or, actually, the very beginning of spring. Or perhaps it wasn't spring at all, perhaps winter had lasted too long and we were just evoking spring without desire. I walked slowly next to Patrik, who was riding in his wheelchair along the Vltava embankment—and we inhaled the fragments of spring from the atmosphere. They were here. In the streets the trams ringing their bells were muddier than ever and the smog exhaled by the cars was thicker and richer than ever; you could actually feel it corroding your lungs. Mud and dust were on the rise in the streets of Prague, smog was on the rise—and there was more and more noise, too: it wasn't just that the conservationists had told me, I could hear it myself. There wasn't a single place where you felt like stopping to rest; if you did manage to take a breath, you couldn't hear your own voice—and the eternally towering wall of sound from which there was no escape stupefied you more than anything else.

I stopped on the two-tone paving stones, right next to some stairs leading down to a little landing. Below us a small, timid steamboat rocked on the waves. Patrik braked a half step away from me and felt the stone railing with his outstretched hand. In the time since he'd been forced to change his life-style, Patrik had become more of a toucher; he could barely take photographs at all anymore. I looked out across his arm at the Vltava and suddenly I was terrified by how thin his hand had become, how long and bony his fingers were (no longer those of a painter), how his disease had entirely changed him, though perhaps only because of his loss of appetite. "You're thin as a rail," I remarked. And Patrik raised his right arm like a prophet, motioned toward me with a long, solemn gesture, and grinned. "It is only the thoughts working in me now, Fialinka, I am only breaking free more and more from worldly chattels, for your information. You, on the other hand . . . the winter has left you somewhat rounder, it seems to me. You should watch yourself, or you won't be doing much hitchhiking come spring. No one will pick you up. Cargo over two tons is bad for gas mileage, you know." I felt the folds of fat under my coat—not folds, really, more like slightly neglected little pockets of skin. "It's not that bad yet, Patrik. It's probably just that as a human scarecrow you can't stand having people around you who are made of flesh, and not just rattling bones and lofty thoughts."

Patrik nodded sagely. "Sherlock Holmes was right when he said you think better on an empty stomach. I've tested his theory. It also explains why most people—including you— love to eat so much, Fial. So they don't have to think very much. The blood is pumped from the head to the stomach."

"And don't you think—" But I stopped. I was about to point out that most people love to have sex, too, because then the blood is pumped even lower. Then I added, "I must congratulate you, Patrik, you must have *all* your blood in your head, because there's certainly no room for it anywhere else."

"That's why I think so clearly," Patrik observed, almost like a priest. "After twenty-seven years, I have finally learned to contemplate."

"I don't believe you."

"But it's true. Remember how you came to me last spring with that beautiful motto, that life is a one-way street with no stopping or standing? Remember that? I thought it was great at the time: you can't stop, you can't turn back—and at the end there's just that wall . . . I've contemplated this very thing, in a kind of half-sleep, see—sometimes at night this damned spine of mine hurts so much—and the pain shoots up so far that I think it's going to shoot right into my brain. Sometimes those flashes illuminate my mind. So one time I saw, as when the road winds around, as when you're going around a curve on a mountain and you can see all the hairpin turns above and below you . . . I saw backward and forward in time. I saw that the road is not just one road but a whole network of roads, every once in a while you stand at a crossroads—and each of the roads leads somewhere different. Not one of them, Fialka, is a dead end, it's our senses that are dead."

I sighed heavily. The stationary air was becoming unbearable. But Patrik obviously hadn't noticed.

"Every once in a while you stand at a crossroads and you have to decide. And for each person, for anyone who has a destination, at each crossroads there's a sign. It could be a moral sign, maybe it has to do with self-preservation—or maybe it's based on what's been pumped into your head from childhood. It might just say SINECURE. Or it might say FAME. Or MONEY."

"Patrik, I really hope you're not planning to add that on the road I'm following there's a great big sign in neat letters saying HELL VIA HANDBASKET."

"Well, I wouldn't argue with that. You could be in Stockholm by now. But don't interrupt me. What I mean to say is this: each life has millions of forks and road signs. There's such a huge number of them, it makes your head spin a little; most people get all muddled up, but I won't let myself get confused . . ."

"And which direction have *you* chosen?"

"*Life*," said Patrik, and he let loose the air in his lungs almost ceremoniously; it was his ancient custom. "I have chosen *Life*. And *Freedom*."

And he raised his hand in front of him, as if about to feed the gulls. It was an old-fashioned gesture, prophetic and summoning.

The birds converged on him.

2

Pieces of ice drifted down the Vltava, and the gulls rode on them all the way from the railway bridge down to the Charles Bridge, where they unfailingly lifted off from their ice floes just above the weir and returned upriver on lazy wings to take another ride. Along the embankment stood people who, like us, had nothing to do, and some of them fed the birds bits of bread. The gulls knew how to show their appreciation. They snatched the morsels out of the air in flight, fought over them, squawking and screaming with that hollow, haughty laughter that always startled me. The swans were still wintering by the landing, and they came joyously paddling over like meek little sailboats when anyone stopped on the bank. The whole population of Prague converged on the Vltava to observe the birds; they fed the gulls as if they were their own chickens and held their breath whenever a white swan, elongated by its long wake on the water, swam closer in expectation. They lived here like ducks on a pond, these white birds who miraculously managed to maintain some degree of their whiteness. The Vltava had an extraordinary power: the power of flowing water that will always have its effect on people, the power of the compact smell of the water, which surprisingly still found its way to your nose amid the dozens of other, far less pleasant odors. I thought of the time when the whole Vltava, still unfettered by dams, would freeze in winter and people could walk across it. This was one of the pleasures our late birth had deprived us of; for years I had suffered nostalgia for time long passed, times I'd never known . . . and never would.

The river also had the power of its sound, which reached human ears even over that ever-rising wall of street noise. I felt half deaf—but still, even way up on the embankment, I could hear the gentle lapping of the river against the stones of the landing, a soft sound but nevertheless dominant, as if lifted up to me by my desire for it alone.

A stooped old woman walked by us, tapping her cane against the pavement. She stopped near us in order to continue her mumbled, almost incomprehensible monologue: "And they never came for her! You see, they didn't save her. They didn't come for her! For whom?" she responded as if we had asked her. "Why, for the swan . . . with a broken leg! If only you had seen her, the way the poor thing was lying there in the inlet, the waves splashing on her—and all she could do was open her beak like this, as if she was crying for help. So I fed her and she ate right out of my hand, she was so helpless. Poor thing! Try to imagine. I called the zoo and even went out there, so they would come and save her, so they would call a veterinarian. And you know what they said to me? They said to me, Sure, ma'am, there are three thousand swans on the Vltava, and if we had to look after every crippled one, where would we be. Besides, soon they're going to have a licensed swan shoot, because the swans are detrimental! Detrimental! Well, what would you say to that? What would you? So these days swans are detrimental, are they, and that . . . poor thing . . . I couldn't find her again . . . God knows what happened to her, so there you are. She was lying right over there, with her leg all broken. Who? Why, the swan, she was just lying there on the landing . . ."

The woman pattered off, clicking her cane on the pavement, repeating over and over all those injustices and stopping passersby to get it off her chest. It gave us both a bit of a shock: in that universal numbness any concern for life was something completely fantastic. For Praguers, the swans and gulls on the Vltava symbolized life. And the woman was a protector of life, even though her focus was naïvely concentrated. The woman wanted to save a swan with a broken leg—and meanwhile ash and soot and carcinogens were showering down on Prague and killing us all little by little. How much better it was not to know about it! How much more comforting! How much simpler!

Isn't that so, Patrik?

3

Dangerous-looking dark clouds were crowding in from the West, promising a wet early-spring afternoon. Patrik was laying out his theories, and the Vltava idled below us, gray and motionless.

"Look here, Fialka, have you ever thought that reality doesn't necessarily have to be objective? What if every one of us sees the world in his own way—and what if there's nothing else? What if the most basic philosophical questions—materialism and God and reincarnation—what if they can't ever be answered? That's why people are always killing each other. As you know, Fialka, I don't try to force anyone into believing anything. Not even you, but at least try with what's left of your brain to understand what I'm saying: Is it possible for a person to be born over and over again? In different shapes? In different times? On different continents, or even different planets? What do you think, is it possible?"

"In your damaged brain," I said. But then I gently added, "No, I do think it's possible . . . a lot of the Eastern philosophies believe in reincarnation. But try to think of it logically, Patrik. Why wouldn't you know about it, if you had been reincarnated? Why couldn't you just simply remember your past lives?"

Patrik roared, "Because you couldn't bear to know!

"Because it would be tedious. Because if you knew your past lives, if you knew everything, if you knew that you'd already been born fifty times before and that you had God knows how many more lives ahead of you, you'd simply be disgusted and cynical from the cradle. And what's more, if anything in life screwed you over, you'd just up and solve it by committing suicide; you'd just throw away that little life like a pair of sneakers that chafe your feet. You'd have no respect for life and you'd get bored with it! That's the principle, the reason you can't know! But there are certain situations that arise, and no, you can't be positive, but still you can get a hint from them." Patrik fell silent.

The smog in the street had gotten unbearable. My hand wandered to my throat to help me breathe—drops of rain were beginning to fall on both of us. It wasn't a refreshing spring shower but a nasty, cold drizzle of concentrated acids the sky could no longer bear. But Patrik still hadn't noticed . . . he didn't seem to pay attention to much lately . . . It seemed to me that his current life was losing its meaning for him—it was chafing him now, like a pair of sneakers one size too small. Patrik was treating the present reality thoughtlessly, carelessly, as if he still had a dozen more realities stored up.

I felt a little sick.

"So you think that when we die we will be born again? Maybe on Mars? Or in India, five thousand years before Christ? Or maybe it will be a more radical change than that, and we'll be born on the Progress Standard Farming Cooperative in Mokropsy, so we can grow up to be good, solid milk cows? To tell you the truth, I don't think I would enjoy reincarnation very much, especially since I wouldn't have any control over it. I'm used to this old body of mine, it's like a pair of jeans I've had for years, I've made my peace with it; I know it's going to wear out someday, but in the meantime, I'm not planning to trade it in. And, seriously, I'm not such a slave to fashion that I need a hundred and fifty bodies and minds, one pair for every occasion, all nicely folded in my dresser. Do you . . ."

"I know perfectly well that you're listening to me, Fial." Patrik looked at me deeply and far too seriously. "I know you understand what I'm saying to you, so it doesn't even bother me when you say such bullshit. You don't want to talk to me about it, because when you talk about reincarnation it's the same as talking about death—and it's hard for you to talk about death with a cripple who'll be kicking the bucket before you even know it . . . Basically you're a terribly considerate person, Fial, and so you don't even talk to me about sex, because you know I'm in pretty shitty shape in that respect. You know how many times I've noticed you—no, don't interrupt me, please—I haven't said anything so bad. Only that from a certain point of view it's necessary to admit that there must be something to reincarnation. That it's possible for you to be reborn, even though you're not conscious of having lived before and—as long as you're living this life, you can't have any influence over what you'll be in the next one. You have to admit that there's a possibility here you can't just exclude."

I could feel the drops getting heavier: the Vltava had started to boil with thousands of small and large rings. The swans hid their heads under their wing. People came back up from the landing—and as they hurried past us they opened their umbrellas and turned up the collars of their coats, shivering. I was starting to shiver a little, and each drop pummeled my head like a brick. We were both wet inside and out, and on the blanket Patrik had thrown over his knees (like a genuine invalid) puddles were forming. Patrik didn't notice. But I was suddenly struck with the fear that he might catch a chill, that he was sick, after all, and that it was my responsibility to get him back to Garden City safe and sound. (Back to the gray prefabs Erik said reminded him of American parking garages.)

Squatting, I raised my eyes to him—I wanted to mention that we ought to be going, so as not to catch cold. Then Patrik said, so quietly that I almost had to read the words from his dripping lips, "I've decided, Fialka, that I want to test it." I knew exactly what Patrik was saying to me—and I just watched as his brow and the corners of his eyes dripped with drops of spring shower, which could as well have been tears, if Patrik still had the ability and desire to cry.

4

I took him home.

Took him—well, he drove in his motorized chair, happily jolting along the pavement and splashing through puddles, betting me that he could splatter various passersby with mud. The passersby, seeing a cripple in a wheelchair, didn't dare protest, and Patrik had a lot of fun watching them. He wheeled his afflicted butt along merrily, giving the chair gas in the most impossible spots, while I stumbled along at a trot just to keep up with him. Patrik was in high spirits, although shivering with cold; he thrashed his arms around in order to generate at least a little warmth. I chattered my teeth alongside; at this point we were talking only about silly things again. We felt good. Patrik sent the gray puddles streaming and we both laughed crazily.

Screw the world.

5

Of course, I understood what Patrik was trying to say, but after that whole speech he gave me, I didn't feel up to challenging him. Patrik was right: it was impossible to live in his condition in that prefabricated rabbit hutch—or at least it was impossible for Patrik. No, it wasn't really important anymore where the truth lay. Patrik had decided on that step into the unknown, into a far darker, denser unknown than emigration . . . He was simply stronger than me. In any case, Patrik had his own truth, which I couldn't disprove even to myself, much less to him. Patrik had made his decision. I didn't think he was bad at making big decisions: he had decided to cross the wall, to start over elsewhere, to start over from the beginning. Perhaps.

Perhaps. Perhaps. *Perhaps?*

That question mark remained for me: I wasn't convinced that Patrik was right about the great unknown. I had always been more afraid of the great unknowns. Every little *perhaps* had always terrified me. Oh yes, our bold Fialka, who had flown for years wherever the devil took her, alone, hitchhiking, was in reality a great big chicken, entirely dependent on the intimately familiar, though perhaps distasteful particulars of her safe little coop: the apartment with Grandmother (I knew I would never move); the Northern Road, where I knew every turn and weathered milestone; and Prague, whose slouching progress toward gray nastiness pained me more and more deeply every year. It had even been that way with love . . . I had thought, Look how transient and free I am, thinking that meant modern. But how long did it take back then, curious Fialinka, to decide to go to bed with someone for the first time? To decide on that step into the unknown that less thoughtful girls leaped into headfirst and without fear? Do you still remember? So just admit it, Fialinka, at least to yourself, you have always feared the Unknowns. Maybe that's even why they attracted you. Oh yes, you loved the little unknowns, particular, unfamiliar regions, because they added a little spice to your life, but you've always wanted to sit firmly on top of what you knew inside and out. Just admit it . . . explain it to yourself: why didn't you marry Erik?

You wanted to, you wanted to desperately—but it would have brought on too many changes. You didn't go off to Stockholm, even though you longed for it terribly, even though you truly loved Erik . . . It serves you right that it hurts you now. You're afraid of unknowns and incapable of making up your mind. You're wallowing in your own accumulation of little certainties, Fialinka—and it is so comfortable to be quietly disgusted by everything. To be quietly disgusted by the world you know and to refuse to look for other worlds.

You envy those who can run and leap.

You envy Patrik.

Yes, you do.

You have no right to try to convince anyone of anything.

6

By the time we got out of the elevator on the fifth floor, a puddle had formed beneath each of us. And when I brought her muddied son to the threshold, Mrs. Fišer didn't even bother with her sociable smile.

In Patrik's cubbyhole, once I'd closed the door, for the first and last time in our lives we kissed.

Later, when I wanted to leave (my heart was pounding), Mrs. Fišer pulled me aside; she had that ear-to-ear smile securely hanging on her face again and she said, "Viola, it would be better for Patrik if you didn't come to visit us anymore."

The corners of her mouth spread apart. "Okay?"

It was like a punch in the teeth.

But in a certain more important sense it didn't bother me a bit.

Not one bit.

It was a matter of the rules of the game. Rules that had now changed for Patrik. It had always been part of the game to discourage anyone who wanted to do anything great, extraordinary, unusual; in other words, something normal people would never do for any reason. It had always been part of the game to tell the person that it would be foolishness or weakness to do such a thing, that he had no idea what he was really suggesting.

If Patrik confided in someone that he no longer loved the world and that he planned to do something about it; it was part of the game to tell him he was being foolish, that he shouldn't give up, that you can find a reason for living in any situation . . .

They would have told him that. They would have made it look as if they were the fount of all wisdom. They would have told him because that's what one was supposed to do.

But such people forget how different the rules of the game were as they now applied to Patrik. Patrik was handicapped, Patrik was experiencing his own disintegration—and he feared it would soon become more than physical. He feared the disintegration of his self, and he didn't know when it would begin or whether he would even be conscious of it. He had no intention of scraping together the remnant of his life and happiness like a child playing in a sandbox, just to show everyone else: Hey, look at me, look how much I still have! Patrik had no intention of accepting the conditions according to which he now had to live; he refused to adjust to them and he refused to learn to be resigned. He didn't accept—and he didn't want to accept—the new rules of the game. Patrik had made his decision.

A normal person would have called this weakness.

I think it was courage. The great courage to leap over the wall.

8

I was taking the Northern Road eastward, and I could already catch hints of spring in the air. It was night.

Our truck—the driver's and mine—panted a little as it cut a path through the darkness and trembled with gentle vibrations that rocked me toward sleep. I knew this truck and I knew this road. I looked out the windshield from the passenger's seat at the headlights licking the silent landscape like two solitary lighthouse beacons on a cliff. I knew. I lay on the seat and I laid out the strands of my hair—now grown out, but still not very long—like a trap across the gearshift. I knew the beech trees near Třebová were coming up soon, the whitest beeches I had ever known.

I was twenty-six.

I was taking the Northern Road eastward, and in that tranquillity of soul, which once more—after nearly a year—had gently enfolded me, only the occasional thought wandered to Patrik.

To Patrik, whom I would probably never see again. To Patrik, who had perhaps this very day leaped over that high wall into the Unknown—and who would (perhaps!) be born again as a completely different self who would nevertheless carry some fragment of Patrik. Maybe in Bulgaria. Maybe in Prague. Or he might travel to another continent: perhaps even now, at this very instant, he had just been conceived somewhere in America. Maybe in America, in that land I would probably never see, never, never, never, because in my fear and indecision I would never be able to leap over that wall.

That wall.
That wall.

The truck came to a stop in a rest area just outside of Olomouc, and in those familiar, endlessly repeating movements, tried and true throughout the generations, we made life.